THE CRY FROM ST

'They call London the Great Whore, and no wonder, seeing so many of her daughters are practising her trade there,' says young Mary Kelly, who returns to London in the terrible summer of 1888. She had fled the horrors of Whitechapel slum life eight years earlier, and triumphantly survived as a brothel-keeper on the Canadian frontier.

Now, a rich and confident woman, she returns to London to find and rescue her two sisters – but she arrives just as the murderer later known as Jack the Ripper begins his dreadful career.

Mary Kelly, searching desperately for her young sister who is still in Whitechapel and is a poor prostitute like all the Ripper's victims, plunges deeper and deeper into the dark side of Victorian London. Gradually she loses all her defences against the life from which she came – until eventually she faces the murderer herself.

Jack the Ripper killed six women in one square mile of East London between August and November 1888. The women were Martha Tabram, Polly Nichols, Annie Chapman, Elizabeth Stride, Catherine Eddowes – and Mary Kelly. Hilary Bailey's powerful and enthralling story of London's Victorian underworld is the story of the Ripper's last victim, who was never properly identified.

Hilary Bailey was born in 1936 near Bromley. She now lives in West London, not far from the Portobello Road. She is the author of about twenty short stories, and her first novel, *Polly Put the Kettle on*, was published in 1975. Her other novels include Mrs Mulvaney, *As Time Goes By*, the bestselling *All the Days of My Life*, and *A Stranger to Herself*, *In Search of Love, Money and Revenge* and, most recently, *Cassandra*. She has also written *Hannie Richards*, a thriller about a woman smuggler, and a short biography of Vera Brittain.

THE CRY FROM
STREET TO STREET

HILARY BAILEY

PAN BOOKS
LONDON, SYDNEY AND AUCKLAND

First published 1992 by Constable & Company Limited

This edition published 1993 by Pan Books Limited
a division of Pan Macmillan Publishers Limited
Cavaye Place London SW10 9PG
and Basingstoke

Associated companies throughout the world

ISBN 0 330 32916 2

3 5 7 9 8 6 4 2

A CIP catalogue record for this book is available from
the British Library

Typeset by CentraCet Limited, Cambridge
Printed and bound in Great Britain by BPC Paperbacks Ltd

The harlot's cry from street to street
Shall weave old England's winding-sheet.

William Blake *Auguries of Innocence*

FOR EMMA TENNANT

The murderer known as Jack the Ripper killed six women in one square mile of East London between 7 August and 9 November 1888. These women were Martha Tabram, or Turner, Polly Nichols, Annie Chapman, Elizabeth Stride, Catherine Eddowes – and Mary Kelly. *The cry from street to street* is the imagined story of this last victim, who was never properly identified.

PART I

I BEGAN my journey back to England, after an absence of eight years, on the SS *England* which sailed from New York on 22 August 1888. I was not going on holiday – I had never had a holiday in my life and would not have known what to do with one if I had. Nevertheless, although my visit to Britain was no pleasure trip, I certainly did not anticipate, as we entered open sea on that fresh day, anything like the events which took place during the first three months I spent in London.

I had a nice pair of staterooms aboard ship, a bedroom and a sitting-room, all brightly polished wood and brass. I took my own things with me and set up a pair of small silver vases, a framed photograph, the glass and silver from appointments for my dressing case. I even had my own bed linen and beside all that, three trunks in the hold containing clothes and property. Though no slave to ease, like some I've known, which often brings ruin, I always travel in the best of style – for the comfort, of course, but also because it appears to be the only way that a woman alone can avoid insult and annoyance. A small fortune takes the place of a large protector in these circumstances. As does a revolver, I have also concluded. Therefore I rely on my trusty Colt for confidence, which I learned to use with accuracy up in the railway camps in my early days in Canada, where a big Russian anarchist, fugitive from his government, supported my trembling arm, as I aimed at a row of beer bottles on a stack of logs. Not, I have to say, that aboard the SS *England* any passenger would ever have occasion to produce a revolver over a foot long, weighing three pounds, though I had it with me, in my trunk, among the French dresses I had bought in New York.

So – the sky was blue, the sea calm and all was well, but for a couple of gentlemen who were pursuing me, whom I avoided as much as possible: a thickset man, Ethan Baverstock, a meat packer from Chicago, and a tall young man from London, Marcus Brown, who had recently been touring the United States for his own pleasure, it seemed, in order to shoot wild animals, encounter wild Indians and mock the manners of those to whom he had introductions. He was full of anecdotes about the primitive customs of the inhabitants, by which I mean the civilized ones – their lack of servants and the democratic manners of those who were employed as help, the strange food and unpolished ways he encountered. He deplored the condition of the South, reduced, he said, to semi-barbarism at the end of the Civil War, had been most at home among friends in Vermont where some culture prevailed. But in spite of measuring everything he'd met against his own standards, which I suppose we all do, he was a pleasant man, kind and gallant, unlike Baverstock, who proposed marriage and bed, in any order, each time he cornered me alone, and fumbled me when he could.

These two men, and the others who paid attention to me aboard ship, did, I think, believe my story that I was the young widow of a Scottish railway engineer from the North-West Territories, but their instincts gave them a different message. You can dress a woman who's led The Life, as we call it, as a lady and still men will follow her like dogs after a bitch in heat. From city father to cowboy they'll come across her, they'll bump and jostle her as if by accident, they'll propose all manner of things without

2

knowing what they're doing or saying. You can put the woman in a sack with a bucket over her head, or dress her as a bishop at the convocation of the Church of England, the result will be the same. It's something in her carriage or manner, maybe an odour she has about her, but I don't complain, since it's been my living from the age of fourteen.

Nevertheless, in spite of the burden of evading these gentlemen aboard a small mail ship carrying few passengers, I was content enough for the first three days of the voyage, though I knew there were considerations I was attempting not to bring to mind. By the time we were only two days from Southampton, where we were to dock, the inactivity a voyage imposes and the memories and anxieties I had were beginning to make me queasy in the stomach, a condition which had nothing to do with seasickness. I was afraid.

It had been eight years since I'd set foot in England, struck the pavements of the London I knew, that warren of dirty streets and passages – Whitechapel – that byword for a slum. I've never seen dirtier, and I've seen many a dirty street since, and streets that were no streets at all, just tracks, muddy or dry between sheds, tents and sod huts thrown up as shelter on the outskirts of some apology for a town, or where the railway navvies made camp in winter snow or dusty summer among bears, snakes and insects. These places were no fit habitations for men. But neither those places nor the Indian quarters on the outskirts of town, where the natives live half-starved, with children playing on the middens, seemed to me as bad as what I remembered about the worst quarters of Stepney and Whitechapel, perhaps because what happens there takes place under clear Canadian skies, near mountains or limitless and untouched prairie, and where at least there is enough space and work for those who wanted to do it.

My heart sank as I thought of those seeping alleyways

and courts, old buildings where families lived, as many as eight or nine to a room, crowded lodging houses at fourpence a night for a mattress on the floor, and the alleyways, railway bridges, courts, where people huddled without a roof over their heads at all. All this on the verge of a great rich city, like a piece of rotten meat hanging in a meat cage outside the window of a mansion. Canada's a rum place enough, but at least wherever you are you can step outside of a morning, maybe, when it's quiet for a moment, and look up at the huge sky and breathe in some pure air. In Whitechapel the air is always stale, laden with smoke, the smell of bad drains, the brewery if the wind's in that direction, and whatever's next to you – tannery smells, the abattoir, 60,000 people crammed into a square mile, all struggling for existence with even the babies coughing like old men. And the air seems dirtier because of the noise, by day costers' cries, people shouting, hammering from cart and barrel makers, clanging from brass foundries and the like, wagon wheels, whipcracks and horses' hooves, and by night arguments, women quarrelling, shouting drunks, pub pianos and singing in the street, while from windows comes the noise of rows between men and women.

Always, all the time, there were babies crying, crying for their lives – small wonder, for who'd want to be born into all that and who'd be the mother who bore them?

From the wooden hut I had first in Calgary, on the outskirts of town – then, all wooden houses (that was before the fire) – I could walk out of a morning, leaving the girls asleep, tumbled in their blankets, and walk up through the pines and look down and breathe freely in the silence. Sometimes I was afraid of the vastness and wildness and the absence of people, aghast suddenly about how far I had come, and how, like most of the settlers, I would never be able to go back. But even when matters went badly, even when I was afraid, I still had little regret for

4

the East End streets I had escaped. And then, of course, civilization in the shape of the railway came to Calgary, I came with it and made my fortune.

So now it had been eight years since I set eyes on London. That was on a winter's night when, under the railway bridge at about two in the morning, I was about to do my business with a slummer from the West End who was the worse for drink. Even as I leaned against the wall, while he fumbled with my skirts, it came to me that in two minutes my pimp Jim Bristow, who had seen me go into the darkness with a customer with a watch and chain and, no doubt, a few guineas in his pocket, would be along to hit him over the head and rob him, and it would be better for me if I acted faster and did it for myself. I was coming up sixteen, and at that age a boy or girl acts on impulse. Only later, when the consequences emerge, does the action make sense, if it ever does. At the time I was angry with Jim for denying me a watch, when he had just mutched a toff I had with me in Hyde Park the week before, and gained a number of guineas, how many he would not tell me. And I had not fancied going out that night, a rainy one, but he had made me, and I suspected he was trying to collect another girl, Rosa, to do his bidding and, as is well known, if a man has his own affairs and a girl who works the streets as well, they are partners; while a man who has two girls on the streets is just a pimp, no mistake about it. I was hurt by this thought of a rival. So, I stooped, as my customer opened his trousers, picked up half a brick from the pavement and, leaning back against the wall, slammed it against his head. I was through his pockets in a trice as he lay on the ground, finding a pocket-book with banknotes in it and a watch across his chest, made, it turned out, of solid gold. Then, afraid of Jim, and afraid I'd killed the man, I ran through the other end of the arch, and helter-skelter down in the direction of the river, with Jim after me, for he had been lurking so near he saw what I did. He pursued me, shouting, 'Hey! Hey! Stop, you bitch!' There were people about, tarts standing on the pavement, sailors, a woman with a pram, an old man on a stick, it was dark and the air was misty so I managed to duck in and out and lose him quickly. Who, anyway, in that neighbourhood, would heed a man shouting, 'Stop, bitch,' after a woman? My feet were wings with the terror of what he'd do to me if he caught up with me.

I went on running and running, but though I'd escaped the man I called my sweetheart, and others might have called my pimp (in fact he was both, a not uncommon relationship in those parts) I'd no idea what to do, or where to hide. It had just occurred to me on the instant that he had less right to that pocket-book and watch and chain than I had. I was the bait and yet again he was about to hook the fish. Then there was the watch he had not bought me, a sign of love withheld, and the business of Rosa and, I dare say, at the back of my mind, other things as well, one of which was the fate of poor little Ginny. She was a little girl of eight or so, blonde, with a cough, whom six months before he'd parted from her mother and sold off to a nobleman he'd met in a pub. He seemed to manage this easily enough. There were six children, Ginny the oldest, in a room in Stepney, the father in gaol for stealing a handcart. I can hardly describe her condition when I came into the lodgings I shared with Jim one night. There poor Ginny lay, on an old mattress in the corner of the room, bruised and bleeding and breathing shallowly. Jim was bending over her in a panic, offering her water she was unable to drink. It seems she'd been flung back at him with no thanks by Lord Pig when Jim – to ask if she'd given satisfaction – knocked politely at the back door of the house in the West End where he'd delivered her the previous evening. No satisfaction, and the girl no virgin, the customer had declared in a rage, when called. Then his

6

manservant had appeared with the tottering girl, and while the lord threatened Jim that if he didn't remove her the police would be summoned, the manservant had thrust this rag of a child at Jim, pushed them both out into the mews behind and bolted the door. All this, while the cook and a scullery-maid looked on.

Jim got her back to Whitechapel in a cab. He was lucky with his driver, for a man of Jim's appearance, a flash cove in white trousers, an embroidered waistcoat and red silk neckerchief, who hails a cab in the broad and well-swept streets of Mayfair, full of gentlemen in top hats and ladies in cashmere and smart bonnets walking little dogs, and demands to be carried back to the slums with a young girl looking something like a broken doll, ought to have been driven to the nearest police station and put in charge by the cabman. But no, Bristow's luck held and he got back without attracting attention. And so I fetched up with the poor girl. I chased Jim off sharply, for she was terrified of him, sent a child on the landing for a pail of water and I bathed and cleaned her as well as I could, put her in an old shift of mine, made her some tea with plenty of condensed milk, with the idea of trying to tidy her up and bring her to herself again and then, when she looked less bad, perhaps call for her mother or leave her at the hospital. I didn't dare fetch a doctor, for fear of the questions about what had happened.

All the while the child just lay there, staring up at the ceiling, incapable of speech. When Jim came back and put his head round the door she shook violently. He wouldn't tell me who the mother was, for fear, I suppose, that the sight of her daughter in that state would arouse some maternal feelings and she'd go to the police and get him into trouble. I made him go again, for the child was so terrified of him I thought she'd go into fits. I called in an old nurse to help with the bleeding, for she was terribly torn inside, I think, and for the next few days I did what I

7

could for her, putting her in the bed, and one morning when I awoke on the mattress and went to look at her, there she lay, cold and dead. She was a weak, underfed child, probably consumptive, and her constitution could not stand the shock and injury, said the nurse, and added I had better sort matters out quickly, or I could myself become involved in a trial over the death of a child and, for herself, she had never been to this room and did not know me and if I tried to say otherwise it would be the worse for me. I took the threat seriously.

Jimmy, frightened by now, had to send for the girl's mother. In the mean while the woman upstairs had dressed the child in a little clean nightdress she'd bought second-hand for twopence, good quality, with a little cotton lace at neck and hem, and by the time the mother arrived, weeping and wailing and tearing her hair, this good woman, who had four children of her own, had done what was right for the poor girl. A scene even now I find horrible to remember then ensued. The child lay still on the bed. The woman sobbed and ranted, talked of Ginny's virtues: 'She was a good girl. She never gave me no trouble. That child was an angel from God, if ever there was one.' She accused Jim of having deluded her into thinking he had found the child a place as a servant in a respectable house. She threatened him with the police. Jim, meanwhile, defended himself and offered money. The deal was struck. Half a guinea for the doctor who would sign the death certificate saying the child had died of consumption, a guinea for the funeral expenses, although both knew the child would go into a pauper's grave and the mother keep the money, and another guinea for mourning clothes for the family, which would not be bought.

I stood in the doorway with the woman from upstairs, who had put the nightdress on the little corpse. Meanwhile, her own children peeped round her skirt as the macabre scene went on, staring in awe at the girl's body. The woman's face was frozen but she said nothing. She was wise. It hardly mattered, I suppose, what was said and done, what money changed hands, for the child was dead.

For a good while few spoke to Jim Bristow, but the matter was overlooked soon enough in the day-to-day, week-to-week struggle to pay the rent, stay alive, straight and out of trouble. But although the affair might seem to have been overlooked, it would not be forgotten in the end. One day Jim Bristow would seek help, or silence, from someone who remembered the matter of the child's death, and not get it. And for me it was a different matter. That was when I found out what Jim Bristow really was. The woman from upstairs called him a devil. He was greedy, lacking in forethought, without any scrap of concern for any creature but himself. Perhaps devils are like that. All I knew was that when he wanted something, when he saw an advantage, he saw nothing else; he grabbed for what he wanted without thinking. He and his brother had scarcely known a home. They'd wandered out to fend for themselves like puppies who stray out of an open door almost as soon as they're weaned, and that street life of living on scraps stolen and picked up, sleeping rough, running with a gang, finding their parents for a night or two only when cold or sickness was too much for them, and not getting much comfort when they did, all that had played its part in turning Jim into what he was.

At that time they were beginning to spend the money subscribed for the conversion of the heathen down in the East End, having noticed there were just as many heathen there as in Africa. But this business of hymns and soup kitchens was too late for Jim Bristow, even if the trick would have worked for him. Anyway, now he had helped

9

to kill a child, and there's nothing worse than taking the life of another. That was one of the reasons why I ran away from him.

A second reason was that having seduced me, said he loved me, then sent me up west to make my fortune, he threatened to destroy me or commit suicide in the name of our love when a lady offered me a position in a house in Mount Street. There I would have been taken care of and could have done well for myself, but by his sobs, promises and protestations he persuaded me not to accept the offer which would have parted us, and so put me back patrolling the pavements and squares of London. Finally, when I fell for a baby, he put me into the hands of an old abortionist near Waterloo Station, who half killed me and made me sick for weeks. This occurred before the death of the little girl, but the memory of that illness also turned me against him. He was kindly at first when I was ill, but after a few days he was gone more and more often and I had to fall back on the tender mercies of my sisters and finally, sick as I was, to look after myself.

He was all over me once I was better but I saw I was in an alley with no way out. I urged him to get a job. He might get a barrow, I said, and set up as a trader, or, I offered, I could work and save up, and we could try taking a front room and sell something, beer, or groceries. I even suggested emigration, little knowing that when I emigrated it would be alone, and from fear of him. But Jim Bristow, though intelligent enough, had no vision. He knew of the profits to be got by me steering men into short-stay rooms round Covent Garden by night, or into the bushes of Hyde Park; knew how to reap the benefit of the fortune between my legs and what he could steal from time to time. He could see a life of taking his ease in coffee shops or taverns by day and visiting the theatre or the music hall or playing cards at Mrs Mundy's at night, and in general living like a Whitechapel aristocrat. His motto was, as they say in the sporting houses, live fast, die young and leave a good-looking corpse – and they might as well, for usually there's no choice.

So there it was: once happy and heedless and feeling immune to any trouble or woe, I had now taken the first bites of the bitter fruit all the women in our neighbourhood had to consume. Those women had looked at me in Whitechapel Road, skipping along in all my finery, jumping on to omnibuses, giggling and laughing, arm in arm with Jim, he, perhaps, with his pockets jingling after some coup he'd made, or a horse had come in first for once, and they'd looked, and how they'd looked, those women in the streets, with cabbages in string bags, or a jug of ale for the old man's supper, all looks sending me the same message, the same chorus of the same old song we all get to know in the end – 'You'll find out. You'll be sorry when you do.'

It could be argued that in the long run Jim Bristow did me a favour, for, it seemed, between the abortion and the sexual disease I caught my body was so mangled, like a country trampled over by an invading army, that I never after that got any pleasure from relations with men, which enabled me to keep my head over them. I was not one to give them gold watches and rings, drink away the sorrows they'd caused me, throw myself off a bridge crying 'Goodbye, cruel world' for the sake of love. I was from then on a whore by trade and a nun by nature, and it was Jim who created me. But I was not so grateful I ever wanted to see him again.

The night I ran away I fled everywhere, not knowing where to go, except out of Whitechapel, and finally dropped down on the steps of a church in Fleet Street, getting woken later by a policeman and told I couldn't sleep there. My heart was in my mouth because I still had the pocket-book and watch and chain on me. The rozzer tipped me the wink I'd be more tolerated, and safer, with the others in Trafalgar Square, so I walked through the dark and finished the night among the people huddling there. At dawn I woke very cold, my head on a man's knees. He was a decent man, thirty years old or so, from the North. He'd come looking for work in London and found little. He said bitterly, 'When I come here I'd a sum which would have paid my fare to America in my pocket, if I'd had the sense to see it. Now it's gone on my keep, and I'm stranded here with nothing. I wish I had that money back. There's opportunities in America. I'd go like a shot.' I pulled out the watch and chain and slipped it to him. 'There's your fare,' I said. 'Never tell who gave it to you.' Then I jumped up and ran for it, thinking he had his chance now to go to America or get taken up for theft of a watch and chain, whichever happened to him. I ran to the river and pitched the pocket-book in, then I hid the three five-pound notes in it about me and roamed about, looking for a place to buy a steamship ticket. It cost me three pounds and fifteen shillings. I hid out for four more long days and longer nights until the boat sailed, afraid Jim would find me, afraid I'd killed the man I hit and the police would be searching for me.

I embarked at Tower Hill, in a big hat I pulled down over my eyes so no one would recognize me, one morning in December 1880, barely knowing to which quarter of the globe I was heading. I had a little bag with me, containing items I thought I would need. It makes me laugh to remember what they were. There was a hairbrush, a lace blouse (I had an impression New York must be in the tropics), a tin of tea, a pair of silk stockings. Then I found myself in steerage, with fifteen adults and seven children, all crammed together and mostly vomiting. A woman lent me a blanket to wrap round myself.

Ten days later, confused and ignorant, sixteen years old and never out of London in my life, I arrived in New York. But I'd had a stroke of luck aboard for although they made every effort to keep the third-class passengers away from the others, I made contact with a first-class passenger, a Mr Geoffrey Bates, a railway surveyor travelling to Canada to assist in the construction of that exciting part of the Canadian railway system which was to travel from the American borders through the Rocky Mountains to the Pacific coast, an enormous and seemingly impossible task, but an effort which had to be made, or the country would remain, in an important way, disunited, like two separate states, divided by the mountains.

This contact I mention began with glances from deck to deck, the first-class deck naturally being out of bounds to third-class passengers, and ended in Geoffrey, a tall, brown man who had been all over the world on his business, even as far as China, meeting me stealthily at night by the lifeboats. This encounter led him to suggest that I might like to travel with him to the prairie where he was to begin his work and I, now knowing better from the talk of the other passengers what I was likely to meet when I arrived in America, and afraid of how I could manage, agreed.

It was in New York that I slipped out of the hotel where we were staying and put myself in the hands of a doctor who half killed me with his treatment of a venereal disease I had discovered on board ship. The pain of the scrapings and ointments was terrible. The result was a kind of mutilation: although outwardly I was a woman, I ceased as far as I knew in most respects to be one. From then on I felt no sexual pleasure. The doctor informed me that I had been a wicked girl and now would never bear a child.

By accident it happened that because of my association with Geoffrey, at that time my only rock and stay in trouble, I became part of an historic event – the creation of the Canadian Pacific line between the years 1881 and

1885. As it turned out, that historic event created my own fortune, too.

It was in the spring of 1881, after a dismal winter spent in a boarding house in Winnipeg, that we set out across the prairie from Brandon in our wagons, Geoffrey being part of the advance party of surveyors and engineers who were to work out the gradients and curves and put in markers for the thousands of men who were to come to lay the track for nearly 700 miles, right to the Rockies.

For those who have forgotten the history of the construction of the Canadian Pacific Railway, the story is this: the task was to link that part of Canada on the Pacific coast through the Rocky Mountains to Winnipeg in the North-West Territories, a total of 1000 miles of railroad track. At the one end the line would be laid across prairie for 700 miles odd, whilst at the other, on the Pacific side, the line would begin to crawl slowly up the mountain, blasting and bridging through the remaining 300 miles. It would be in the heart of the Rockies that the two lines would be joined together – Canada, as a country, would become one. In fact, even when the track through the prairie was half completed, they had still not even found the pass through the mountains on the other side. This lack of foresight on the part of the engineers was only equalled by the heroism of those small parties of men who tackled that part of the range known as the Selkirks again and again in an effort to get through.

And so, off we set into the limitless prairie. I posed as Geoffrey's wife, Mrs Bates, in this situation, for the navvy camps were full of clergymen. The truth is that Canada, as soon as it got shot of the infamous Yankee traders, began to work hard to become a highly respectable country. The men could escape this to some extent, there were so many of them, but there was no room for irregularities among the officials. I don't know whether this story of my marriage was believed. It was plain Mr

14

Bates was a gentleman, and I was no lady. Nor was I at that time capable of posing as one – this was an art I learned later, through necessity. Still, it might be said that three years on the prairie were the real test of who was a true gentleman and who was not. And Bates failed the test in the end, while many a less promising candidate succeeded.

I believe now that it was a privilege to be one of the first, and last, people (excluding, of course, the Indians) to set eyes on the prairie as it had been for countless thousands of years before and, due to the coming of the railway, was never to be again. As we moved along, always some twenty to thirty miles ahead of the navvy gangs, I saw the great plain from spring to fall, three times over, from the coming of the coveys of geese, snipe and duck after the winter and the springing of the great tall grass, the bursting out of willow and balsam, the daisies, tiger lilies and purple sage right to the coming of the first snows. I smelt the scents of this untouched land, saw the great herds of antelope and buffalo moving across the landscape.

At the place called Pile o' Bones Creek, which is now Regina, thousands of buffalo bones and skulls lay all along the river banks in the pens the Indians used to drive them into for slaughter. As the railroad moved forward, it broke the plain in two and drove all the existing life before it, not merely the animals and birds, but the Indians too. It was not just the army of men 12,000 strong, living in tents or whatever squalid shacks they could construct for themselves, nor the tiers of railroad cars, kitchens, offices and the like at the end of the track, but the noise breaking a thousand years of silence, the shouting and clanging as the track was constructed, the singing and swearing of men, steady hammers going down on ties and rails. Small wonder all the former residents of the prairie, from frog to wolf, ran ahead of it, as if it had been a prairie fire.

The horizons, as we moved, were seldom empty of a herd, a solitary animal, or a long line of Indians, the braves with their women and children and the horses they obtained from the white man carrying their tepees, cooking pots and the rest. Other Indians of course hung around at the end of the track where the lines stopped. These had already been corrupted by the American traders at places like Fort Whoop-up (now soberly named Lethbridge), who bartered guns and whisky for their skins and furs. These traders had been cleared out by the North-West Canadian Mounted Police ten years earlier, to the great relief of the Indian chiefs themselves, who saw the Mounties as the lesser of the two evils. But they had left evil knowledge behind. The Indians, too, knew well what the price of opposing the white man's advance truly was from the experience of the other tribes in America. News travels fast in these places, as it does everywhere. Also, the buffalo were dying out and the Indians knew in their hearts they were dying too. It was all good luck for us, otherwise we would have been faced with attacks from the Cree and Blackfoot of the plains. As it was, I was never confident, our party being small and ahead of the main body, that I wouldn't wake up one night to hear whooping and hollering and end up minus my scalp. I carried a pistol all the time, whether going to the creek for water, building a fire or whatever. But we had no trouble.

The Government had wisely decreed that the whole territory should go teetotal, chiefly on account of the Indians' shocking predilection for alcohol. Many's the man, of course, and woman too, who has lost employment, home, family and friends through this vice, but with the Indians, unused to alcohol, this fatal craving caused collapse immediately and almost universally. It took little for the noble savage to become an inebriate who would do anything for a drink, and this caused them to be much despised by the whites, who said that they would sell their women for whisky, a thing no white man would ever stoop to – yet I've seen many women, high and low, sold in civilized surroundings, so I thought this just hypocrisy. These natives had been fierce and warlike only years before; but now the buffaloes whose meat they ate and from whose hides they made tents and clothing had been slain, they were hungry and often ill. It was a pathetic sight to see the women with their infants begging for food.

Meanwhile, some 12,000 hardened navvies, men who had taken the railroads across America and often many other countries too, worked hard, got high pay and were faced with the prospect of nothing at the end of a hard day's work but a cup of tea. It would not do. Human nature being what it is, there was a big trade in the smuggling of alcohol and the making of it, too. The home-made hooch was very sinister stuff. However, this state of teetotalism throughout the territory was to help me greatly later. Part of my arrangement with Mr Hamilton of the North-West Canadian Mounted Police in Calgary was that I would supply my customers with drink as long as matters never got out of hand. That way, I profited and he knew where his problem lay, so we were both content.

And so we moved on, for three years, in rain and storm – the spectacle of lightning over the prairie, mile on mile of electric swords flashing down over the landscape, disappearing, then flashing down again elsewhere, was impressive. Alarming, too, since we at that time were the highest feature of the landscape, most likely to be struck by lightning, until the engineers improvised a lightning conductor to protect us. The spectacle of the early snows, too, turning that world to white, was equally astonishing. There were times when, rising and looking at the great arc of the eastern horizon turning red, the great sky overhead coming blue, I felt so pure I was like a saint. There were far more times when the emptiness and stillness made me feel I might go mad, the company of Geoffrey likely to make me kill him or him me. Then I was desperate to escape. The hardships were awful, too – the washing, the cooking on an open fire, the fuel-gathering, the lugging of water, and worse, even, the moments when we ran out of water and did not know when we would find more. There was a perpetual battle with the weather, mud when it rained, boiling heat in summer, the cold of the first snows and the dread that we would not get back to base before a chance blizzard struck us. I was desperate, as I say. I might have turned back, but what had I to go to except life as a whore or a servant in the little glum town of Winnipeg? The truth was, I was afraid to go on and just as afraid to turn back. Yet I survived it all.

Geoffrey, my prairie husband, did not. He did not die, but he degenerated. He held it against me, anyway, that I had infected him with gonorrhoea, which had necessitated a trip back down the line for painful and humiliating treatment. I denied the charge, but I don't think he believed me. The isolation, the responsibility for keeping the gang together in such primitive surroundings, had turned Geoffrey to drink. By the time we neared Calgary he had added opium, the use of which he had learned in China, to the recipe. This was brought to him over the mountains often in conditions of great hardship by the Chinese working at the Pacific end of the line.

The other two engineers of the team tried to control and hide his excesses, but he grew worse and worse, more brutal with his work-force – and with me, too. It was not far off Calgary when he beat a Sarcee Indian worker so savagely that the Irish foreman, seeing the madness in him had to drag him off the man, whereupon Geoffrey dismissed the foreman on the spot. The Irishman's wife, who had just come out to join him, did her best for the Indian, but he died. Savage fights, beatings and violence of every kind were not unusual on the line, but this episode was one too many: Geoffrey was becoming dreadful to all, as a man can become when he is powerful and living in areas where no white man ever put his foot, where there are no towns or cities, settlements, law or any civilization at all. He had become a tyrant, that is all, and made the mistake of showing it too close to a settlement where the men knew there was law and order administered from a fort, run by the North-West Canadian Mounted Police. Feeling against Geoffrey grew. There was nearly a riot.

So it was in the summer of 1884 when we reached Calgary that I jumped ship. We had been gradually approaching the Rockies. Their great forms stood out against the landscape and, looking over the prairies at them day by day, their snow-covered tops growing bigger and bigger as we advanced, I realized I could never tolerate railroad life as it began to penetrate the mountains, nor would I be able to live any longer with Geoffrey. He was getting to the point where a man turns on a woman and kills her. Her death might take only two minutes to accomplish – but the woman who does not see those moments coming and escape in time is nothing better than a fool. As we moved forward, I concluded that Calgary, then a mere matter of one fort, two missions, a store and a hotel, would soon become a town. Anywhere the railroad stopped became a town. They sprang up behind us. At that point the railway gangs would be in the mountains for years, work would be slow and each winter the gangs would have to retreat, leaving only a few hundred men up there to cut timber for ties and fuel for the engines. So the rest would come down into town in search of liquor, women and entertainment. (There was no future in the settlers. At that time I doubt if there were twenty homesteads along the whole track, so hard and dry was the land and so severe the winters.) But the railroad-men could be detained and the cowboys, loggers, trappers and the rest would all be attracted to Calgary once it became a railhead town. Why, while the town was still a tent-city two men set up a local newspaper, in which they instantly began to denounce me! This sign of progress and civilization convinced me. Here, I realized, lay my future. Here was my end of track.

I must admit I hesitated in my plan when the Blackfoot Indians mustered under their chief and said their lands were being taken away and destroyed by the railroad's progress. In the end good old Father Lacombe, who had lived with them, nursed them through epidemics and all for twenty years, went up the hills with a cargo of sugar, tea and tobacco and persuaded them they'd do better to arrange matters with the iron horse than foolishly try to fight it. This they did. It was just a last moment of rage – they were in no mood really to quarrel with progress.

That difficulty easily settled, there was a bright future for saloon keepers and whores. So, at the tender age of nineteen, I landed in Calgary, then set up shop in a wooden shack near the Bow River, just outside of town, with the help of one of my first customers, my friend and secret sleeping partner the Mr Hamilton of the North-West Canadian Mounted Police I've already mentioned.

Little arrangements of this kind are common in every society and in every country where the white man has set his foot, thank God, and in this way, only a few short years later, I had my lovely wooden house, which I christened Esmeralda's, with its verandah, on the outskirts of Calgary where it would not offend the respectable. Downstairs, a bar and space for dancing. Upstairs, for the girls, bedrooms done up in the very best of style. I also owned a piece of well-watered land further off which I rented for grazing to cattlemen bringing steers to the railhead. Hard work and useful tips from the customers made me a wealthy woman – a far cry from the East End where I was born and where I was nervously returning, not because I wanted to, but because I knew I must.

I was not born in Whitechapel at all but in a small, yellow-brick house in a respectable street in Hackney. All the houses were joined together. There was a patch of garden at the back where my father, a railway signalman, planted potatoes and cabbages, and an even smaller patch at the front, where faded grass and a rosebush grew. A feature-less street, dry and dusty in childhood, or cold, or hot as you dragged back with mother, and the shopping, baby sister whimpering in the pram. Then we would re-enter the house, to a well-banked fire in winter or lemonade in summer, read, play in the garden, be calm and safe. I was the oldest, Marie Anne; next down, a year younger, was Marie Claire; then, after that, eighteen months younger still, the baby Marie Jeanne (my mother was French and had been a seamstress with a famous dressmaker in the West End before she married). When we went to school, of course, in the classroom we became plain Mary Anne, Mary Claire and Mary Jane.

We grew up pretty, intelligent, lively girls, two of us resembling our mother, dark, with dark eyes and slender bodies, Marie Jeanne blonde and ruddy, resembling my father, a big, fair Irishman. Leading us all to church on Sundays dressed in our best, he would call us the Big Frog and his three Little Frogs.

It was indeed a dull street we lived in, one of many long, straight streets, all new yellow houses, a Baptist church on one corner here, a little grocer's there, quiet pubs, a drab little park – nothing special or remarkable about it at all. The man next door worked as a tram driver. The man on the other side left for the West End each day in a dark suit. He worked in the gentlemen's

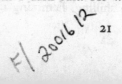

21

section of a department store, selling shirts. He was Mr Lloyd. Mrs Lloyd was a jolly woman, with five children. The oldest, Alice, had golden ringlets, and was my friend. If we had stayed there, I suppose I would have become bored in the end, but it soon ended, so I never got the chance. I remember the winter evenings with father reading his paper in a chair by the kitchen range while mother ironed, or mended, or made a little dress for one of us, her three Marys.

We were Catholics, my father Sean, or John, Kelly having come over as a boy from Ireland during the dreadful famine. My mother had prosperous grandparents, it seemed, Calais merchants, but her mother had run off and married a French seaman, and the family had rejected her. The seaman had given up the sea when four children were born, and gone to work in a small brass foundry in Kentish Town. My parents had met when my mother was taking her father his dinner and a jug of beer there and Sean Kelly had come in to ask them if they could knock out the dents on a much-prized brass plate, crushed by a door falling off its hinges in some farcical domestic episode. They often spoke of this fallen door, without which, they argued, they would never have met.

Then when I was eight, Mary Claire seven and Mary Jane only five, my father began to have pains in his abdomen, dying, in the end, of a growth in his stomach.

The operation they gave him to get it out when it was large enough to feel, and be identified as the source of his trouble, killed him. His pension was small, only ten shillings a week. We were forced to move from our house into lodgings. My mother took in sewing to try to keep us, but things nevertheless went down and down. We moved into worse rooms, then worse still. Mother had herself and three growing children to keep, and work as she would, with the sewing machine going day and night, making men's shirts for a shilling, hemming mounds of

22

sheets for ninepence each, the work was never sufficiently well paid or regular enough to provide. We continued the downward spiral, ending up in one garret room in White-chapel, with three beds in it and everything else we needed. If my mother had had some luck, or some harder determination, if she'd been prepared to find me employment in a workshop where children illegally rolled cigarettes or made string or buttons, if she'd even grieved less for my father, we might have survived better. As it was, man's oldest enemies, poverty, hunger and cold, were bound, pretty much, to win in the end.

My mother found something to keep her on her feet during this unequal battle and what she found was a pint of porter or a threepennyworth of gin of an evening. The pint inevitably turned into two, the threepennyworth into sixpennyworth and so on and so forth, until the drink ceased to help, and started to hinder. Not that she ever sank to the level of those hatless, dirty women, staggering and shouting, singing in the street or just silently reeling on from corner to corner, not knowing where they were going. Still, you may picture our little family at that time, just like a sentimental picture in a magazine. In our clean garret – for at least it always was clean – there would be mother, sewing, two pretty little girls, cleanly but poorly dressed, quietly helping with their needles, while the littlest plays with an old doll. The last of a dozen soldiers' tunics must be made by next day, at tenpence each, the work given out by a man who has to deliver four score by Tuesday, at one shilling each, and so thousands of tunics back to the fat man in Manchester, who spun the cloth and will deliver them to the War Ministry at five shillings each.

The pretty pictures never depict true want – the cold in winter, heat in summer, the weight of the buckets that had to be hauled upstairs to clean the floor, the fight against bugs and lice, the pain in the fingers forcing a needle through serge. They don't even show the beds, stretched across the room, and with the table, leaving hardly room to turn round. Nor do they (unless in another picture) show the weary children in bed, waking to hear mother's unsteady footsteps coming up the stairs, later on her body stretched across her bed in her clothes in the morning. What mother did, drunk or sober, was get us, even if hungry, to school. She always spoke to us gently and never struck us. She fed us when she could. In the end she had worked and worried herself into the grave. At twelve I was apprenticed to a milliner and at fourteen I had abandoned a life of making hats for fashionable women in favour of making money for myself, in the only way I knew. Ably assisted, I hardly need to say, by my good friend Jim Bristow, at the time only seventeen himself, but old in the ways of the world.

A year later my mother died – she said, of my disgrace, but I think of work and worry. At any rate, when she died she died in a clean bed, with a doctor calling and food in the house for her and us girls, all purchased with the good coin of my disgrace, the wages of sin.

I remember a Salvation Army band coming down our way one afternoon, and once they'd collected a crowd, listening to the music, a woman in a blue uniform and bonnet stood up on a box and addressed a drizzled-on crowd of respectable women with shopping, urchins who should have been at school, street corner layabouts and costermongers. She said, I remember, 'Though some of you are besmirched, you can be clean. The Lord Jesus will cleanse you white as snow.' A trader cried from his stall, 'Cockles and mussels, alive-alive-oh, penny a cup, halfpenny to pretty girls and sinners.' And I reflected that smutted and besmirched was only the half of it, or a quarter. If that woman but knew it, much of the crowd were filthy in and out.

I felt low after that, for a few days, and considered

changing my ways for the better because, after all, I was brought up religious, but I was not persuaded enough. In the end, we needed money, and the price of a woman's snow-white soul worked out at about a shilling a day while I could get half-crowns, five shillings and half-guineas by pulling down my drawers. Later I heard that General Booth, the man who set up the Salvation Army, concluded, and said, that the choice for us girls was to starve or sin, which showed he knew a lot more than his missionary woman on her box in the street. He was right. The same is true for men also, half the time. Looking back, I resented his dispatching a woman who had never known want in her life to Whitechapel Road to stand up in front of all and sundry and address us on the topic of sin.

My Russian, Ivan Somethingovich, the man who taught me to shoot, told me life was a matter of who had money, and who not, and God had nothing to do with it. He was by way of wanting to shoot and blow up the wealthy, had escaped the Tsar who persecuted him for these views, and joined the railway gang, where a strong back is enough and you can say what you please. He might have offered to marry me, he said, but would not, since marriage was against his religion. I responded that it was also against mine, as it seemed to me all too often for a woman it was a kind of respectable workhouse.

As we drew closer to Southampton I grew more nervous. I stayed in my cabin a fair amount, to be alone, and without my suitors, Baverstock and Brown. One morning, made restless by the confinement, I went on deck to sit and look out towards England, hoping to be soothed by sight of the sea, but always wondering how matters would go for me when I arrived. I wore my white dress, with lace insertions in the neck and wrists, white shoes and big shady hat, and felt every inch a lady.

As I sat, I tried to read, but my eyes kept wandering to

the horizon, and the sight did not soothe, for I was bursting to arrive, restless, after a week of inaction, and yet I feared what I should find on my arrival. Then a lady joined me, and asked if she might sit beside me, which I welcomed to some extent as I knew her presence would deter my prowling suitors – men, like lions and tigers, prefer to hunt prey when it's out of the herd.

The lady, Amanda McKay, was middle-aged and got up too warmly in an ugly coat and skirt, made, she told me, out of her family tartan, or plaid. She was returning from a post as governess in the household of a Member of Parliament in Ottawa to nurse her widowed sister in Aberdeen.

I encouraged Miss McKay to talk, having no wish to answer any questions from her side, for my story aboard ship was that I was the widow of a Scottish engineer, a Mr Frazer, and was returning to live with his parents in Scotland after his untimely death of fever. Largely ignorant of Scotland, except for what my patron, Mr Hamilton of the Mounted Police, had told me, I did not want to discuss too closely any details of the situation of my imaginary parents-in-law, so I encouraged her to speak of her own history. I heard much of her three brothers, one a minister, one a ship's engineer and one an officer killed at Omdurman, fighting against the Mad Mahdi. She spoke also of her sisters, their confinements, children et cetera et cetera, and of her childhood, glum enough, it seemed to me, but without want as my own had been. I remembered the blue dresses mother had sewed for the three of us before father died, while he smoked his pipe and drank a glass of beer and read to us from Dickens, for he was a book-loving man as the Irish often are, and I imagine it is from him I get my habit of persistent reading.

As we ladies both watched the smoke from another ship on the horizon, Ethan Baverstock came up bringing a deck-chair so that he could sit with us. He told us of his business, meat packing in Chicago, flourishing more and more now the cattle could be shipped by train rather than arriving thin and worn after long cattle drives across country. I responded with my tales of the encampments on the prairie as the Canadian railway was built (my imaginary husband, Mr Frazer, standing in for the gentleman I had actually accompanied).

I did not, of course, tell them my real history or reveal that my present prosperity had begun with bringing whores in wagons to the navvy camps in the Rockies. They were fearsome journeys, especially at the beginning of winter, when the snows began, and hard going when we arrived, but there was money, a great deal of it for all, and as we departed, the women flat out in the carts, we jingled as we went. The lonely men would stand on the track a mile from their camp, cheering as we arrived, running down to try to jump on the wagons for the rest of the journey, but we were guarded by a big half-breed called Johnny, with hair to his shoulders, and a small strong Irishman, Pat, both with rifles, so no disorder arose. In other places the whores came into the camps by train along the existing track, but out of respect for my erstwhile lover, even though he was sadly deteriorated by his drink and smuggled opium, the other engineers in charge would not offer me this facility. Though half the time they were doing his work as well as their own, they still supported his cause, feeling that by abandoning him to set up in business as a whore I somehow degraded him. So our journey was far longer, more uncomfortable and dangerous than it needed to be. But it's natural for men to stand by each other, I suppose.

Anyway, it was from those journeys that I made enough money to build my new house, outside of town, and buy out my partner, Mr Hamilton, to his profit, whereupon he purchased from their landlord the humble croft in the Highlands in which his parents lived, though I don't suppose he told them where the money came from. Just before the journey became too long and difficult for us, before the two sides of the railway joined up at Eagle Pass in 1885, a sickness hit the camp and we took it, too. The Irishman, Pat, and five of the women died within days of each other on the journey back. They were the Indians, Betsey and Flora, the half-breed, Hannah Long, who sang like a bird, Josephine O'Mahey and the woman from Bath, Nellie Rose, who had come out as wife to a track layer and fallen on hard times when he was killed in an explosion. The news went back to the camp and some of the men came down to help with the burial and make markers for their graves among the trees in the foothills of the mountains. When we arrived sadly back in town only I, Dolly Halloran, Frenchy Stillwater and the silent half-witted girl we called Vanya were left in the two wagons. It was a sad blow, and I wondered what to do next, with my big house half built, including a bathroom a duke would envy and a piano coming in all the way from Winnipeg and with women, especially white women, like gold dust in those parts. And white women are an attraction in a house like mine, that can't be denied.

Naturally, as I told Mr Baverstock some tales of the building of the railway, I did not say any of this. Nor did I tell him that part of my reason for returning to White-chapel was to recruit ten or fifteen pretty young women for my house in Calgary. In fact, if I got enough, I was ready to start up a new saloon in Regina or Medicine Hat in due course. I even dreamed of a theatre, too, for men in those parts crave entertainment, which I love myself.

Meanwhile Marcus Brown, the tall Englishman, joined us, revealing for the first time that he was returning to England after the death of an uncle. I think, from sheer nervous anxiety and restlessness, I must have begun to make eyes at him – in a polite way, mind you, more like a widow aboard a ship than a tart in a saloon wearing a red petticoat and no drawers. Nonetheless, I did it. The danger of our trade which I know but sometimes cannot avoid is a craving for attention, excitement and excess. In that life there is always something doing – a row between women, hair pullings and petticoat tearings, drunk men acting flamboyantly or violently. In my house I make them give up their guns at the door, but men used to a hard life can still make plenty of trouble without firearms. There's always movement and event in the life of a whore, drinking and gambling, wins and losses, rumours of theft, murder and hold-up and, at the back of all, always, fear of violence offered by the men. We are always over-stimulated, our nervous systems always strained, our senses agitated and in the end, unless careful, we come to demand excitement as some crave drink or laudanum. It takes one's mind away from the dismalness, the discomforts of the trade; and the contempt. In any case, we generally have short lives. We depend on youth and good looks for our trade and lead the life which destroys both. By and large, we live hard and die young and for us an early death may be a blessing. To consider that life in cold blood while you are leading it is unbearable. So, as I spoke to Brown, that old, vicious mixture of boredom and agitation overtook me. All this, taken with my anticipations of the future, made me so restless that, as we steamed steadily over the calm sea to Southampton, I forced myself from my seat and, saying I felt the beginnings of a headache, took to my cabin. Mr Brown, stimulated by my unsuitably challenging demeanour, was, I knew, disappointed by this departure.

I lay down in my bunk, thinking of my sisters, Mary Claire and Mary Jane. 'Look after your sisters,' my mother had told me before she sank into a final coma. They had been almost her last words, and the most important. I had been fifteen, Mary Claire fourteen, a fairly sober girl, though pretty and with many sweethearts, working selling hats in a shop in Mayfair, and Mary Jane had been twelve, and even then given to disappearing and coming in late without explanation. And I had not looked after my sisters. I had excitements and problems of my own. I saw that the rent was paid. I spent a night now and again in the two small rooms we had then. I lectured my sisters, lost my temper and went out again. I was not a good girl looking after my sisters and they were not good girls either. They resented me, stole my silk stockings, called me a whore and refused my orders to scrub the floor and the like. So things were bad and got worse between us, and in the end, of course, I ran away to America. I thought nothing of this for years, but when I became rich and settled I began to ponder about them and about the broken promise to my mother. Now I was going to find them, if I could. I feared the worst, too, that perhaps through my abandonment of them, one or the other, or both, had died or got into bad trouble.

I had sent a message to Mrs Mundy, a fairly trustworthy woman who ran a beerhouse in Commercial Street, asking her to get news of them and tell them, if she could, that I was coming. I had requested her earnestly to tell no one else, except her son, who for the neighbourhood was a strangely contained young man, not kindly or sympathetic, but intelligent. I hoped she was keeping to my instructions for I did not want to find Jim Bristow or any of the old lot at Mrs Mundy's as soon as I arrived, their hands out for Canadian gold.

Fearful as I was, as the voyage came to an end I began to look forward to my arrival. I wanted to set foot on solid pavements again, not wooden boards above a dirt street. London! Pavements! Gas-lamps! Theatres, music-halls, bookshops, department stores! Buses! Oh – the wonder of it all.

I began to remember one of the frightening times in

Canada when we were stuck on the mountain with an axle broken, just the Irishwoman, Dolly, the half-breed and me, while Pat, the Irishman, slogged off to the camp five miles away to borrow a wagon. The dark was coming down, a sprinkle of snow, too, and there was only one little lamp and a small fire we'd made beside the line to fight the solid darkness and the wild beasts in the forest. We sang every song we knew to cheer ourselves up and ward off the bears and wolves, though many of Dolly's own songs were so mournful and eerie I soon had to ask her to stop. When I tuned up with 'God Save the Queen' she protested that this was a song she could not abide, seeing our soldiers in Ireland as an army of occupation and the English as conquerors of her native land. Pat got through to us not long after dawn, by which time we were frozen and tired and reduced to chewing strips of pemmican, the dried buffalo meat the half-breed had in his pocket. This was a delicacy to him, so many of the buffalo being gone. But he had been reared in winter on it as a boy and it's the food of childhood you crave. Approaching England I couldn't wait for some good old cod and chips, piping hot and wrapped up in newspaper to keep in the warmth. Endlessly eating river fish got on my nerves and I yearned for a taste of that deep-sea fish they brought into the docks on North Sea trawlers.

Excitement gained on me. Whatever you think about London it's the hub of the universe, and if you're brought up near the docks you know it. Everything is sent to London – wood, gold, fruit, tobacco, rice, cloth. The dark warehouses of London docks suck it all in. It's as if a great pair of hands reached out from Britain, one holding a gun and the other seizing things from all over the world, grasping them and carrying them back to deposit at home. If you have money there's nothing in that city you cannot buy. If you have not got money, of course, it's God help you, but that's the same wherever you go.

Now, on my bunk, my head filled with scenes from the world I was returning to – the lights at night from gas-lamps and houses, the sounds of dogs barking at daybreak, cocks crowing, women quarrelling at the pumps in the yards, then wagons passing full of beer barrels, rolls of hessian, or piled high with bananas, with children leaping on and off, risking death to grab one.

In my head I heard costers calling 'Fruit, hardly bruised', 'Cockles and mussels, alive, alive-oh', the barrel organ playing, and at night, pianos in the pubs, people singing, footsteps – staggering drunks, strolling tarts, people going off to work at all hours – the voices of straying gangs of sailors calling out to each other in foreign languages, men and women shouting and always, at all hours of day and night, crying babies. What an anthill it is, always stirring, not like Calgary. Apart from my own establishment, and some like it, or the odd mounted policeman riding in late, this town mostly closed down early, started up in good time and had, all around it, the quiet of the prairie and towering above it the silence of mountains all untrodden except for generations of redmen. It is a frightening, empty feeling you get under a huge sky in landscapes so deserted, mile on mile of waving grass and rivers. There were times, especially in the railway camps on the prairie, when I'd have given my soul for the sight of a crowded pavement, a pub, a woman coming out of a fish and chip shop with the family dinner, a boy selling matches, a couple of girls, arms linked, walking along singing, some boys sitting with their feet in the gutter playing cards, while an omnibus rattled past. In Canada, sometimes, I've felt as if I were living on the moon.

PART II

We DOCKED at Southampton on 29 August and I took a first-class ticket to London, sitting in the compartment reserved for ladies only, together with my governess friend and a severe-looking lady in mourning. I planned to avoid Baverstock and Brown, since both had said they were travelling to London. Both had, in fact, separately asked me where I would be living after my arrival. I had answered both, shortly, that I should be spending only a day or two in London, then going directly to Scotland. Both, in fact, turned up in the corridor outside my carriage: Baverstock smiled and raised his hat, but dared not approach because of the other ladies; Brown actually put his head round the door and invited Miss McKay and myself to have tea with him in the restaurant car. I refused, Miss McKay accepted, which I think must have been a disappointment to him.

The fields, with their hedges and small clumps of English trees, seemed very small, the little villages we passed very permanent, as if they had rooted into the landscape, like the trees. In Canada I had heard exiled men talk nearly in tears of the fields, the old country churches, the brooks and streams of home, but like any slum girl I had barely seen any of this before I left. I saw the beauty of it now. They were harvesting the corn. Big horses were pulling reapers along the fields; one farm had a steam engine pulling. Puffs of smoke hovered over the yellow field of corn, half reaped, while men in open shirts and women in sun bonnets were tying sheaves and loading them on to carts. A woman sat under a hedge, feeding a baby.

We arrived in London in time for me to find accommodation in Fleet Street, which I did by the simple expedient of taking a cab there and entering shops asking if respectable lodgings were to be found in the neighbourhood. I had a job to keep calm and sober, as befitted a widow, because the short journey from the station to Fleet Street in a cab, at dusk, just as the lamps were being lit, the sight of the crowds, shops, restaurants and all the advertisements excited me so much.

I was directed by a Jew who owned a leather shop selling boots and bags to a place some doors up, a tobacconist; and so, just as the woman in charge, a Mrs Isabella Cooper, was closing her shop, which purveyed superior tobaccos and pipes, I arrived and asked for accommodation. She offered to rent me her own rooms above the shop, which consisted of a bedroom, parlour and a small room for luggage and boxes. I agreed and took the apartment for three months, saying that I had business to attend to, and friends to visit in London before joining my late husband's parents in Scotland, and that I wished to have my own rooms as I had a good deal of luggage and did not want to be a permanent, over-encumbered visitor in other people's houses.

My landlady was the plump and respectable widow of a captain of merchant ships plying between Liverpool, Africa and the West Indies, carrying cotton, tobacco and slaves, and, she confided, often outrunning the guns of the Royal Navy ships after trafficking in slaves was outlawed by Parliament. She had invested her husband's savings in this shop, dealing in one of his late commodities, after

34

he'd died of a fever in Kingston, Jamaica. She was delighted to let her rooms to a respectable widow like herself. I explained my lack of mourning clothes as I had done to others: my husband, I said, had implored me on his deathbed not to wear black for him.

I was pleased to obtain the apartments, which suited my requirements exactly. They were conveniently near to the East End where I would be looking for my sisters, but well inside the City, on the right side of London Wall. That is the city frontier, originally made by the Romans, which these days separates the world of riches and order from the world of grinding poverty and lawlessness. I knew enough about the latter not to want to live in it while I conducted my search. I was pleased, too, that after eight or nine o'clock at night the shop would be shut and there would be no one on the premises except for the servant girl to note my comings and goings.

And so I was given keys to the door at the side of the shop which would be my entrance, sent a cab to the station for my trunks and settled in, having first asked my landlady to place a bath in the boxroom, for I am always keen on cleanliness, probably because I have experienced so much of the opposite. I then got some tea sent up from the kitchen behind the shop. The maid of all work was a skinny London girl, Dora, underpaid, underfed and over-worked, I guessed. I drank the tea, unpacked a few of my books and personal items and hung up some of my dresses. Mrs Cooper then entered with her brother-in-law, who was to assist her in carrying her own effects to his house, where she would lodge while I was occupying her rooms.

I was raring to go after several days aboard ship, quickly changed from my travel-weary clothing, put on a simple rust-coloured cotton dress and matching bonnet and left, saying I was invited to supper at the house of a friend near Hyde Park and would get a cab in the street. I had become accustomed, I told her, to a greater degree of independence than might seem usual, because frontier life demanded this of women.

As I left I observed the servant girl, still at the mangle, wringing out sheets. I thought the less she knew of me the better. She was a sharp-faced girl, no more than sixteen and about five feet in height, thin as a rat, with a transparent, pale skin, like a ghost, fair hair scraped back over her forehead and bundled into a wispy bun at the back. Her pale blue eyes had flickered round the room quickly taking in everything when she brought up the tea. Her appearance, as much as anything else, reminded me of where I was going. So far I had only travelled through the better parts of London, where the more affluent were to be seen. This girl was a city rat. Children born in Canada, if their parents have any luck at all, grow tall (I have seen ten-year-olds as big as their own immigrant mothers) and their skins take on a healthier tinge. This girl looked like a stick of celery, reared in soot; her legs, under her skirts, were bowed; everything about her appearance spoke of London streets, including those sharp, pale eyes, for however much that poor upbringing damages the body, it sharpens the wits. Babies like Dora are born in a leaky room, with the others sitting on the stairs outside, put all day in the care of the oldest girl, who may be no more than five or six herself, while the mother works. They learn to play on the pavement, see what's to be seen, hear what's to be heard, keep away from the traffic on the road. Those who survive accident and sickness do not thrive well, but they come out of childhood with unequalled mental agility, though it is not of the kind an Oxford professor would recognize or commend.

I dodged past Dora without attracting her attention as she sang, rather wearily, 'Ta-ra-ra boom-de-ay', and slipped out, marching past St Paul's, just to look at it, treading the mile through Threadneedle Street and Bishopsgate to quieter streets of banks and the premises of those dealing in all commodities, mostly closed now. Lights still burned in a cobbler's windows, and there was the tap–tap–tap of his hammer.

It was nearing ten o'clock by then, but I knew that unless Whitechapel had changed a good deal since I was last there, the streets would still be full of people. At Liverpool Street I crossed to Spitalfields Market, where people were still rummaging on the heaps of discarded fruit and vegetables, even as the men were trying to put the refuse on the rubbish carts. 'Hurry up, mother,' a man said, leaning on his broom, as an old lady picked up a few leaves of cabbage or some such and put them in a sack for her rabbits or herself, I don't know which. I tripped across, avoiding the stares and trying to keep my kid boots clean. People were huddled around the big, soot-blackened church there. As I slid past down the street beside it a black shape rose up and a woman with a baby at the breast, barely covered by a shawl, said, 'Lady, have you anything for a poor woman with a baby?' and launched into a tale of a husband injured at the docks. I sped up, knowing that if I stopped and produced so much as a penny I'd be mobbed in a flash.

I cut away down the streets towards Commercial Street, moving fast, but not too fast, which would attract attention. I became more vigilant. I was a stranger, like an animal that's been away from the pack too long. I knew I must look and smell unfamiliar now to the inhabitants of those streets. A young drunken man, cap tilted cheekily over one eye, swayed up and offered me his arm. 'Might I escort you, madam, to wherever you are going? A lady such as yourself is in need of protection in an undesirable neighbourhood such as this.' Knowing he'd have his hands on my bag in a flash, then wrench it out of my hands and leg it down an alley, I gave him a violent jab in the ribs with my elbow and marched on, hearing him gasp out satirically behind me, 'And I thought you was a lady.' I threw my head up and sniffed, Whitechapel-style. I had my gun, of course, in the large black leather handbag I carried, although it wouldn't save me from a sudden mobbing, or a crack over the head from behind. But the narrow streets were crowded, as usual, which is a defence of a kind. And so, a little the worse for wear, I reached my destination, Cora Mundy's alehouse, which she had always kept in the front of a two-up-two-down on the corner of Brushfield Street and Commercial Street. A cage bird hung in a wicker cage out of an upper window, next to a drying petticoat. And what a smell in the street! That real smell of poverty, made up of overflowing privies at the back, broken drains, damp houses, cooking, unwashed bodies living at close quarters. Even the soap used to try to keep floors and stairs clean mingles with the other odours, making them somehow worse. How it all came flooding back – but I stepped boldly into Mrs Mundy's, putting a good face on things, and there she was, just as before, still standing there behind her trestle, a barrel on either side, tankards across the front. She was pulling pints for a couple of men in collarless shirts and heavy boots, who had, I guessed, just finished work. Out of necessity people work all hours in Whitechapel.

In Mrs Mundy's cramped front room there were three small tables in the middle with chairs and benches all round the walls except for the wall behind where she stood. There a door behind her led into the back kitchen. There were only three customers – the two men, and a woman slumped half asleep on a bench in a corner. There were gas mantles burning on either side of the empty fireplace but the woman was in the shadows so I could not see her clearly. Poor old cow, I thought, and went up to Cora Mundy. 'Hullo, Cora. Recognize me?'

She was a big, shapeless woman in an old black dress with a cameo at the neck and she wore a sacking apron because I suppose she'd been bringing in a new barrel from the yard at the back. Her face was big and pale and she looked at me shrewdly from two little black eyes, like currants in a suet pudding, the eyes revealing nothing of her speculations, although I knew their nature. Had she seen me before? If she had, was it wise to admit it? If she had not, what did I represent? What use could be made of me? Was I bringing good luck or bad? After a pause she said, 'Can't say I do recognize you. You put me in mind of somebody, though. Now, who is it?' Then she pondered, or pretended to.

'Come on, Cora. Think. You know me.'

She looked again and laughed. 'Oh, my Gawd – it's Mary. Mary Kelly. I spotted that little mole on your neck and suddenly it came back to me. Well. . .' she said on a long note, regarding me, 'you look fine. You've come to no harm since you took off.' The little currant eyes went all over me. 'You never got that dress here, nor them boots. Where you been? Not up north? You'd never have got that stuff there. Don't tell me – let me guess – that dress is French,' she concluded triumphantly. 'But,' she added, 'that makes no sense because we know you shipped out of St Katharine's Dock, third class for New York.'

I nodded. 'Right on all counts, Dora.'

'There was a man scouring the streets for you for days after you left so sudden. You know who. In quite a state, he was, saying all kinds of wild things. He was like a wild man when he found out. But,' she said quickly, seeing my expression, 'that's all in the past. Here you are back again. Married well, too.' She had spotted the outline of my wedding ring under my glove.

Whether she believed I had really married or not I don't know. I didn't contradict her. I did say, 'There's a certain person who I don't want to know I'm here. The individual just mentioned.'

'Of course,' she responded promptly. 'Say no more.

It's understood. Let the dead bury the dead, that's what I say. Now then. What will you have? A nice glass of ale? Or . . .' She winked at me.

I nodded. She wasn't meant to sell spirits for she had no licence, but she kept a bottle or two of gin under the bar for favoured customers. She tipped some in a beer glass and handed it to me, helped herself and made me a toast, 'England, home and beauty.' I drank to it. 'Though,' she said, 'you've been well away from this place, in my opinion. Glad you left, I expect, and finding things no better now than when you left. They're worse in fact. Trade's worse. Folk flood in from all over – Scots, Irish, country bumpkins, not to mention the Jews, they're all over the place, and the Chinks, they're everywhere else, so the rents go soaring up. Times must be mighty hard where they all come from, I say, if they want to come here and help themselves to the little we have.'

'More trade for you,' I ventured.

'Trade?' she said disgustedly. 'The Jews don't hardly drink and as for the Chinks, gambling's their game, that and sitting about fuddling their brains with opium. Well,' she added, on a less bitter note, 'it's good to see you back, and looking so bonny.'

The rumour was that Cora Mundy had a small fortune in gold hidden away somewhere on the premises, but such stories are common in poor places. Many an old man's had his head bashed in by some villain, or desperate soul, and floorboards pulled up to find the gold he never had. Myself, I think half her profit went to her pet son Harry, a giant even bigger than she was, who spent most of his time sitting idle in an armchair in the back room, reading the paper and marking up his bets in the *Sporting Life*. She needed him for moving the barrels, though half the time she did it herself, and sorting things out when it got rowdy in the alehouse and even her strength was not enough to stop the fighting. A fight at Cora's was worth running to watch. A crowd would gather to laugh when one occurred and the Mundys started throwing out drunks into the street like so many rag dolls.

Anyway, as she praised me for my looks, clothes and prosperity, she was still eyeing me speculatively. I told her my usual tale of widowhood and then got down to business. In a lower voice I said, 'I've come looking for my sisters, Mary Claire and Mary Jane. I think you knew them both. I want to help them if I can find them. Can we go in the back for a private talk?'

She brightened. It was a common dream, the dream of the relative back from making a fortune in the colonies, ready to save the family from want.

She looked round at the customers and pulled another couple of pints for the men easing their tired bones at one of the tables in the middle. The woman was still slumped in her corner. Cora Mundy beckoned me through the door into her private room.

Inside, a door at the back gave on to a small dirty yard where the privy and the beer barrels shared most of the space, except for when Cora let the butcher next door store an overflow, when it was also full of carcasses or the waste meat.

The only time I'd been out there a cat had leapt off a pile of bones and offal with a rat in its mouth. Mercifully the view of all this was obscured because the small window beside the door was too dirty to see from. At the back of the room was a dresser where cracked cups and unmatched plates stood in disarray. In the middle was a table covered in newspaper on which stood a pewter tankard and a plate, which had no doubt had on it Harry Mundy's supper. Harry himself was sitting in his torn armchair, from which the stuffing poked out in places. His feet, in slippers, were inside the fender of the fireless grate and he was reading *King Solomon's Mines*. Beside him on the floor lay the *Sporting Life*.

'I'd offer you a cup of tea, dear, but as you see the fire's out,' Cora said comfortably. 'Take a seat at the table, do. More gin?'

I shook my head and sat down on the wooden chair at the end of the table.

'Mary Anne Kelly, as ever was,' observed Harry Mundy, putting down his book and picking up his paper. 'Where's you sprung from, then?' He looked me up and down. 'City clothes and a country face,' he observed. There was nothing wrong with Harry Mundy's wits. I've known plenty with half Harry's brains in a much more prosperous way of business. His weakness was idleness, not stupidity. And being born poor, of course.

'Calgary,' I said shortly. 'I'm here looking for my sisters, Mary Claire and Mary Jane. Do you know where they are?'

'Mary Claire went up to Liverpool with a sailor a long time ago – five, six years ago. What was his name now? Sugden, I think. Edward Sugden. Right, ma?'

'Yes, I suppose so,' she said.

'Wilmot came by,' he told her, 'by the back way, while you were out front.'

'You told him no, I hope.'

'Didn't I?' he said with satisfaction, shaking his paper to get rid of a couple of flies. He took a short length of pencil from his waistcoat pocket and began to note something in the margin.

'As to Mary Jane,' Cora said, 'she's around and about.'

'To and fro,' added Harry, jotting down a calculation.

They were telling me Mary Jane, now twenty, was on the streets, getting her living from prostitution just as I had. I assumed Mary Claire was in the same game, if she'd gone off to Liverpool with a sailor. This news came as no surprise.

'What's a poor woman to do?' Cora remarked.

'Not marry a bishop, that's for sure,' I told her. 'Do you know where I'll find Mary Jane?'

'She's not been here for a bit. About a month,' Cora said. 'I'll put the word about you're looking for her. Am I to say she'll hear something to her advantage?' She looked greedy.

'No fear,' I said firmly. 'I'd have the whole of Whitechapel round me like flies. My circumstances aren't bad, but they're only modest.'

'Yes, my dear,' nodded Cora. 'Well, in your shoes, if I had anything, this place would be the last where I'd reveal my good fortune.'

'Seen any Indians out there?' asked Harry. 'Any squaws? Cowboys? Totem poles? Any scalpings and all that?' He must have been at Bill Cody's Wild West Show. I never told him how Robert Ford, who had shot Jesse James, had been two days at Esmeralda's.

'Hundreds,' I told him. 'But it'll have to wait. I'm pressed at the moment. And I'm eager to start finding Claire and Janie. For the rest,' I added, giving the words some import, 'keep mum. Not a dicky bird. I'm going incognito for my own purposes.'

Harry gave me an incredulous, sidelong look from his chair. Cora also nodded. 'Please God you find them poor girls very soon,' she said piously.

As we walked back into the other room she took off her sacking apron, dropped it behind the bar and addressed three Russian sailors who had come pushing through the door, arms linked. 'What's it to be, gents? A nice glass of ale?' To me she muttered, 'Do you want news of Jim Bristow?'

'Only if he fell under a brewer's dray,' I responded.

'I've got to disappoint you, then,' she said. She was pulling a pint as she spoke. She put it on the bar. 'Here you are, Ivan,' she said. 'That's tuppence. Two pence,' she added, speaking loudly and clearly, holding up two fingers. He put his hand in his pocket and pulled out some coins. 'What ship are you off?' she enquired, quickly taking a shilling and a penny from his extended palm, putting the coins in the till and closing the drawer.

He searched for the words. 'Murmansk. *Ekaterina*, six days,' he announced. 'Pretty girls,' he concluded, looking at me.

As she pulled the next two pints she muttered to me, 'Ask in the corner if she has any news of Mary Jane. She's an unfortunate by the name of Cath Eddowes, but you've got to start somewhere. Give her a shilling,' she appealed. 'She's down on her luck.'

And she'll spend the shilling here afterwards, thought I, so you'll benefit; but I went over to the slumped figure leaning into the corner, motionless, barely detectable, for the fizzing gas mantle cast some light into the room, but not on to her.

I went up close and sat down on the bench beside her. I looked at her. She was quietly asleep, a woman of forty to forty-five with a big, tired hat with cherries on it askew on her dark hair, which had streaks of grey in it. She wore an old grey cotton frock, partly rucked up so you could see her legs were splayed, and a good length of leg, in wrinkled black stockings, from knee to ankle, ending in a shocking pair of black boots, the leather all wrinkled up, several buttons missing. Her mouth was open; she was breathing heavily, nearly a snore. In spite of all that, she wasn't too bad considering everything; she had nice high cheekbones and a well-shaped mouth, and if her hair under the bonnet was falling down, it was abundant and curly, which counts for a lot in a woman.

I picked up the thick, work-worn hand from her lap and pressed a shilling into it, 'Mrs Eddowes,' I said in a loud voice, 'can you help me? I'm looking for my sisters, Mary Claire and Mary Jane Kelly.' Perhaps, I thought,

Harry Mundy was right in saying that Mary Claire had gone to Liverpool. But perhaps she had not, and was still in Whitechapel. Or perhaps she had gone, then come back again.

Catherine Eddowes came round a bit when she felt me pushing the coin into her palm. Her fingers tightened over it, and she muttered, 'Kelly – yes. That's me.'

'Mrs Eddowes,' I said, 'it's my sisters who are called Kelly.'

She opened her eyes, large and dark, and answered, 'Find your sisters for a shilling, is it? I've done worse, for less.'

I had no doubt of it. She mumbled on, 'I'm Jane Kelly, sometimes. I'm married to John Kelly – sometimes.'

I hoped I wouldn't have to hear one of those long, complicated Whitechapel sagas, full of husbands, children, beatings, landlords, accusations made and refuted, quarrels and the like. I hoped, but I knew I might have to listen. She hailed from elsewhere, this woman, Kelly or Eddowes, or whatever. She had a touch of the North in her voice. Half Whitechapel, at that time, came from somewhere else, as if they came in on the Thames tide, along with the household rubbish, broken casks, bits of wood, discarded paper. What was her story? A marriage failed, so out into the world alone to pick up with some other drinker and start a new little home, just the two of them, a bottle of gin between? Or a solid tart's career starting as a pretty girl, worth half a guinea picking up clients on the promenade at the back of the music-hall, then, a few years later, down to five bob in the West End, and so down, faster and faster until it came to a fourpenny stand-up in an alley, enough for a bed in a row in a dosser, or a good, long drink (planning to use the money for the first, then being tempted and using it for the last). And then, she'd be lucky not to catch pneumonia on a cold wet night, get picked up and die in the hospital. It was to prevent all this I wanted to find Mary Claire and Mary Jane. That life was nothing. It meant grim city streets from which the only relief was drink – or the dream. This dream was of true love, of a rich kind protector, of being taken care of, but as the streets and the men wore you down and down it grew harder and harder to believe in, and, when it finally went, so did you.

In any case, whatever Cath Eddowes' life had been, it had come down to this, now – snoozing, half-drunk in Cora Mundy's alehouse. The Russians were getting noisy, first shouting, then laughing, then bursting loudly but sadly into a melancholy song. The young one, seventeen or so, with red cheeks and a blond fringe, was crying, I think.

Cath Eddowes had gone into a daze, the fine black eyes were staring into space. I squeezed her hand firmly to bring her round. 'Well, dear,' I said, 'can you help me?'

'The police,' she mumbled.

'Do I look like a policeman, my dear? I'm just a woman such as yourself looking for the only relatives I have left in the world.'

She rallied a little. 'I know. I know,' she said. 'I had a sister once, a pretty, kind girl. But she went wrong –'

'Yes,' I said, trying to keep my patience. 'Not the only one, I dare say, the world being as it is and men what they are.'

'And now she's no more.'

'Very sad.'

She spoke, as if in a trance, of the country, open fields and rivers, the maypole dance on May Day. 'Then, ruin,' she said. 'Love, but it was not fated to last.' Whores are sentimental, or else as hard and tough as railway ties. Thinking of this, and a shilling wasted, I was about to leave, when she said, 'What are their names, your sisters?'

'Both Mary Kelly,' I told her, again. 'Mary Claire and Mary Jane.'

'There was a Mary Kelly had a room in a house where I lodged.'

'What street? When?' I urged. 'I'd be most obliged if you could tell me.'

'Mm,' she said. Her eyes closed and she threw her head back, singing very loudly and in a nice contralto:

'Father, dear father, come home with me now.
The clock on the steeple strikes one.
You promised, dear father, you would come home
As soon as your day's work was done.
Our fire has gone out, our house is all dark,
And mother's been watching since tea,
With poor brother Benny so sick in her arms.'

She concluded with some satisfaction:

'And no one to help her but me.'

Her speech was clearer when she sang. I was desperate. She might have been mistaken about a Mary Kelly at her lodgings, or even if she was remembering accurately, the woman could have been another Mary Kelly – it's a common enough name, God knows; apparently even Cath Eddowes herself claimed it from time to time. Yet I didn't want to depart without finding out what, if anything, she knew.

I tried another shilling, pressed it into her palm again. The fingers closed, then opened. 'No, no, dear,' she said. 'I don't need payment. This Kelly, a fair woman, quite young, was at Mr Murgatroyd's, near Goulston Street, in a room, with a feller, I think. She left – well, before Christmas, I know.'

'Thank you, Mrs Eddowes,' I said, rising.

'The landlord cut up rough. She did a moonlight flit, two months' rent unpaid. You might ask how she got away with two months in the first place.'

'You might,' I replied. 'Well, good luck to you, my dear.'

'Yes, yes,' she replied wearily, now looking me muzzily in the face for the first time since I'd approached her. Those tired eyes told me that very little hope of luck remained in her. There was just a spark, though. 'I'm going down to Kent with my man, hopping.'

'Nice to get into the country.'

'Nice,' she said. She started a song about a blackbird on a twig.

As I left, Cora Mundy called out, 'Where shall I find you, if I get some news?'

'I'll let you know soon,' I called back. I did not want to give her my address. I didn't trust her not to send all and sundry to my lodgings to see what they could get.

I turned back to the woman as I went out, calling, 'Good-night, Mrs Eddowes,' but she did not respond.

And of course I never saw Catherine Eddowes again, for a month later she was murdered.

It was late now, too late to take dark streets to Goulston Street, walk up crumbling stairs, bang on doors in an unlit building, waking tired children and men who had to get up at four next morning. I had another reason for getting back to my lodgings in Fleet Street, too: upwards of £2000 in share certificates and notes, a bag of gold nuggets and some jewellery I'd brought across the ocean in a strongbox in one of my trunks. I planned to entrust all this to a London bank. The colonial banks had a habit of going bust or getting robbed, held up or absconded from by dishonest employees. There were solid Canadian banks, it had to be said, but I wanted my cash safe in good old England, and the sooner the better. It was my savings and hoardings, enough to buy me a big spread in Canada, a large house with a couple of acres here in England, to keep me in modest comfort, invested at 3 per cent.

I walked wearily back to Fleet Street, satisfied that after

48

only a few hours of investigation in Cora Mundy's ale-house the word was out that I was looking for my sisters and I had even had rumours of them – of Mary Claire in Liverpool, Mary Jane in the very locality where I was searching.

It was, indeed, very strange, letting myself in through the side door of the tobacconist's, walking upstairs and, alone, entering my apartment. Carriages came past in the street below. People went by talking from time to time. Nevertheless, it was a far cry from the singing, the noise in the bar, the piano, the men's feet up and down the wooden stairs of Esmeralda's, the laughing, shouts, noise all night till dawn and beyond it.

Tiredly, I took off my bonnet, flung it on a chair in my sitting-room. I let down my hair, took off my clothes and boots, washed in the basin of unfamiliar-smelling water, put on my nightdress and sank into bed. Sleep overcame me as soon as my head was on the pillow.

Dreadful nightmares ensued. Only an hour or so later, as the clock of the church nearby struck one, I was awake in the dark, wild-eyed and sweating. I'd found myself in a court, big dark buildings all round like black walls, running towards one of the alleys. At the bottom of the alley lay a road – I could see the street lamp at the end. I was being pursued. If I could get to the road where there were lights and people I might be safe, but my feet were sliding on the slick of filth lying on the stones of the court and he, my pursuer, was gaining on me. He caught me, cornered me against one of the black walls – that was when I woke, terrified, sat bolt upright as you do when afraid of a dream.

At first I did not know where I was. The curtains were drawn, the streets outside dark and silent. A carriage with jingling harness went past. Then I remembered where I was, back in London, far from my house in Canada near the river, with the forest rising in the distance. I breathed

49

deeply, became calmer, and told myself the strangeness of everything had disturbed my nerves. I went back to sleep. And yet, again came dreadful dreams of being pursued through narrow, empty streets. Broken gutterings dripped on my head and I knew the drips were blood. In a panic, still with the monster behind me, I reached the waterfront, where dark ships lay at anchor. A huge sky of scudding clouds moved overhead. And on the deck of one of the ill-defined craft were two girls in short dresses, hand in hand. In my dream I thought they could save me, or I them, I was not sure which, if only I could cross the water to the ship. Scanning the edge of the dock in terror, I could see no companionway to the boat, only a gap too big to jump, with murky water swirling below. I knew behind me my attacker, with what I saw as a wharfman's hook in his hand, was coming up to me. And I knew suddenly, when he had killed me, he would get on to the ship somehow and kill Mary Claire and Mary Jane.

After that, tired as I was, I dared not go to sleep again. I lit the gas and sat reading a novel by Emile Zola about a whore, Nana, whom he calls the Gilded Fly (how such as us do fascinate the men); dawn came and the street below began to start up for the day with the sound of horses' hooves, wagon wheels creaking, footsteps and voices.

At six I went down in my wrapper to the kitchen, intending to make myself some tea. There I found the girl servant, Dora, in her nightdress, letting out of the back door a young ruffian with a head of blond curls and his shoes under his arm. Saying nothing, I filled the kettle and put it on the kitchen range. She hastily rebolted the back door and set to riddling out the range and opening up the draught so the fire would come up. I leaned against the sink, waiting for the kettle to boil. 'I'll say nothing about this for the present,' I told her, 'but don't let me catch you at these tricks again.'

She stood up and faced me, looking sullen and washed

out, but I knew I had her where I wanted her. 'Go upstairs and tidy yourself,' I commanded. 'I'll make my own tea. I'll need my bath at eight, plenty of hot water, and breakfast after that.'

She slipped off. If I had secrets to keep, or needed any errands run, I could be sure of her co-operation. One word from me to her mistress about her carryings-on and she'd be turned out without a reference, and what would she do then? In fact, I thought, I might as well offer her the chance of coming back to Canada and working at Esmeralda's. She was well on that path already, the chit, at less than sixteen years old, so she might as well try it in a place where a whore can find more opportunity. There's a woman famine out in those frontier-lands and many a whore has married an up-and-coming man and eventually found herself wife to a rich rancher, or a man in government, and nothing said, even if it's known, about how her career began.

I spent the next hours unpacking and making up an advertisement for the Liverpool newspaper and *The Times*. The message read, 'If Mary Claire Kelly, otherwise known as Marie Claire Kelly, late of Whitechapel, London, will communicate with Messrs XYZ of ABC, she will hear something to her advantage.' I would add the name of my solicitor in London when I had appointed one. The final words, about something to someone's advantage, will, I know, get any message to the person for whom it's intended, over mountains and plains at the other end of the world, though it take half a year.

Earlier than eight a subdued Dora was carrying up pails of hot water for my bath and before nine I was dressed and out, my sleepless night only affecting me by making me quicker and more energetic, though I imagined I would pay for it later.

First, I went to the bank with my box of valuables, well received by the manager, who then made some effort to establish, since I was a widow, what other man – father, brother, uncle, reliable friend – was responsible for me and my fortune. Perhaps because of my bad night I did not give him my usual soft answer, but told him I believed I had heard that, thanks to the Married Women's Property Act of 1870, I was now responsible for my own money and property, being over the age of twenty-one, and that I had no need of other help.

'I hope so, my dear lady,' he responded, a warning in his tone. 'I do sincerely hope so.'

'Thank you,' I replied and, as they say, swept out with my nose in the air.

To the solicitor, Mr Ratcliffe of Ratcliffe and Ratcliffe in Mitre Court, I was more civil. I went there simply because I had heard Ratcliffe's name used by one of my old customers in Calgary, poor Joey Fitzgerald, who had died of consumption. It was Mr Ratcliffe who forwarded from London the money he was always awaiting in Calgary. His family, he sometimes said when drunk, paid him to stay away. Sometimes, again when he was drunk, he wrote to them, pathetic scribbles of apology, asking forgiveness for some unspecified crime. They never wrote back. So that there would be no contact with him at all, they employed Mr Ratcliffe to send him remittances.

The frontiers have their complement of these young men from prosperous families, sent out to make a life for themselves because there is no future for them in England, or sometimes, like Joey, because they have done wrong. Only when they have been dispatched thousands of miles can the family again hold up their heads, their disgrace being well away in desert, in jungle or on the prairie. These poor fellows succeed or fail – or just die like poor Joey, killed as much by homesickness as anything else, I daresay. What terrible crime he had committed I never found out – gambling money he didn't have, getting a girl into trouble, something like that. Whatever it was, I don't suppose it was much by Whitechapel standards. Well, so be it. He had died one winter in his shack, snow coming under his door, fire out and a bottle of hooch to hand. And I had come back alive.

Ratcliffe was a calm, thin man of forty or so, behind a mahogany desk in a solid but dusty office. He had a young family upstairs, I guessed, judging by the sounds. I explained I had heard of him from a certain Joseph Fitzgerald, whom, I claimed, my husband and I had tried to assist in Canada. Ratcliffe agreed to take care of the deeds of my house and farmland and to act as my man of business in London if necessary.

I told him the Scottish widow story briefly, but although he had a long, grave, thin face very suitable for a respectable solicitor, he had quick eyes, and a trick of raising his eyebrows in enquiry which made me suspect a sceptical, and tolerant, turn of mind. He was barely worth trying to deceive, but I felt it was only civil to seem to try. I explained that adverse circumstances, family difficulties, the long distance between us, had caused me to lose touch completely with my sisters, and that I was now attempting to find them. Would he, I asked, accept letters and messages for me, as I was not sure what my movements would be? He suggested newspaper advertisements, an approach to the police, and, if that failed, he thought a private detective might be of assistance. He could recommend a reliable man. I told him that if my own enquiries failed I would certainly consult him.

'If you feel equal to the toil and difficulty . . .' he said uneasily.

'A duty,' I assured him, 'I am happy to undertake.'

But he still looked doubtful.

I thought, as I left, My God, pretending to be a member of the weaker sex, while still managing your own affairs, doesn't half take it out of a woman. Then, full of excitement, I jumped on a bus for the first time in eight years, paid my twopence, sat down beside an old man in a silk hat and was carried off through the wide busy streets of London, not knowing whether to laugh or burst out crying.

Only a few miles from the slums of the East End, all was prosperity – shining carriages waited outside large shops with gleaming glass windows; ladies in large hats and gentlemen in toppers strolled along; servants in trim uniforms did errands; clerks in bowlers hurried with messages; boys on bicycles with big baskets in front ferried meat and fish to big houses. Who, in these broad and open tree-lined streets, under a blue sky and in late summer sunshine, outside these well-kept houses where the letter-boxes, knockers and bells had been brought to a high polish – who could believe there was anything wrong with the world? The country was at peace, a third of the map was red, we were at the hub of a mighty and benevolent empire. Down Whitehall the Horse Guards stood firm, great ministries ordered the affairs of state and as soon as the members had returned from their holidays, the Mother of Parliaments would be in session. And the theatres would put on new plays.

I began to consider staying in England, setting myself up at ease, where there were no bears or Indians, snow-storms or droughts, where there was plenty of hot water and servants, and a lady was not required to do anything. Indeed, she was under strict orders to do nothing. If that were my choice, then I would marry to make myself respectable, though I was not sure whether, after my independent life, I would be able to submit to a husband in all affairs, nurse him when sick and keep his house as a matter of love, and duty.

I took myself off to the Army and Navy Stores and had a cup of tea in the restaurant. There, I glanced about at the other patrons. There were two respectable middle-aged ladies, both in mourning, with a girl, daughter of one, perhaps, in blue; two dressy ladies with tight waists and high feathers in their big hats; a gaggle of suburban housewives; an old lady in black, with a pale woman in grey, her paid companion, I guessed. The only man there was a ruddy-faced clerical gentleman, free on a weekday of course, and his wife, a bitter-faced matron, a stranger to any joy if ever I saw one.

As the waitresses moved to and fro with their trays, I felt becalmed in a sea of women sheltered from all harm. They were calm-faced, mostly, but it was the calm of an opium addict with his pipe, and, under the calm, as with the addict, who knew what dreams, fevered, mournful or terrifying, swam about? The society ladies in their big hats looked a little more alert; one laughed at something said by the other. One other patron, in a corner to which the waitress was going with a tiered cake-stand laden with confections of every kind, had a cheery look. She stared out the vicar's wife, whose glance suggested repressively that cream cakes in mid-morning were unsuitable fare, and then turning her glance, caught my eye and gave me half a wink from under a grey silk bonnet, which matched her coat, both items French, if I knew anything. She had rosied up her cheeks, too, though it would have taken a keen eye to detect it. An actress, or a singer perhaps, with a rich protector, or just a girl who'd fallen on her feet? At any rate, being of the same general species, we knew each other. I dropped an eyelid at her, returning the wink, and she settled to her éclairs. Concluding that it was too late for me to join the lady class, I finished my tea. At that moment those worthy ladies, my fellow customers, appeared to me to be only one step up from so many Mohammedan wives, made to wear veils and live behind a screen. I knew I could never manage it, however hard I tried. I might succeed for a while, then I would break out again.

So I set off over the carpeted floors of the vast

emporium to get my shipping order for the Villa Esmeralda settled. A bolt of red silk, a bolt of red taffeta, two of red flannel, two of white, for the realities of a cold climate have to be accepted; a new piano and a pianola and many rolls of music at ten guineas, so we could have tunes when we felt like it, even when the pianist was drunk. I bought two brass bedsteads, a wagon of bed linen, a bale of new chemises, drawers, stockings, lampshades, lamps, canned food of every description. There were times, in the snows, when we'd had to eat moose, and I do not recommend it. Worse if anything, in times when the trains were not getting through, we came close to scurvy for want of fruit and vegetables. I bought netting against insects, netting for the windows. I bought fans for the ceilings, medicines, bandages, splints. (In Calgary we had a doctor, funnily enough, a woman. The Canadians make few difficulties for lady doctors, only too pleased, I suppose, to have one at all in the wilderness.) I bought facial lotions, hairbrushes, toothbrushes, a gallon of lavender water, and rouge and powder from a discreet lady assistant in a corner. I bought insect killers of every kind, candies for the girls, a fancy dog-collar for Dolly Halloran's mongrel dog, the only creature she loved in the world, and bangles, beeswax, new pans for cooking, a patent bottle opener, louse combs. In short, I bought everything necessary for a large household, if of an unusual kind, situated in a wild place where the railway had only just established itself.

I had seen some time ago that I would have to establish a superior sort of business. Because of the railway a higher kind of civilization and better standards of life were emerging. My clientele was changing and I sensed would change further. There would be more lonely clerks and storekeepers, and unsatisfied respectable farmers married to wives in their sixth pregnancy, fewer trappers, loggers and cowboys, no railway navvies at all. The last had been all too ready to take a squaw on a blanket at the back of a barn, if that was all there was on offer, and at the start of my career that often *was* all. In any case, many of them were fit only for those conditions, being dirty and lousy and uncouth after so many years away from any kind of civilization. But times were changing fast. I dreamed of discovering a girl here who could play the piano well and sing. Even if she had a wooden leg and a glass eye, I'd import her, along with the beds, the rouge and the pianola.

For my loyal half-breed I ordered a full dress suit: trousers, stiff shirt, silk hat, tail coat, even down to the white kid gloves and silk-lined cloak. I knew he would like the suit, for he'd often pored over the picture of a gentleman going into an opera house in a story in a magazine we had. On the other hand, when he put it on he might find it enormously restricting, after his buck-skins. And I knew he would wear all this finery with moccasins, for he couldn't wear shoes. If he would not wear the suit in the end because it constrained his move-ments too much, I would make him do so on special occasions, for I couldn't resist thinking of the impression he'd make, a giant, with his long black hair coming down from under a silk hat, perfectly dressed for a West End evening (but for his moccasins). The assistant who took the measurements from me scarcely believed the size of the man and thought, I believe, I had made some mistake.

I bought a new, splendid mouth organ for the Negro who hung around the place, sometimes singing his plan-tation songs for the customers and doing that lively nigger dance they call Jump, Jim Crow. To be quite candid, this was the purchase I most enjoyed making, when all else was done, for at night he would sometimes sit alone on the verandah in the dark, playing and singing sad, barbaric songs I found most affecting. In spite of their strange rhythms and tunelessness they seemed to call up and yet soothe pains and troubles I was not conscious of in my daily life. They were quite different from the songs with which he used to entertain his masters, when he was a slave in Mississippi as a young man. Freed, he became a roamer, and washed up on my shore, old and broken. What had happened to him in life I don't know. He was nearly beyond all speech. He mumbled. His sentences were confused and sometimes meant nothing to me. He could still sing, play phrases on the piano sometimes. It was as if the music was more deeply embedded in his mind than speech. Perhaps this is so with all of us – drunks and small children, beyond or before rational speech, still sing, or try to.

Sometimes, his discordant songs, which must have had their origins long ago in the jungles of Africa, became unbearably painful to me. I would shout, 'Shut your row, nigger,' and pretend I hated it, but I think he, whom we called Blackie, knew better.

So from there, my commissions done, I skipped luncheon and left the busy but orderly streets full of wealth and luxury and took a bus to Whitechapel High Street, passing the stalls, selling vegetables, fried foods, old clothes, and turned off up Commercial Street. There were warehouses on either side, two churches, the Baptist facing the Anglican from opposite sides of the street. From the Jews' school came a high-pitched chant as they recited their tables or whatever inside. Then I went down Goulston Street, crowded and full of smells, rubbish, children and dogs, as it had been when I left, only now it was worse, if anything, and asked at the Bull's Head for Mr Murgatroyd's. There was a big house, claimed the barman, on the next corner, and that was Murgatroyd's. He gave me a curious look, which changed into an ugly one. He told me, 'No point in asking him for lodgings.'

'Why not?' I asked.

'He don't take Jews. He can't abide them.' His expression told me that for his part he endorsed Murgatroyd's sentiments.

'I'm not a Jew,' I said.

'That's your business. I'm just warning you, Murgatroyd's got no time for Cohens and Levis.'

It seemed a good idea to leave, so I did. It was probably my dark hair, oval face and pallid, or ivory if you like, complexion which had made him think me some Jewish woman. The native East Enders are of course often golden-haired, with blue eyes, and call to mind the old Roman declaration about the British captives in Rome: 'These are not Angles, but angels.' This helps them detect strangers in their midst and persecute them. Their attitude is best summed up by the cartoon in *Punch*. Two hobbledehoys are standing shoeless in the street. ''Ere, Bert,' says one to the other, 'there's a foreigner. 'Eave 'alf a brick at 'im.'

Nevertheless, when I got into New Goulston Street I saw that since I was last there it had become partly a Jewish colony. Dark children played in the street, their mothers, outside on chairs, sewing for dear life, making cigarettes or preparing food, called out to them in German. A lot of the shops had foreign names, Nathan, Stegenburg, Zuse. The houses let out the smell of foreign dishes. But it was still the same old place, people coming out of the fried fish shop with newspapers containing their dinners, a boy struggling along with a bale of striped ticking for his mother and sisters to sew up into pillowcases and mattress covers, a girl of ten, carrying a baby in the crook of her arm, holding a shopping bag with her hand and leading a toddler with the spare one, a mouldy-looking dog nosing in a gutter where sat a dirty child with blonde curls and an equally dirty one with black curls, the black-haired one jabbering away while the blonde one, sucking

59

her thumb, stared, wide-eyed, probably wondering why she could not understand a word of the other child's speech.

A young, fair man with a horse and cart stood talking to another at the end of the street. I could tell from the tension in the first man's manner that, although he liked the other man, a dark Jew in a black jacket, he was trying not to, was trying to keep a distance between them. Come nightfall he and a band of mates would be roaming the street looking for a Jew to beat up, on principle, and he wouldn't want to look down in the darkness and notice he was kicking in the ribs of a man he'd been speaking to in a friendly fashion earlier on in the day.

As I approached I could see the house outside which the men stood was bigger, not like the narrow two- or three-storey houses on either side of the street. It was a wreck now, with green slime trailing down where the gutters had broken, and cracked windows wedged up with bits of wood. The peeling front door was propped open with a big stone from another part of the building. A prosperous home once, it was now falling to pieces. Inside it would be a kind of crazy-house, where large rooms had been split up to make several small ones, people were living eight to a room, and any garden there once had been would be filled with shacks, sheds, and outhouses.

By now I was quite excited, thinking I might find Mary Jane inside, or at least get recent news of her.

'Is this Murgatroyd's?' I asked the man with the horse and cart. I was not dressed for this area. I was very clean. My complexion was fresh as no London complexion, even a well-tended one, ever can be, because of the smoke and grime. He looked at me stonily, thinking I had come to interfere about something or other.

I just stepped into the hall where, on the cracked tiles, a lean dog was scratching itself vigorously. The hall itself was broad, with a battered, once imposing staircase up the middle, banisters missing, used for firewood no doubt; on either side of the stairs at the back of the hall, two sacking curtains hung down. In the space behind them someone, or several, were living. I saw the sacking bulge out as a body came against it. I was probably under observation. There were doors to right and left. I planned to begin by knocking on the nearest, but having seen three children, the eldest a girl of about seven, sitting half-way up the stairs, I paused and said, 'Good-day.' They stared back at me doubtfully. The girls had boots. The boys, about five and two, wore plaid bedroom slippers. Their little legs were thin and pale, like stalks. They were clean, wan, underfed children, and probably their mother was trying to keep them good, not allowing them to play in the street alongside the shameless, barefoot lice-ridden urchins who roamed around in packs, getting into bad ways. I pitied those children. My mother too, before overwork and drink broke her down, had tried to keep us respectable, made us stay in the house within call, while she sewed, and sewed and sewed. As I came through the door I'd spotted the big sister trying to amuse her brother with a cat's cradle made out of yarn, heard her singing, with the little one, 'Humpty Dumpty sat on a wall', seen her eye attracted by something happening in the street outside, where I'd heard a child's voice call, 'Come on, Tom. Hurry up!' Now they sat silently, looking down at me.

I said, 'I'm looking for a lady who lives here. Mary Kelly. Do you know anyone who could help me?'

Seemingly not hardened to Whitechapel ways, where a child's first lesson is never to give information to a stranger, the little girl responded, 'No, miss. Never heard of her, miss.'

'Is your mother in? Could I talk to her?'

As I said this a tall, thin young woman appeared on the landing, her head tied up in a scarf, white threads on her black skirt. She demanded, 'What is it?'

'I wonder if you can help me?' I said. 'I'm looking for Mary Kelly.'

'Gone,' she responded. 'Nearly a year ago. We've got her room.' She gave me a hard look. 'What do you want with her?'

I could tell she'd heard tales of her predecessor, from the rent collector or another neighbour, and did not approve of what she had heard.

'Was she Mary Jane Kelly? A fair-haired woman?' I asked.

She nodded reluctantly. 'Sometimes she called herself Marie.' She added, 'French,' with all the disapproval an English person can impart to that word.

'Thank God!' I found myself crying out. 'It must be my sister. Can you tell me where she went? Will anyone know?'

Her mouth closed tightly. She glanced at her children, back at me. She said, 'She didn't stop to let anyone know where she was going. She left no address. The rent collector's still looking for her.'

'Can I speak to him? Where does he live?'

'Mr Brewer. He lives in Doughty Street,' she told me. She couldn't wait for me to leave.

'Are you sure there isn't anyone here she was friendly with?'

'No,' she said firmly. 'I keep myself to myself. Try the police station.' Arms folded, she guarded her landing, her stairs, her children. The battle to stay decent, the daily struggle to avoid hopeless poverty takes its toll. She tensed as I ran upstairs to give the children sixpence each, tucking each coin into a surprised little hand, and then watched me like a dog as I left. I hoped the children would get toys, but thought most of the money would end up in the hands of Mr Brewer in Doughty Street.

Some shaven-headed boys were playing on the pavement outside with a stick and ball. I asked them if they knew of Mary Kelly. Of course they denied it, would have denied it if she'd been their own sister.

'Say her sister's looking for her,' I then told them. In Whitechapel the system of street communications is faster than the telegraph.

They brightened up. 'I'll find her for a shilling,' asserted one.

'There could be something in it for the person who finds her and tells Mrs Mundy at the alehouse in Brushfield Street,' I remarked. 'There might be five shillings.'

This quickened their interest even more. 'I know where she is,' claimed one boy.

I didn't believe him. 'Tell Mrs Mundy,' I told him and walked away.

I was pleased. Admittedly, the news of Mary Jane was old, but she'd been here, in Whitechapel, last year, and I thought she might still be. And at all events, she was alive and thriving.

I spoke to Jack Armitage at the Lamb and Flag down Thames Street, and left word at the herbalist, she called herself Old Mother Hardacre's, in Aldgate. These were the only two people in all Whitechapel I could trust to keep their eyes and ears open and their mouths shut. To Whitechapel, in my character of the wealthy sister back from Canada, I would look like the answer to everyone's prayers. The good news would travel swiftly. Within twenty-four hours half the district would be swarming all over me like Cornishmen on a wrecked ship. I'd be besieged with Mary Kellys and tales of Mary Kellys, they'd try to sell me their children, offer to become my servant, errand boy, fancy man, anything I pleased. They'd swear eternal loyalty, and plan to rob me. Even to Jack Armitage and Old Mother Hardacre (by a message to the man she called her husband) I did not reveal my address, just asked them to leave a message with Cora Mundy.

Tired of walking, I went into a respectable-looking café west of Aldgate, then went by cab to Doughty Street. By now it was about five o'clock. A postman directed me to Mr Brewer's residence, a lean, three-storeyed house with a plane tree outside. The tree had some brown leaves on it. Autumn was approaching.

A little maid answered the bell and I looked into a narrow hall with flowered wallpaper. There was an unpleasant smell of old roast lamb and cabbage mingled with something else. I gave my name, Mrs Frazer, and asked if I might see Mr Brewer.

'He's at his tea,' the maid reported discouragingly.

'May I wait?' I asked. She looked me up and down, but I was too ladylike to be summarily ejected on to the pavement.

'I'll ask,' she said.

Brewer then came out, a short, thickset man with a heavy black moustache. He looked like a man with a ready temper, controlled but ready to leap like a tiger. I took an immediate dislike to him there and then. I had seen my mother begging such a man for time to pay the rent and weeping when refused. It is not a pleasant job, taking rents from the very poor, for such housing as they can afford. They do not employ pleasant men to do it.

I stood calmly in his hall, my bag on my arm, my gloved hands clasped loosely in front of me.

His manner changed when he saw a pretty, well-dressed woman, bearing about her, as I knew I must, an air of authority normally found only in the womenfolk of the mighty of the land. This air I had achieved by running a bad house, with all the responsibilities and dangers that such a life entails, but he was not to know that. I apologized for interrupting him at an inconvenient time and said I would be glad to return at a more suitable hour.

He had already adjusted his jacket, which he had plainly put on in order to greet me, and 'Not at all, not at all,' he

64

said. 'Perhaps you'd care for a cup of tea. But I'm afraid you'll have to take us as you find us, in the dining-room. There are workmen in the drawing-room and everything's topsy-turvy.' He looked cross about this as he led me into his dining-room. As we were entering, two big lads in caps, one with a boat under his arm, and a little girl of about five, her loose hair held back by a ribbon gone awry, came in through the front door, accompanied by a maid.

'What's this?' he asked in agitation. 'And you're putting water on the floor.' A few drops were falling from the boat on to the tiles.

'We've been to the park, papa,' the older of the boys told him.

'Very good,' he said. 'But Maria must take the boat into the kitchen. And,' he told her, 'get Jane to clear the table quickly.'

His tone had been sharp, but 'The cares of a family man,' he remarked more jovially as we went into the dining-room.

It was a biggish room with some large, dull paintings in oils on the walls and a window which must have looked out on to the garden, though the thick net curtains obscured any view. At a mahogany table, laid only at one end, sat a young woman, seeming to be in her early twenties, heavily pregnant. Opposite her was a young man with a pale face and red-brown hair dressed in a stiff shirt with a bow tie and a brown jacket, which appeared a little short in the arms for him, as if he'd grown after it had been bought.

Brewer introduced me. 'My wife. My clerk, Mr Henry Churchill.'

Churchill, I supposed, would be one of the chief rent collectors for properties managed by Brewer; Brewer would only step in where there were complications or difficulties. Or something else. Young Churchill, in his stiff collar and starch-laden shirt, had the air of a young man whose laundry was still being looked after by a devoted mother, who sent him off each morning 'tidy for business'. A pimple on his neck, sign of a poor diet, I thought, threatened to burst, nigh to the collar. A strictly-brought-up widow's son, I decided. Congregational, probably.

I looked warily at Brewer, a man who would take advantage of an attractive tenant in trouble with the rent. Comprehending such things by instinct is, after all, part of my trade. Mrs Brewer – the second Mrs Brewer, I assumed, for she was not nearly old enough to be the mother of either of the boys, possibly not even of the little girl – would naturally know nothing of his exploitations. She drooped a little in her chair, perhaps in need of rest.

The servant who had opened the door came in with a tray and began, hurriedly, to clear the dishes on the table, a cake, bread and butter, a dish of junket and Mr Brewer's plate. He had partaken of a piece of smoked haddock, I noted, and this accounted for the confusion of smells in the hall.

'Forgive this informality,' he said. 'And please sit down.' He took his own chair at the head of the table. I sat beside Henry Churchill.

'Now, in what way can I help you?' He hoped, I expect, that I wished him to manage some large property of mine. This, at any rate, was the impression I had tried to convey, otherwise I do not think he would have seen me so quickly. I leaned forward past Churchill to see him better. 'I've come to ask your assistance, in a family matter. I've only recently returned from Canada after the death of my husband.' Condolences were murmured, for which I thanked them. 'The reason I impose on you so inconveniently is because I'm trying to discover the whereabouts of my sister, lost to me because of some family difficulties. I've visited some lodgings of hers which she used to have, and a lady there said that you were trying yourself to find out where she now is. I believe', I said, dropping my eyes to the lace cloth on the table, 'there were some arrears of rent due to you which, of course, I would be more than glad to settle on her behalf.' I returned my eyes to his face. 'I have come to help her. Can you assist me in finding her?'

He was looking disturbed. I now came to the difficult part of my story. 'Her name', I said steadily, 'is Mary Jane Kelly. The house I visited is in Goulston Street, Whitechapel.'

At this, Brewer flinched, scarcely perceptibly, and glanced at his wife as if assuring himself of something – that she did not know of anything like Goulston Street, or the Mary Kellys of the world, their lives and trade, or perhaps merely that she could not read his guilty conscience. His gaze returned to me; a less obliging expression came to his face. 'She was there last Christmas,' I said.

'Elizabeth, will you leave us?' he asked. She stood up immediately, said goodbye to me and left. Brewer leaned back in his chair now, clasped his hands in front of him, became familiar. Churchill followed suit, tipping his own chair back and turning his head towards me. A kind of taproom atmosphere, initiated by Brewer, and picked up by his clerk, began to prevail. Any respect I might have got from them as a lady had evaporated now they knew I was the sister of a common prostitute.

They say there are above 60,000 prostitutes in London. As it's a city of three and a half million that's one in thirty of all the women and girls there, and one in twenty if you exclude those too young or too old for the game, though in Whitechapel it's hard to be either. They call London the Great Whore, and it's no wonder, seeing so many of her daughters are practising her trade there. Anyway, by arithmetic there's a whore for every twenty men in London and though not every man in the city makes use of them, many do — or many a poor woman would be hungrier than she is. This Brewer was a whoremonger — it's a habit which leaves its mark on a man, for those who can spot it. I was sure he'd introduced his overgrown-schoolboy clerk Churchill to his nice practices. Thus the relaxation of manners in his dining-room, now I had slipped, in his eyes, by my connection with Mary Jane. He could probably smell me, anyway, as I smelled him. I played the ignorant to make him uncertain of the position, knowing that otherwise I'd get no assistance from him, merely insult.

'Have you any information to help me?' I asked in an even tone. 'I have offered a reward for anyone who finds her.'

He looked at me insolently. 'I shall have to consult my books,' he told me. 'They are at my office.'

'May we make an appointment to meet there?'

'I shall be back there at seven this evening, briefly,' he said. 'Would that time suit you?'

'Indeed, it would.' I stood up to leave. He stood also, ready to see me out. He had fallen for me. He desired me, but thought me too proud, thought he couldn't have me, so he attacked. 'I must advise you — you must prepare your mind for disturbing news about your sister.'

'What news?' I cried, turning round in alarm.

He shook his head. 'Her life . . .' he said. He hesitated, to make me even more anxious. Was Mary Jane ill? I wondered. Diseased? In the workhouse? In prison? 'Her life', he repeated, 'is not a blameless one.'

I tried not to look too relieved. 'Whatever her case, I only want to help her,' I said gravely. 'This city is dangerous in many ways for a young woman on her own.'

I hot-footed it then to Whitechapel, taking the Aldgate route, best avoided by the squeamish, for that's where the slaughterhouses are, the streets full of castaway innards, which the poor pick over for their food. The walls around the slaughterhouses, when they're killing, are lined with boys and girls, the little fiends, clapping and shouting at the squeals and moos of the scared animals, relishing the throat-slittings and stunnings and the sight and smell of fresh blood. It's considered cowardly to flinch. Those who don't enjoy it have to pretend. Then the pious, leaving their own children in their nurseries with their peep-shows and fairy-stories, descend on the East End to lecture us on depravity. What chance could there be of finding virtue, sensibility, Christian charity in children over-stimulated in that way? The miracle is that any grow up decent, as some do.

I cut through the stalls of Whitechapel Road and went to Mrs Mundy's to see if there were any messages and to tell her the name and address of my new-found lawyer, Mr Ratcliffe. I was not going to tell Cora where I lived.

'No messages,' said the fat woman. 'But a boy came in and told me you'd asked me to give him half a crown for information supplied. I knew he lied, clipped his ear for him and sent him packing.'

'Quite right,' I told her. 'Nothing, then?'

She shook her head. 'Not a whisper.' Her little eyes seemed to cloud. 'God, Mary,' she said, 'I don't half suffer with bad dreams. I'd hardly a wink last night.' She shook her head again, trying to throw the spectres from her mind. I wasn't the only one tormented by nightmares. 'What's it all about?' asked this woman, who had, in her time, probably broken every one of the ten commandments, and would break them all again next day for sixpence. 'Here we are, the Queen's on her throne, God bless her, the country's at peace. Yet look about you, there's misery and want everywhere. Only last night a poor old woman round the corner was half beaten to death in her own room for the little she had. They say she'll lose an eye for sure. Sad and miserable days, Mary. Thank God I've got my Harry to protect me, that's all. It makes you feel heavy, things are that bad.' She sighed.

I knew she was given to these fits of gloom. 'Soon you'll hear a shilling ring on your counter,' I told her. 'The sound will revive you and make life seem worth living again.'

She disliked my tone. 'Jim Bristow got to hear of your return,' she told me, scanning my face to see how the news affected me. 'He dashed round here to ask where you were.'

'I don't want to see him,' I said. 'What did you tell him?'

'Nothing,' she answered, quite annoyed. 'You indicated you wanted nothing to do with him. Still . . .' She sighed a sentimental sigh. 'Poor Jim. Things haven't gone well for him recently.' She stared, to see how I would respond to this news. I took care not to, and saying I had an appointment to meet someone who might tell me where Mary Jane was, I departed politely, leaving five shillings on the counter, to keep her sweet. I could not afford to fall out with her but I did not trust her where Jim Bristow was concerned. Some women, as they grow older, develop a weakness for these cocky young villains, and Cora was one of them.

For the excitement of it, I descended into the bowels of the earth at Whitechapel, and took the new underground train to Baker Street. I stood on the platform and saw a train come in through a tunnel from the centre of London, flinging out smoke and disgorging people. And it was not seven o'clock yet, so many offices and shops would not yet have closed and released the workers. Even so, what a gang was rattling through the underground tunnels of London! These were clerks, a street-sweeper, a gaggle of shopgirls, women with packages, a girl with a tray, who had been selling flowers judging by the big red rose in her hat, two women of the streets with painted faces, a couple of old rabbis with beards and big black hats, a group of bad lads you could swear had been pick-pocketing in the West End crowds (one to distract, one to pick the pocket, the rest to pretend to give chase to the villain and trip up the real pursuers as if by accident).

I ascended my noisy train most nervously considering I was a woman who once found a bear snoozing on her porch in the snow on a winter morning and took it quite for granted. I was then whisked to Baker Street, first in the open, then under London's streets. I marvelled at the development. From there, being short of time, I took a cab to Sackville Street for my appointment with Mr Brewer. I was received by a clerk, then asked to wait on a chair in the big room where six men in black coats sat working at large ledgers. Half an hour elapsed awkwardly for us all as I sat in the overcrowded, hot room, covertly assessed by the men working there.

When, finally, Brewer put his head round his office door and invited me to step inside, I found myself in a long room with large windows at the end. Brewer did not offer to shake hands and got quickly behind his heavy desk, on which were silver inkpots and a silver-framed photograph with its back turned to me. I guessed it was a family portrait. In a sad and patronizing tone he said, 'Well, Mrs Frazer. I have checked the details in the case of Miss Kelly, your sister. They may not be pleasant to your ears.' I think he found the details very pleasant and the chance of humiliating me through Mary Jane even more so. I could tell the contemplation of all this had stirred him up. He looked at me as if I were about to lead him off up an alley, or he wished I would.

'Intimations of my sister's way of life have reached me, Mr Brewer,' I said. 'But blood is thicker than water, as they say. So it's her whereabouts I'm most interested in.' I was trying to be civil, but the little toad was angering me.

He would not to be cheated of his fun. 'The neighbourhood in which she lodged is not a good one. Many unfortunates dwell there.' I nodded. 'Sadly,' he continued, 'this city is full of them.' He would have been delighted to expand on the subject. Men like nothing better than to talk of sin to pretty women. For some, it's better than the act itself.

'Just as sadly, these unfortunate women find many men to take advantage of their plight,' I countered, to cool him down.

He pulled himself together a little and said, 'Yes, yes indeed. A deplorable situation all round, I'm afraid. Anyway, to the matter in hand. Your sister, if indeed the woman concerned *is* your sister, lived at the premises known as Murgatroyd's in Goulston Street, for which I'm responsible, from August to December last year. I believe she was living with a man, I don't know his name or his trade – I believe he had no trade. Disputes arose between them and he left, according to neighbours. Now, by December she had paid no rent for two months, and I decided it was time to confront her about the matter, and invite her to leave if she could not pay. When I arrived, she'd been gone for several days, and, of course, had left no address, in order to prevent me from finding her and demanding the arrears of rent. Doing a moonlight flit, this is called in local parlance.'

'I know the term,' I responded soberly. And had done the deed, more than once, I thought.

'Local rumours enabled my clerk, Mr Churchill, to track her down to Gun Street, at the back of the old convent, if that's any help to you. A building run by a Mrs Smith.' He paused. 'Her lodgings aren't becoming any more select, Mrs Frazer, I'm afraid. The arrears of rent amount to four pounds and ten shillings.'

Brewer had had her, I was sure, in lieu of rent. Otherwise, how could she have stayed in Goulston Street for two months without paying? Perhaps Mary Jane preferred it that way, I couldn't tell. At all events, he was a dirty dog, Brewer. I think he was feeling his private parts behind his desk. I stood up.

Some anger must have shown on my face. He knew I had found him out and quickly realized I was not going to pay Mary Jane's outstanding rent. 'If you find her, tell her Brewer has her best interests at heart, will forget the past and if there's any service he can render her, in her misfortunes—'

I left. At the door I said, 'Mr Brewer, do you take me for a fool?'

'I take you for one of the same sort as Mary Jane,' he snapped.

I opened the door. 'And that is a sort you must know well. Indeed, know intimately.'

I stamped angrily, leaving the clerks goggle-eyed in the office, and walked off in a rage, heading blindly for Fleet Street. These hypocrites! First they took what they wanted, then condemned it. Perhaps they really believed as they spoke, the way children sometimes do, that they were the men they claimed to be, and lived as they said they did. And how they hated those who tempted them, whether they succumbed to the temptation or not. How they tried to humiliate the women they could not resist, but by whom they felt humiliated. How they blamed them, how they whitened themselves by blackening them. And my sister had pulled up her skirts for that man! What disgrace, even if she'd thought it worth the price to get her lodgings free. What a place this was, I thought, as I stomped through Trafalgar Square, where the people were already, like so many roosting birds, settling down for the night, and the whores starting their early shift round St Martin's, down the street to the Strand. What a place of smoke and smells, beggars and drunks and people toppled in doorways, where a girl would sell herself to the landlord for five shillings' rent. What chance had a poor woman in this city? Where were my sisters? What had happened to them since I'd shipped out eight years earlier, leaving Mary Claire, a hard-working, quiet-living fourteen-year-old, and Mary Jane, only twelve, getting jobs in shops or factories, stopping one, starting another, abandoning that one also, growing saucier, bolder and stronger by the day?

Back in Fleet Street I stretched out in the chair in my lodgings, quite worn out, and considered my course of action. I recognized I might have to go deep into the East End to find my sisters – if Mary Jane was there at all now, for I had as yet had no reports of her. I fell asleep, and dreamed of a red room, where a terrible event had taken place, a warning I could not properly hear, a threat to myself. I woke after only a quarter of an hour, terrified, wondering if I, who had slept soundly all my life, would ever enjoy quiet rest in this city again.

It was a hot night. Tired as I was, I had street fever in my veins. At half-past eleven I was trying to pick up news in one of the many lodging houses in Flower and Dean Street. How many were there – five, eight, ten? One thing was for sure: there were no flowers and precious few deans in that street. There were bedrooms upstairs at number 5, or mattresses anyway. The place acted as a lodging house, brothel and thieves' kitchen all at the same time. By the fireplace a man was pushing scraps of food from his pockets into a dented saucepan, his two children standing by, staring hungrily. He pushed his hand into the boy's shirt, pulled out a potato, shoved it in the pan, put the pan on the fire. A man in rags, feet stuck out, sat propped against the wall, head back, tilting a bottle towards his mouth. In a dark corner a man opened his jacket, slid in his hand, pushed what he took from it into a woman's open palm. A mangy puppy lay in the arms of a skinny boy. He was feeding it with the heel of a loaf. There must have been fourteen people in that hell-hole of a kitchen, less than sixteen feet square. I was in a corner with three women. A middle-aged one, with dyed red hair and very bad teeth, sat against the wall in an old wooden chair. Young Kitty was on the floor with her spindly legs, ending in cracked boots, stuck out in front of her. The other woman and I leaned against the filthy wall. We were all sharing a bottle of gin I'd brought in with me. I'd pulled my hair about, wore a shawl instead of a bonnet and an old grey dress, but I still didn't fit. The gin helped, though.

Suddenly there was the erratic clatter of feet on the stairs, and a tipsy girl in a short scarlet skirt, scarlet and black hat, a man's jacket draped round her shoulders, came through the open door. She leaned against the wall laughing. Heads turned.

'Hey!' she called. 'Any of youse in here seen Liam Flynn? Come on now, Flynn's the name. Have you seen him?'

'Has he got a wooden leg?' enquired a thin, pale girl near me. There was some hope in her voice.

This made her laugh more. 'He has not. Ah – no point in asking here, yez all dead here, but you don't know it. Christ!' she cried out, as the big black cat who lived there stalked up to her. 'What in God's name is that – the devil?'

'Oh, clear off,' shouted Bess Watkins, the woman I'd been talking to. 'There's no Flynn here, as you can see, so just get out.'

The drunk girl made a tottering curtsy. 'Your wish is my command, my lady. I wish you well of your castle, so goodbye, chimney sweeps, goodbye.' She burst out laughing again and departed.

'Get herself murdered one day, running about like that,' grumbled Bess. 'Skirt half-way up to her knees, bosom there for all to see—'

'Leave her alone, Bess,' said skinny, red-headed Jane. 'She's no different to what we were at her age. Let her enjoy herself while she can.' Rouge stood out on her cheeks. She looked ill. 'Give me another drink, dear, my teeth are torturing me. I'm in agony day and night. Why did God give us teeth?'

'Get them drawn, my darling. Get them drawn,' advised Bess, whose front teeth were lacking top and bottom. 'What ain't there can't hurt you.' She grinned, to demonstrate. She could have been a pretty woman once. Now, with her straggling hair and veined face, her looks had gone. 'Swallow your gin down, Kitty love,' she advised. 'Did you take the powders the woman gave you?'

'I did,' said the young woman on the floor. 'They're not working.'

'They will, believe me,' the other advised grimly. 'Poor girl,' she told me. 'She's in a bit of trouble. She had to run away and come here or she reckons her brothers would have beaten her, nearly to death. Now she's trying to get shot of the baby.'

There was a silence. I had to speak. 'I'm in no danger of that,' I volunteered. 'I'm scarred inside.'

'Oh,' Bess said, understanding. 'Like that, is it? And you so young.'

The girl, Kitty, didn't seem to follow any of this. I don't think she understood half of what was going on. Her eyes were rolling round the darkness of the room in panic. She was like a lost dog, which has been running about fearfully trying to find home, and when it stops all of a sudden realizes that, after all that effort, it's even further off, in a strange place. Shadowy figures leaned, lay or sat in the gloom, one bolting down scraps of food from a handkerchief he'd pulled out of a pocket. A woman had crept in and sat by the door, suckling a child. Two boys played knucklebones on the floor. A thin voice, a man's, started a song – 'A-roving, a-roving, I'll go no more a-roving, For roving's been my ru-in' – but no one joined in and he broke off with a terrible graveyard cough which went on and on.

It must have been a pretty fair version of hell for the girl, who, a month ago, must have been looking out over empty fields and a long white road stretching for miles with not a soul on it. Not hell; perhaps for her it was a limbo. She was stunned. She'd had the strength to leave but I doubted if she had the strength to survive here.

'Even so,' Bess said after a pause, 'I wouldn't regret those scars if I was you. Look at me, married at thirteen, I'd four youngsters by the age of nineteen. Five before I was twenty-one.'

'I don't know why you don't go to a mission, say you've been a bad girl and promise to reform,' I told Kitty. 'They'd feed you, at any rate, and take care of you till your troubles were over.'

She didn't respond. Perhaps my words sank in, to be remembered at a later date. Perhaps not. I turned to my own business. 'I'm looking for my sisters, Mary Claire and Mary Jane Kelly. One's twenty-two, one twenty. I left them here eight years ago. Mary Jane was in Goulston Street, then they're saying she may be living down by the old convent, but I daren't go looking at this hour, by myself. You wouldn't have heard anything of either of them, would you?'

Red-headed Jane just stared at me, with some hostility, I thought. She guessed I was only slumming. Bess was softer-natured. 'No, love,' she said. 'Can't say I've heard anything about either of them.'

'If you hear anything would you leave a message at Mrs Mundy's, in Brushfield Street?'

A man stumbled through the door. He was a surprise in that dismal room. He wore a clean white waistcoat, a white shirt open at the throat, a fresh red neckerchief and black trousers. He had on his head a round black hat with a brim. The boy holding the puppy gaped. The men in the corner summed him up and evidently dismissed him as a threat. But the woman, Jane, shrank back against the wall, 'Oh my God,' she said, to me, and Bess, I suppose. 'He found me.' I thought her fear was mingled with excitement, that need to figure in another chapter of the romance unfortunate women write for themselves, to make up for having no work and no position in life. The pimp in this novel is transformed into an ardent lover, the whore is a much-courted virgin. Thus a spangled veil is thrown over squalor.

The man spotted her, cried out, 'Jane!' and came forward, stumbling through the others as he went. He was a bit drunk. 'I've been searching hours for you. You come along of me, Jane. I need you.'

I did not stay for the drama to follow, her cries and reproaches, his threats and protestations. I nodded to Bess and Kitty and got up out of the pit by the wooden steps into the fresh air. It was fresh enough for me anyway, after that kitchen.

It was by now midnight, for I heard the church clocks striking, and I made my way from Flower and Dean Street, with my shawl over my head and dangling down to conceal the bag at my side, across Whitechapel High Street, which was even now fairly crowded. The pubs were still open, smoke and music coming from the doors, and scores of children waiting outside for their parents.

> 'Come where the wine is cheaper,
> Come where the beer is free,'

sang a man coming past me, up close, with a gang of others at his heels. I snarled the East End response to this, 'Garn.'

'Lady, can you spare a copper for a woman and her baby?' said a wan woman with a very rosy baby, goodness knew how it could be, under her old plaid shawl. Then,

'Bitch!' she shouted after me as I walked swiftly on, jumping on the last tram down Leman Street for the docks.

There were seamen everywhere, of course, and tarts moving like moths round the street lights, and people carrying around bundles of this and that, anything from a baby to a sack of coconuts pinched from a ship.

At the seamen's home by Dock Street twenty sailors got on. They found they were going the wrong way and jumped off again. There were warehouses on either side. I got off in the looming shadow of the tea warehouse and turned on to the street running parallel with the river. Here, there were warehouses on the other side; the docks lay beyond them, and there was a pub every 200 yards, and a whore every ten paces. I walked past these women, staring in each face. They stared brazenly back. A whore can get killed, slashed, filled with disease, but she'll never cast her eyes down. That's for the respectable woman.

'Move along, darling,' said one, painted to the hairline and old enough to be my grandmother. Pocked, too.

I looked at this travesty of a visage and said, 'I'm looking for my sister, Mary Kelly. Do you know her?'

'Just move on, will you?' she demanded, and I did, for a woman like her will fight you for twopence and God knows what diseases a bite from her wouldn't convey to you. Such a brigade of faces, old, young, sick, well, novices and old hands. What risks didn't they run, beside warehouse walls, down behind pubs, in the dark, with the smell of the river in their nostrils? But I was getting the scent of the life now: river smell, beer, the cheap scent they wore, the sitting on his knee in the pub, singing, then the darkness, the fast money from his pocket. I knew how it ended, too – rotting in a basement room without food or fire, raving mad with disease in the Lock Hospital, or just jumping in the river to finish it all.

I had to move quickly. The women didn't want me

standing about gossiping. I might be after their pitch; I might deter the clientele. So I went, getting no good answers and some bad ones from all and sundry. All the time, I could smell that black and stinking river, the tide rising now, hear it slapping the dockside, hear the cables of ships at anchor grinding and straining.

Then I heard hooves and wheels behind me and turned. The carriage stopped a little way off and two men in evening dress got out and began to move along the pavement looking into the faces of the women, who spoke to them in the usual cant, 'Hullo, my dear. Do you want a nice time?' and the like, while they, not responding, patrolled on. All the while the carriage kept pace with them on the street, for fear of toughs and robbers. It was the custom, I knew, after dinner at the club, instead of a game of billiards or cards, for a man or a party of men to go whoring down at the docks, for the novelty of fucking dirty women, is how they put it to themselves, the same as cards or going to the theatre. Never believe it! They need what we have to offer more than that. There's talk now of the destruction of pure women by the diseases caught by their husbands, or bachelors who've been sowing their wild oats and bringing the harvest with them on their honeymoons. To tell the truth, I've little sympathy with these pure women. It seems to take too many whores to keep them unsullied and unseduced before marriage and unburdened by children or lustful demands afterwards. You'd think they could endure from time to time just a particle of the risks we have to take to keep them pure. Still, that's our living. And if the likes of us weren't guarding their virtue with our bodies we'd be working in their kitchens. The rich will use up the poor, one way or another, that's always true.

Anyway, the gentlemen moved on. I was under a lamp with a rosy girl in a big flashy bonnet. They stopped, one middle-aged, red-faced, the other a bit younger with straw-coloured hair. I moved back into the shadows, but the straw-haired one spotted me. 'Aren't you in business then, my dear?'

'Not tonight, guvnor,' I whined. 'I'm sick.'

He looked disconcerted, but plunged on, saying to the rosy girl, 'What about you, my darling? What's your name?'

The rosy girl said, 'I'm on my way home, sir.' A likely story.

The men moved on and apparently made a bargain further up, for they went off with two women into the shadows. The coach waited for them. The rosy girl spat discreetly in its direction.

'Do you always turn down wealthy customers?' I asked.

'The young one's the barrister who prosecuted my dad down in Kent,' she said. 'I knew him the minute I clapped eyes on him.'

'I'm looking for my sister, Mary Kelly,' I said.

She summed me up. 'I worked with a girl called Kelly in a hat shop,' she told me. 'She looked a bit like you. She run off with a sailor. It's a few years ago now.'

This was the second time now I'd heard the same story about Mary Claire. 'Thank you,' I said.

'What do you want her for?' she asked. 'Anyway, you'd never find her down here. She was a good girl.'

I told her I had two sisters, Mary Claire and Mary Jane. I told her about getting news to Mrs Mundy, if she heard or remembered any more. I asked for her address, saying I might be able to offer her employment in Canada later on. Of course, she refused to give it, but she did give me the address of a big house in Kent where her sister worked, and said a message sent there would find her.

I tried a few more women, but a Chinese with a pigtail came out of the darkness, said I was disturbing trade and threatened me, so I wandered off back to the Lamb and Flag, thinking I might find a cabman there, prepared to take me back to my lodgings. I felt too tired to walk there. I could have slept on a stone, but I still dreaded the bad dreams I was having in my lodgings. I wondered if the rooms were haunted. At all events, I would have to move elsewhere if the dreams continued. Strong as I was, I could not go on like that, night after night.

At the Lamb and Flag a man in an Arab robe and a bowler hat was playing 'The boy I love is up in the gallery', singing in a falsetto, and a group was joining in. It wasn't very full now. Many of the customers had retreated to get some sleep for work next day. Jack ran a respectable house.

He was drying glasses at the bar. He looked less cheerful than usual.

'Anything wrong, Jack?' I asked.

'No,' he said. 'Well – it's the old woman. She's expecting another kid and she don't seem too well. The doctor says it might be a hospital job. Now she thinks she's going to die – and she's bothering on about not letting him send her to the London Hospital. Make sure it's Bethnal Green, Jack. Make sure it's Bethnal Green, she keeps on pleading.'

'No one wants to go to the London Hospital,' I pointed out.

'It's nearer,' he said.

'Safer to go further and fare better,' I told him.

'I suppose so. I've promised her over and over I won't let her go anywhere, especially there, but will she believe me? No. Pregnant women are funny. She must think I've got it in mind to polish her off. Anyway,' he said, leaning forward, 'as to that other business you mentioned, try them old Jews over there playing dominoes. They might help.'

I pushed past a group of navvies and stood by their table. They both had big black hats on, and greying beards. They looked as old as the hills. They knew I was waiting there, but they wouldn't look up from their game.

Finally I said, 'I'm Mrs Frazer. I'm looking for my sisters, Mary Claire and Mary Jane Kelly. Can you help me? Do you know anything of either of them?'

One of the old men, not so old really when you studied him, looked up after a pause and asked, in his thick accent, 'What do you want with her?'

'I'm her sister. I've been away for eight years.'

He took another long, cautious look. At the end of it, I think he'd decided I was genuine, but to make sure, he said, 'You don't look much like her.' He looked again at me, screwed up his eyes and finally said, 'I took a girl of that name on for shirt-making. She was very good. Fast. A clever girl.'

'When was this?'

'June, July. At the end of July she said the room was too hot. She'd work faster at home with the window open. By then I trusted her. I'd had a big order in. So – she left one evening with twenty yards of best striped cotton to make up, swearing she'd be back in five days with the shirts. I smiled, she smiled, that was the last I saw of her, or my best cotton. When I went to the address she gave me,' he shrugged his shoulders, 'she'd gone.'

The other man muttered something in Hebrew, or whatever he spoke. The robbed Jew replied in the same language.

'What are you saying?' I asked, thinking they spoke of Mary.

'My brother told me it was my fault if I trusted her,' he said. That wasn't what he said, and I knew it.

'Where was she living?'

'She wasn't. She gave me an address in the Old Nicholl. I had to go there with my sons for fear of trouble and after all that they say she'd only lived there for one week, on the run, they said, from some trouble.' He paused, then said quickly, 'If you're her sister, you should cover her debt.'

'If I find her and she supports your story,' I said.

'You tell me I lie.' Suddenly the other man had me by the hand. 'My brother is an honest, hard-working man. Your sister has robbed him.'

I began to scream and yell. 'Honest man? Don't make me bloody laugh. Twenty women in a space ten feet by ten, working all hours for dear life at two bob a day and he calls himself an honest man? Sweat-shop owner, killer, more likely. Let me go, you bastard!'

Of course, people began to turn round and of course they'd side with me against a Jew, whatever I'd done or not done. That was taken for granted. A big man in shirt-sleeves, another only slightly smaller behind him, came up. 'Let her go, Ikey Mo,' he threatened. The Jew let go. They went back to the piano. I sat down at the table. We looked at each other.

'Did you swear out a complaint against her?' I asked.

'I did. They'll never find her now she's disappeared into the rookeries.'

Jack called, 'Cab's here, darling,' and I got up.

I sank back, looking out of the window, when I spotted a lot of huge German sailors, about seven of them, staggering along the darkened street. Two of them had hoisted up a kicking figure. Her black stockinged legs came turmoiling out through ruffled petticoats, her hat was askew, and even from behind the closed windows of the cab I could hear her shouting. 'Here you – Hermann – let me down. Bastards! Police! Help! Kidnap!' Then she began yelling in another language altogether.

With difficulty I stopped the cab. The cabman didn't like the idea. One of the Germans laughed when I opened the door. He tried to grab me. 'Let her go or I shall go straight to the police station,' I commanded, very much the outraged lady.

They sobered a bit and put the woman down. She looked at me and cried out, 'Mary, my duck! I don't believe this,' and fell into my arms. The sailors milled about on the pavement. One grasped her. She gave him a backwards kick in the groin, jumped in the cab, fell into the seat, slamming the door at the same time. She cried, 'Whip up the horse, my man.' Then, turning to me, laughing, she said, 'Phew – my honour saved again.' The cabman's horse set off, slowly, leaving the sailors milling about on the pavement.

Rosie Levi was wearing a bright green taffeta dress, cut very low, a lot of rouge and a big hat with a feather in it.

'Mary – I don't believe it. How are you? Where you been?'

The cabman, who had had no instructions, turned round, asking, 'Where to?'

'How about Mrs Mundy's?' I asked. 'A drink after your ordeal.'

'Blimey! Those Hermanns don't half get boisterous,' she said, unpinning her hat, settling it back on her head at the right angle and pushing the hatpin through again. Then she pulled at her décolletage to order her bosom correctly. 'Well, Mrs Mundy's it is. You can tell me where you've been and what's been happening. I could do with a break. It's been a night and a half, I can tell you. Them sailors was just the last straw. I had two jockeys earlier. Two at the same time, I ask you – I think they were twins – and the man before that was less than five feet tall. I got to feeling like Snow White and the Seven Dwarves.'

The cab horse was still plodding slowly forward. 'Well, where d'you want to go?' the cabbie asked impatiently.

'Brushfield Street, my man,' ordered Rosie in a haughty tone.

He stopped the cab and turned round. 'No, lady. I'm not going there. Don't ask me.'

'I'll double the fare.'

'Not for a fortune,' he told us, and got promptly off his box into the road, opened the cab door and said, 'Sorry, ladies. I've got a wife and children and I stick to the main thoroughfares in this neighbourhood. Either get out or go somewhere else.'

I shrugged at Rosie. She shrugged back. 'We'll get out then,' I said.

'Rather you than me,' was the cabman's comment.

'So what turned you into a lady?' she enquired once we were out on the pavement and the cab was moving off. 'Did some rich gent adopt you and put you in a finishing school in France? La-de-da, la-de-da,' she carolled, adopting the walk of a woman too good for these streets. Then I felt her shiver.

'Cold?' I asked.

'No,' she said. She dragged me off the street, through a dismal court I couldn't remember. One gas-lamp shone weakly down on to its paving, slick with dirt and grease of every kind. The dark houses loomed on all four sides. A few windows were lit. A baby cried, high up. On another floor a couple shouted at each other, a candle flickering behind them. In doorways against walls were the dark bundles of sleeping people. One stirred, groaned, scratched, went limp again. There were footsteps behind us, a weary working man's tread. Rosie hurried me down the alley at the end of the court, between high walls, with privies behind judging by the smell. Then she crossed another street, went rapidly down another alley, into another court – I was lost by now. At the end of the next alley three men stopped talking to each other and watched us as we stepped quickly past them. In the next street a big pack of dogs, about seven or eight of them, rampaged past us. Then we were in Brushfield Street. Keeping up with Rosie's pace had made me breathless.

'What's the matter?' I asked, as we went into Mrs Mundy's. I sensed a desperation in her.

'I don't know. Things are getting worse. You have to

keep moving. How long since you were here? Seven, eight years?'

I nodded.

'That's what I mean,' she said.

I wondered what had been happening to her. She was twenty-three now and losing her freshness, a fast-perishing commodity in those streets.

Mrs Mundy's was empty, except for Cora herself, of course, and a man asleep at one of the tables in the middle, a tankard by his side.

'Hullo, girls. A reunion is it? What's it to be?'

'A pint of milk stout,' declared Rosie.

'The same,' I said. 'Any messages?'

She shook her head and poured the pints carefully. I ought to have known from her silence that she was hiding something, but at the time I thought nothing of it.

'So,' said Rosie, when we were seated, 'where have you been? Somewhere far off, judging by your complexion.'

Her own, I noticed, was blotchy under the coating of white powder. She had always been very fresh-looking when I'd first known her, with big brown eyes, fluffy pale brown hair and a healthy flush beneath her skin. Now she was wearing a lot more rouge and she looked tired. Beneath the gaiety which was so natural to her that, as she said, she thought she must have been born laughing, some stale current ran. Still, life as an East End tart isn't like being a patient in a sanatorium. I told her my lying tale of Canada, marriage, widowhood, the coming trip to Scotland. After eight years you don't tell a friend everything. You never know what they might have got up to in the mean while.

She took a long drink and said, 'Pull the other one, Mary, do. There ain't no husband, is there, and never has been? I believe you're in the same old game and doing very well. How's that?'

87

I didn't answer.

'Look here,' she said. 'If you're on to a good thing and there's room for one more inside, share your secret.'

'Perhaps I will, later on,' I told her.

She leaned back in her chair and stared at me. 'You're a hard one,' she said.

'Perhaps I am. I've had to be. Apart from anything else, a doctor in New York made a mess of what was left of my inside.'

She looked at me in alarm. Rosie never got anything wrong with her inside, to my knowledge. I don't suppose she'd ever even had the clap. She kept herself very clean and ate a lot of fish, which might have helped. I went on, 'Never mind that. Something's worrying you, I can tell. What is it?'

'Bless you, nothing worries Rosie,' she said. Then, 'It's nothing – it's everything, I suppose. Times are hard. I'm not getting any younger.'

'You're only twenty-three?'

'I'm not advancing myself,' she proclaimed.

I stared at her. She was a funny girl, Rosie, or perhaps it was just being a Jew. They have a different way of looking at things. Where the English'll stand in a pub spending the rent on beer and singing 'God Save the Queen' a Jew's more likely to be found in a synagogue or a political club. Even in their own back kitchens, boots off, drinking tea, and smoking pipes, they're having long discussions, while the old Jewess stuffs a few more coppers in the mattress, cooks up something smelly on her fire, and starts scrubbing and scouring all the pots.

Rosie's father was a cobbler who worked for another Jew in the city and she had three brothers and three sisters. From what she said, this was the form in her home, endless tea, religion and discussions of this and that, nothing practical, just God and the nature of man and putting the world to rights. The English don't go in for all that. Not being English myself, but half French, half Irish, I understand the Jews a little, for the French believe in education and, however ignorant an Irishman may be, or drunk, he usually respects a learned man.

So, Rosie being a Jewess as well as a tart, I wasn't completely surprised to hear her speak of progress in a measured and dignified way, as if it meant something, which it couldn't in her case. The average East End tart doesn't make progress – remorselessly down, from bad to worse, is the usual route.

'I wouldn't talk like this to anyone but you,' she further confided, 'only I can tell by looking at you that you've bettered yourself and, well, you know it. Now, look at me. For me, there's nothing. Only the hope of rolling a sailor for his pay, a toff for a few sovs, and how long do they last? I'm not one to dream of a duke or an earl taking a fancy to me, true love, or whatever. What I've got is what I've got and there isn't any more.' She paused, and added, 'And now I'm in fear.'

'What of?' I asked.

'I don't know.' She thought, then said, 'Mary – you know there's always trouble round here, plenty of it, but now, I don't know – I feel bad, as if the whole neighbourhood was rotting like a piece of old meat. It's full of people trying to save it, closing brothels, rescuing orphans, saving fallen women, handing out soup. But they've come too late. They can't stop it. It gets more crowded and dirty and broken down every minute. Rents keep on going up. Trade's in a slump. The kids are getting more wicked and bold, got to, poor little buggers. Mary,' she appealed to me, 'you know how it used to be – up with your skirts, huff, puff and it's over – he felt better, you took his money, that was the way. Now – and it's not just the East Enders, it's the others too – they're getting horrible. They want to hit you, spit on you, talk filthy talk to you. That used to be rare, now it isn't. And they're more after the little girls and boys now, there's more of that kind of nasty business going on. Tell me, Mary, am I imagining it, am I going doolally, or what? Is it all in my own head, or is it this place? Sometimes I feel so bad . . .' Her voice shook.

I was staring at her. I didn't know, either, whether she was describing something true, or whether it was all fantasy.

She continued in a more normal voice, 'I'm wondering if it isn't because of these God botherers, saving souls all over the place. You'd think it'd improve matters, but maybe telling men all the time how evil they are turns them worse. There was a horrible murder of a woman just three weeks ago in George Yard Buildings, not a quarter of a mile from where we're sitting now. That woman, an old whore of forty-five, was found on a landing, poor cow, stabbed thirty-nine times. It must have been a madman. They were that worried they called in the CID but they never caught the man. That was round Thrawl Street. That's why I raced you through at the charge. Now you know why. And she's not the only one.'

Horrible as this crime had been, the murder of a prostitute was not unusual in Whitechapel. There would be one or two a year, women killed by a rival, a pimp, a customer, maybe by one of the gangs of young men who used to rove about, preying on prostitutes.

I asked Rosie what had become of her protector, a tall, handsome Swede who had jumped ship at Tilbury and taken to living off women.

'Someone cut him up bad in a pub fight,' she told me. 'You remember how he used to drink. While he was in hospital I had other offers, but I thought I'd go it alone. They don't like it. I don't like it much myself. It's lonely, but it's helped me to save a little money.'

'What about the danger?'

'What danger? That Lars was never there – he used to wait in the Lion for us to bring the money to him: we used to look after each other, as much as we could. In the end it looked as if Lars couldn't even protect himself. He wasn't half a sight in the hospital, all done up in bandages.' She burst into a roar of laughter. 'I'm telling you he was so wrapped up it could have been anybody. Sal knocked on the bedstead and said, "Is anybody in?" God, how we laughed. Hey, Cora,' she called out, 'fetch us a couple of gins.' She leaned forward now and said, 'Come on, spit it out – what are you here for?'

'I'm looking for Mary Claire and Mary Jane,' I explained. 'I told my dear mother before she died I'd look after them. But of course, I cut and run from Jim, so I lost them. So – I'm better off now and I've come to see how they're faring. I've heard Mary Claire went to Liverpool some years back. Mary Jane's in the neighbourhood, they tell me, but I haven't caught her yet. I only arrived yesterday and as it seems she stole some cloth from an old Jew, she won't be showing her face much. She's been in Goulston Street, the Old Nicholl, all over the place, always in rat holes of one kind or another. Have you heard anything about her? Or Mary Claire?'

Rosie shook her head, making a face. 'The Old Nicholl. Blimey.'

'I'll go and look for her.'

'Not at this time of night,' Rosie exclaimed. The Old Nicholl was the worst part of the East End slums, full of gangs. Policemen there patrolled in pairs.

'No – not tonight,' I said and yawned.

Rosie stood and stretched. 'You're tired and I must love you and leave you, as the soldier said. I've promised my room a good turn-out tomorrow. Will you come and visit me?'

I said I would. 'It's nice to see you again, Rosie,' I said, as we went to the door.

'Likewise,' she told me. 'Cheerio, Cora, my darling. Don't do anything I wouldn't do.'

We parted in the street, she strolling off in her tatty finery as if she hadn't a care in the world. 'Cheerio, my dear,' she called. I heard her singing as she walked alone up the middle of the dark street. 'Ta-ra-ra boom-de-ay, my drawers flew away, They came back yesterday, let's hope they're here to stay.'

'Shut up,' called a voice from an upper window.

'All right, my dear,' Rosie called back confidently.

I, more sober, walked back to my lodgings, reflecting that, though less cheery, I had fewer burdens than Rosie. For one thing, she'd been cast out by her family on account of her way of life. They'd even read the Jewish funeral service over her, which meant she was dead to them henceforth, and I know this upset her. Still, I reflected, she would make a most promising recruit for my Canadian enterprise. She was clean, sober on the whole, sensible and energetic and I now knew she wanted to leave the East End.

I was extremely exhausted when I reached Fleet Street. I'd only arrived recently, had slept badly and had been running round London all day and now it was the early hours of the morning. My only hope was for a long, undisturbed sleep, well into Friday morning. I washed, brushed out my hair, got into my nightdress and lay down. I was asleep as soon as my head touched the pillow – but not for long.

A voice, in my dream, kept singing jovially, 'Good for any game at night, boys, Champagne Charlie is my name. Good for any game at night, boys . . .' I gazed at a sickly ape in little red trousers and a red fez perched on a barrel organ in a crowded street. Oh, the horror of that little creature. Its eyes watered. 'I'm going to marry Yum-yum,

yum-yum,' it sang. 'Going to marry Yum-yum.' The barrel organ ground out a tune from the music halls, 'The boy I love is up in the gallery'. Then a creature caught me against a wall in a square of black, blind-eyed buildings. A hand, a paw, came over my mouth; a face, or a muzzle, was pressed to mine in a reek of liquorice. I woke, suffocating. It was no dream, I quickly realized. There was a hard and heavy hand over my mouth. My eyes darted from side to side round the dark room. Only a little light came through a crack in the curtains. The rest was pitch black. And above me was a dark figure, with one knee on the bed, I guessed, and one hard hand pressed over my mouth, while the other was on my shoulder, holding me down. I began to toss my head violently, attempting to dislodge the hand enough to get my teeth into it. A familiar voice then said, 'Don't thrash about so, girl. It's only me. If I take my hand away, will you be quiet?' He released the pressure on my mouth enough to enable me to nod.

The hands were removed from my face and shoulder. I struggled up. My attacker now sat near me on the bed, near enough to fall on me and silence me, or prevent me from moving, if he wished. I stared, in the dim light, at the man who had apparently got through the locked and bolted doors downstairs (I had seen to all this myself when I came in). Unless that silly Dora let out her lover later and left the back door unlocked, he would have had to climb the drainpipe at the front in a city street, seldom empty, then swing off it to get on to the bedroom windowsill four feet away, push up the bedroom window silently, and climb in without waking me. Jim Bristow could have done such a thing, had done such things in the past – and had done it now.

I suppose it was a relief the intruder was Jim. Unless things had changed much for the worse, he wouldn't murder me for my hairbrushes.

'Well, Jim,' I said in a low voice, for I did not want a disturbance, 'this is an unusual way to call. Couldn't you have knocked at the door, like anybody else?' As I spoke, and he listened, I snatched my Colt from under a pillow to my right (I was sleeping on the left side of the bed) and at the same time rolled over and out, which left me standing beside the bed aiming my gun at him. This he had not expected. Men of Jim's kind expect coshes or knives, not guns, which are for the gentry. And none of these weapons in the hands of a woman.

He recovered quickly and said, 'Don't shoot. I don't mean any harm.'

I kept my finger on the trigger, so he could see it, though. I had no real idea of shooting. I did not think he meant to attack me. The Jims of this world do not harm women, unless they have said they love them. As for me, I had no wish to kill him. It would only have been for revenge and he had done to me no more than what thousands and thousands of men have done to women. If all women with no more grudge than I took to shooting their menfolk, they would have to recruit all the others as gravediggers.

'Why are you here?' I demanded.

'Let me light the gas,' he said, 'so we can see each other.'

'I don't want to see you, Jim,' I told him. 'Leave now and we'll say no more about it. Otherwise, I'll raise the alarm and say you came to rob me. How did you find me, anyway?'

'Followed you from Mundy's,' he replied promptly.

That was the reason for Cora's shifty looks. The old bitch had told him how to find me.

'I only wanted to talk to you,' he said, 'for old times' sake.'

And all the more, I thought, now he'd looked round the room, spotted the silver appointments of my dressing-

94

table, the long string of amethysts I'd taken off the day before, and looped over the side of the mirror before I set off for the East End. Not that Cora Mundy, during her revelations, wouldn't have told him 'an old friend of yours, Mary Kelly's, back', without adding 'done very nicely for herself, by all appearances'.

'Old times' sake, eh, Jim?' I said. My tone must have been grim for my finger suddenly began to itch on the trigger. He'd taken the money I'd earned dropping my drawers in the dark for all and sundry, sent me off to Old Fanny Baines for a dirty abortion and abandoned me when it nearly killed me, and from this, or from the disease I'd caught, I'd fetched up half a woman, lucky not to be dead. For a moment I thought it might be worth shooting him, purely for the principle of the thing, and putting up with all the trouble of appearing soberly costumed at the Old Bailey, shaken and sobbing, claiming I'd woke up to find a burglar rifling my jewellery box. Anyway, he caught the hanging judge note in my voice and said, 'Come on, Mary dear, let me light the gas.'

'Light it then,' I said.

He took the matches from the mantelpiece and stretched up to light the gas mantles. When he turned, he flinched a bit, seeing me clearly with my hair down, in my night-dress, holding a gun pointed at him, with an expression on my face, I'm sure, like the statue of Justice.

In my turn, I saw a figure in a greasy-looking black waistcoat, bright bandanna round his throat, shirt not fresh for a week, black trousers and patent leather shoes, somewhat cracked and dirty. A moulting peacock, Jim was not tall, though he was strong as one of those weeds which put down obstinate roots in city soil. His dark hair was a stubble, which probably meant he'd been in gaol and had his head shaved. His face was pale and plainly his last bath had been months before. As Cora Mundy had put it, things hadn't gone well for him recently.

He shifted uneasily in a way I remembered, but demanded boldly, 'What's going on? I'm not a bloody Indian tribe you need to hold off with a gun.' (So Cora had added even more information, I noted, such as where I'd been.) He continued, 'It's me, Jim, and I've come to help you. Put the pistol down and let's talk.'

I didn't, so he went on, rapidly, 'See here – Cora Mundy tells me you're wandering Whitechapel at night, looking for Mary Jane. For a start, that's dangerous. You need a man about you for work like that, as well you know. And, moreover, I can help you track her down. Gun or no gun, Mary, you need some help and protection. God knows what life you must have been living,' he added piously, 'to have to sleep with something like that under your pillow. But the point is, if you really want to find Mary Jane, you need a man who knows what's what to go about with you and protect you.'

Yes, I thought, a half-breed Indian six feet tall, paid to do so. With him, I felt safe. With Jim Bristow, never. The fact was that even crouched in the steerage of a ship beating up and down in the Atlantic, on my way to a place I knew nothing about 3000 miles away, I'd felt easier in my mind than I had in London with Jim. His eye quickly lit on the silver-framed photograph of Esmeralda's which stood on the dressing-table. It showed the house with tall pines behind. The Indian was standing barefoot on the verandah with his shotgun. Jim glanced back at me quickly, smiling his charmer's smile. 'Anyway, like it or not, there was always something between us,' he told me.

He had not come up a drainpipe at two in the morning to persuade me to go to church. He hoped to seduce me, thus the liquorice he had chewed to disguise the smell of tobacco and whatever he had drunk, perhaps even the empty-belly reek of his breath.

I said, 'Whatever there might have been between us was

a long time ago. I don't need you, Jim. You'd better get out.'

'Charming woman you've turned into,' said he, going out of the room and across the sitting-room as if to the door. Half-way across, he turned. 'I know where Mary Jane is.'

'I don't believe you.'

'Don't, then,' he advised with his hand on the door-knob. I dropped my hand, with the gun in it, to my side.

With the door open he turned again, to face me. 'If you want to find out where Mary is, meet me at the Ten Bells at ten o'clock tomorrow night.'

He was grappling, like a wrestler for a good hold, one that would make me feel the pain of it. He had planned to catch me at a disadvantage, alone, at night, in bed, and take advantage of the apprehension any woman must feel in that situation. If it led to some love passages between us, so much, he would consider, the better. His aim would be to make me fear, or love him – or both – for that was the way of it between Jim Bristow and the women he knew. My producing a gun had overturned his plans, yet I knew in the end I would get nothing from him unless I played the part he expected – I, powerless, begging and imploring, he powerful, giving or refusing at his discretion. So I agreed to meet him. 'Leave your lover at home,' he told me, nodding at my revolver, then left.

I went down some minutes later, to lock the door and draw the bolts after him. I came up again and slammed and bolted my bedroom window. If I had not left it open, Jim would not have been able to ease it up and creep in.

Then I lay down on my bed, and found myself drifting off into a kind of stupor. The room still smelt of Jim, his unfresh clothes and body, and behind that unmistakable odour, the very essence of Whitechapel poverty. With it came over me the old Whitechapel fatigue. This is caused by men and women eating and sleeping when they can, not when they ought, by being kept awake by lice, bedbugs, crying babies, shouting drunks, or hunger, or rolling home drunk at three, or by rising at three to queue for work – in docks and markets, unloading a wagon of threshing sheep or bucking cows, brought in late at night – or by walking the streets till dawn, or rising all night to tend fretful children. This fatigue, and the depletion of body and mind it brings, is one of the faces of want. The well-off take their rest, the poor doze when they can, and are often startled awake; the well-off have stocked larders, the poor shop ten times a day, for tea in a screw of paper, a gill of milk, a herring, a slice of soap. The well-off clean their homes, the poor pick up a rag, try to wipe a floor clean, the baby cries, they tend it, tire, forget what they were doing. The well-off go to their regular employment, the poor hear of a job, run to get it, may fail and walk home again. If they get the job, it lasts only a day, perhaps only half a day. So each day, each hour of each day is unpredictable, confused, a battle. This weary, chancy way of life is one of the real hardships of poverty and one of the reasons why it is so hard to rise from it. Unsuspectingly, I was re-entering this world.

I cursed Cora Mundy. She had deliberately given Jim a way of finding me and, by hinting at my prosperity, a reason for making the attempt. Did he know where Mary Jane could be found? Or was it just a trick to capture my attention and find out what I was worth to him?

Finally, I fell into a nervous, restless sleep, full of dreams, and woke, unrefreshed, in my stuffy bedroom with the maid, Dora, standing beside me with a cup of tea, and glancing round the room. She had heard a man's voice that night, I guessed, and caught the sound of bolts being drawn and pushed back. Now, because I had caught her with her lover, she would watch me carefully, and try to get evidence of guilt.

Even before Dora had gone, or I had begun to drink the tea, the day began with a vengeance. There was a ring on the bell outside. Dora went down to answer. There were feet on the stairs and, as I got up and put on my wrapper, the parlour door opened. A little child's voice, northern in sound, moaned, 'I want home, mother,' and I opened the bedroom door to find in front of me, fatter and dressed in heavy serge, with white piping, a dreadful bonnet on her head, my sister, Mary Claire. By the hand she had a little boy of about eighteen months, in a dress and blue serge coat, a hat pulled down over his brown, curly hair. There was a young man behind her in the doorway.

I cried, 'Clara!' for that was our name for her in the family, and ran to her. Her body was stiff as I hugged her. She moved away from the embrace, pecking my cheek. 'I've found you!' I exclaimed. 'Thank God you're safe and sound!'

But the smile she gave me was restrained. Her eyes took in my nightdress and ruffled peignoir, travelled uncertainly round the room.

The man behind her, whom I recognized as Mr Ratcliffe's clerk, stepped forward. 'If you've no more need of me, Mrs Frazer,' he said, 'I'll go off and leave you to your happy reunion.'

After he had gone, Mary Claire, still standing in the middle of the room, said, in a rather cold voice, 'I read your advertisement. I'm pleased to see you looking so well. And this is Thomas, my boy. There's baby Andrew, also, but I've left him behind with mother.'

'Mother?' I asked. It began to feel a little like a dream. Here stood Mary Claire, a little stout, in her navy dress with the small, blue-ribboned straw hat skewered fast to an uncompromising scraped-back bun, holding by the hand a little boy, my nephew, and now speaking of mother, when our mother had of course been dead for nearly ten years.

'Mrs Sugden, senior,' she told me. 'I am married to Mr Sugden.'

'Oh, yes,' I said, confused now. 'Well, sit down, Clara, do, and tell me how you are.'

'I can't stay too long,' she told me. 'I must be back in Liverpool at seven.'

'So soon?' I asked. 'You shouldn't have come all this way with the child. I could have come to you. Why didn't you write?'

We'd been merry girls, as girls are in spite of hardships. I could remember Mary Claire, my Clara, dancing about in boots and petticoats, hair flying, singing silly songs. We'd been pretty girls, too, with a taste for finery, forever quarrelling over who was to wear the nicest stockings, blouse or hat. This Mary Claire, the new one, eight years on, was vastly different. I was beginning to feel awkward and discouraged. I said, 'You must want some breakfast after your journey. And Thomas must have some milk.'

I told Dora, inside the doorway and staring hard, 'Will you get us some breakfast?' But Clara interrupted, 'We had breakfast at the station, thank you. I was not certain I'd find you. Fortunately, Mr Ratcliffe was at home when I called, and asked his clerk to conduct me to you.'

'Tea, then,' I said to Dora. 'And a glass of milk and a biscuit, if you can find one.' Not without a backward glance, she went off.

I leaned forward in my own chair, as Mary Claire sat there with the boy in her lap, and said, 'So, I have two nephews. And how are you, Clara? I'm so happy to find you. I'm searching for Janie, too. Do you know where she is?'

'I don't,' she told me. 'I've had nothing to do with her since I left London. You seem well and prosperous, Mary Anne. Where have you been? We worried when you disappeared.' She had been glancing at my hand. 'Are you married too?'

I shook my head. I knew I ought not to tell her how I had led my life since I'd left London. Clara bore all the signs of respectability, her expression was so restrained as to constitute something like a warning. She did not want to hear my story. I ought, I knew, to resurrect poor Mrs Frazer, the youthful widow, with the respectable family awaiting her in Scotland, because that was what she wanted to hear.

Instead, I told the truth. 'I had to run away, Clara, believe me, being so abused and mistreated by Jim Bristow. Since then I have become prosperous, running my house in Calgary. Don't judge me, Clara,' I added, like the heroine in a sentimental play, as her expression hardened. 'What choice did I have, arriving penniless and alone?' She did not soften. 'At all events,' I said, 'I came back when I could to make sure you and Mary Jane were safe and sound, and to help you if I could.'

She had looked from me to the child and back, as I spoke, as if to see how much he was taking in. I'm sad to say that as I spoke, her face was not only unfriendly, but dour, as if she heard news no better than she expected.

She responded, 'I've no need of your assistance, thank you. Though Mary Jane might be glad of it.'

'Have you any idea where I might find her?' I felt I was pleading.

'Let me be quite plain with you, Mary Anne,' she told me emphatically, like a woman many years older, 'and let me tell you once and for all. I have no wish or desire for any connection with your affairs, or Mary Jane's. When I left for Liverpool with my fiancé, Mr Sugden, you were long gone and Mary Jane' – and here she glanced at the child – 'was going her own way, had been for many years, lacking the care of either parent, and perhaps not much improved by the example of her oldest sister. Mr Sugden was then a seaman, but being married got employment ashore, as a clerk with a large shipping firm. We're not wealthy folk, but we're comfortable in a modest way. My husband was born a Baptist and though he lapsed in his seagoing days he found the faith again. I am baptized now. I have found true faith, Mary Anne, and set aside the error in which we were reared.'

'You've put the past behind you?' I said flatly.

'I have. It scarcely exists for me any longer.'

'No pity, no thanks for your mother, who tried to rear you?'

She looked at me, remembering, I have no doubt, that stumbling, defeated woman coming home with uncertain, tipsy steps to the room we all lived and slept in, recalling, perhaps, her unhappy, sodden muttering sleep, the grey-faced beginnings of another toilsome day, those helpless, anxious eyes which sometimes went over us, her daughters, as we went about our daily business, the excuses and tears to the landlord coming for the rent – our mother's errors, her weakness, her loneliness, and struggle. She may even have remembered her love. But she could not afford those recollections and resented me for forcing them on her.

'I have pity – yes,' she responded.

'A grain of pity, but, it seems, no more. Have you even that much for Mary Jane?'

Her face unstiffened for a moment. 'What do you expect me to do?' she burst out. 'Take her in? I don't want it and Mr Sugden wouldn't stand for it. Why should he? Mary Jane's life is her own. It has nothing to do with me.'

The room was warm, but it felt cold. My sister sat solidly in her unbecoming hat, worn like a crown, condemning me, her mother and sister for their lives. I could not blame her, but it was not what I expected when I had begun my voyage to find her. She had fallen silent as Dora came in, all eyes as usual, and set down the tray with a pot of tea and a mug of milk on it. Dora left. My sister had composed herself after her outburst. 'Suppose you discover Mary Jane, what will you do?' she asked me.

'Take her back to Calgary, if she'll come,' I said.

'To that . . .' She could not bring herself to pronounce the word 'brothel'. 'To that place,' she finally said.

'It's better than Whitechapel, Clara,' I told her.

She flinched even at the mention of the name, then set down her cup resolutely and delivered a statement. 'I'm very glad to have seen you again, Mary Anne, and to know you're alive and well and prospering. But it was in my mind as I came from Liverpool last night that we came to the parting of the ways many years ago – your doing, not mine. And that it wasn't likely we could mend matters. I want no part of that old life. I have a new one now. I have written out the address of a good woman nearby to me on this card and you may send letters to me there, only if essential.' She took a card from her handbag and gave it to me. The address on it was in Fleetwood, some way from Liverpool.

'So I'm not even to know where you live?' I said, stung.

'It's better not,' she replied firmly. 'I must go now. It's a long way back.' And she set the child on his feet and led him from the room. She did not even turn in the doorway to wish me goodbye and good luck.

I sat on for a few minutes, quite stunned, then was on my feet in a rage, pacing the room, furious at, yet wounded by, this cold rejection. To be considered too wicked and corrupt for the rest of the world is one thing, to be treated like a leper by your own sister is another. Hadn't I brushed her hair every night when she was young? Hadn't I taken a comb and vinegar to it weekly against lice, given up my wages, whether of virtue as a milliner, or vice as a tart, to help put food in her mouth and boots on her feet? Hadn't we gone out hand in hand on cold days when we were short of coal, to collect scraps of wood, chair legs, bits of rotten skirting board, for burning? Hadn't I taken her to *Robin Hood and his Merry Men* at the Pavilion Theatre one Christmas when I was in funds, on a tram to Victoria Park to hear the band (though, come to think of it, Jim and I had run off somewhere and she'd had to find her own way back, with only sixpence in her pocket)? And now I was not even to be allowed to know where she lived, had to correspond with her through a stranger, and, she'd made it pretty clear, only in emergencies. I had become, it seemed, my sister's guilty secret.

Spite and thoughts of revenge filled my head. When the day dawned that that eminent shipping clerk, Mr Sugden, lost his employment or fell under a Lime Street tram, I thought, and a letter arrived in Canada, via Mr Ratcliffe my lawyer, appealing for assistance, what rough answer wouldn't I give? I knew what happened in such cases. Dolly Halloran had many a letter about the poor harvests and drowned pigs in Donegal from a family which would not speak her name, because of the disgrace she'd brought on them in earlier days. Many a now-prosperous rancher, shipped out as a failure, or to avoid scandal, had found himself the cornerstone of a family which had as good as disowned him in the old days. So, I thought, when the tale of outgrown shoes and day-old bread, or the funds suddenly needed for my brother-in-law to seize a business opportunity reached my ears in Canada, Clara need not expect a kind response from me.

After half an hour of raging, a kind of pity for her came over me. She had lost her mother and her oldest sister, who should have taken care of her – small wonder she'd become bitter. Now she had obliterated her family and her past, no doubt had a false tale she told her neighbours, kept a silence even with her husband about where he'd found her, and what her circumstances had been. The truth was between her and God, now, and, as we know, He is often lied to, puts up no arguments and never tells.

What sort of a life had she, hating her own past life, forced to lie, clinging righteously to her dreary familiar things, a small cold house, an ugly chapel at the end of the street, embracing, sober-faced and sadly clothed, the dull routine of Sunday psalm-singing and Monday washday, through to the Saturday whitening of the front step, the scrubbing, polishing, cooking, shopping, ironing, black-leading and holystoning?

As I stood, thinking all this by the fireplace, in came Dora to collect the tray, but goggle-eyed.

'Mrs Frazer,' she told me, 'the baker came with such a horrible tale – a woman foully murdered by some stables right off Whitechapel Road, just opposite the hospital.'

All my blood seemed to drain away. I stood frozen, one hand on the mantelpiece, just strong enough to stand, but not speak or move. She went on, relishing the tale, and its effect on me, 'They found her early this morning, two men going off to work in the market, thought at first she'd been ravaged, then her throat cut. But when they come to undress her in the mortuary, oh dear, oh my, didn't they find she'd been horribly mutilated, ripped right open like a pig, with big slashes down her belly, torn up you know where. Ain't it horrible?' Her big blue eyes were wide and frightened, yet she enjoyed the fear. 'There's a monster at large,' she concluded.

My first thought had been for Mary Jane and Rosie. 'What was she called?' I managed to bring out.

'They don't know, says the breadman. It sounded like some poor old tart, from what they're saying in the neighbourhood – begging your pardon, ma'am, a poor unfortunate, I should have said. Well, that's the most likely, ain't it, unless he knew her, the murderer, I mean. Perhaps it's his wife, though. Wicked villain. He must have been covered in blood, after hacking her about like that. It made me come over quite faint when I heard.'

As she spoke I had turned and gone into my bedroom,

begun to splash my face with water, brush out my hair. I got out of my wrap and nightdress and put on my chemise. 'Help me,' I called. 'I have to go out. I'm in a hurry.' Her face full of curiosity, she tied the string of my petticoats, buttoned my boots as I did up my hair. While at work with the buttonhook on the floor she said, 'Mind you, there was another woman killed round there only a fortnight ago, stabbed over a hundred times, they said.' She looked up at me. 'Do you think it could be the same man?'

'I don't know,' I said, feigning indifference, but I had already thought of Rosie's story about the woman who had been killed three weeks earlier, and the fear she'd said she had begun to feel. 'It's as if the whole neighbourhood was rotting like a piece of meat,' she'd said; and then she'd gone off, drunk, alone, singing. Dora handed me my hatpins as I put on a bonnet and so, uncorseted, breakfast-less and poorly washed, I rushed into the street, found an empty cab and went to Mrs Mundy's.

I banged violently on her door to make her open up. It was just after nine o'clock. A man with a handcart stopped to watch me beating on the door. A woman came out on the pavement and said, 'She's up. I've heard her moving about.'

Finally, Cora opened the door in a huge unclean night-dress, like a tent, and a shawl over her shoulders. Seeing me, she tried to shut the door again. I'd have none of it, and stuck my boot in the crack. A couple of women with baskets joined the man with the handcart and the woman who lived next door to watch. 'Let me in, Cora, it's not what you think,' I said loudly. She was forced to open the door.

'For God's sake,' she protested, 'what is all this?'

In the bar, which smelt of last night's beer and tobacco, I asked her urgently, 'The woman who was murdered – who was she?'

'Murdered?' she exclaimed in confusion. 'What murder?' She must have guessed Jim had been to see me (or knew he had) and thought I'd come to row with her.

'A woman was killed last night,' I said. 'She was cut up and mutilated near Whitechapel Road, opposite the hospital.'

Cora stared at me. I even had a moment of doubt. Perhaps it was just a silly rumour; Cora usually knew everything which happened within a mile of her alehouse, almost before it happened. She seemed to pluck information from the air, like catching flies.

'I don't know what you're talking about.'

Harry opened the door at the back on cue, an enamel mug of tea in his hand. He was unshaven, wearing shirt and trousers, and slippers on his feet. He filled the doorway.

'That's right, ma. I had it from her next door.' He nodded in the direction he meant. 'She put her head over the fence while I was in the yard. They found a dead woman up against a stable doorway in Bucks Row, round Durward Street, all cut up. Ask me, I'd say it was the same bloke who killed that tart, Martha somebody.'

'What was her name?' I cried.

'They don't know her name or who she was. Why come here? Oh . . .' he said, understanding. 'You think it might be Mary Jane. Well, I don't suppose so. If you're going to go running through the streets with your hair hanging down every time somebody cuts up a tart you'll soon be skin and bone. Still, it's not nice, I'll give you that, especially if one man done both crimes. But they've probably got him by now anyway. You'd better go to the police station.'

What he said steadied me. At least Harry was always sensible. Even so, as I turned to go I felt dizzy. Cora spotted it.

'Oh, sit down, Mary. You look all over the place,' Cora

said impatiently. 'I'll get you a little drop of gin to steady your nerves. How can it be Mary Jane – she's not reduced to going down the back of the coalyard in Bucks Row with men she doesn't know, is she? That's for the lowest of the low. She'll turn up,' she assured me. 'If she's still here she'll soon get to hear you're asking for her. You'd do better to go out shopping, go to a play, enjoy yourself a bit.' She shook her head compassionately. 'Your nerves'll go completely at this rate. You'll get ill, that's a fact. Find yourself a sweetheart and go down to Brighton, get some sea air. You used to be giddy enough. You never stopped laughing and kicking up your heels. Now look at you—'

'I suppose you've got Jim Bristow in mind to restore my lost gaiety,' I interrupted. 'Well, I don't want him and you had no right to point him in my direction.'

'What's wrong with him?' she said angrily, feeling in the wrong, prepared for a quarrel. 'He's a lively sort.'

'Lively?' I said. 'He turned up last night looking like a three-day-old corpse. Where's his hair? It hasn't been long since he got out of prison, that's my guess.'

She didn't answer. 'You've got very fussy since you left,' she began.

'Hah!' I told her. Harry Mundy was laughing. 'Listen, Cora,' I said, 'I'm here for a purpose, and that's all. I don't require a pimp or a sweetheart, and if I wanted one, or both, Jim would be the last man on earth I'd pick—'

'You're a silly old cow,' Harry Mundy told his mother unsympathetically. To me, he said, 'Anyone can see you're well above all that and as for Jim, she may love him, but I don't. He's a fool, and if he don't end up on the gallows it won't be for want of trying, and as for gaol, well, you're right there, six months for being caught breaking into a pawnbroker's.' He paused. 'Only thing is, he may know where your sister is.'

'Why do you say that?'

'Just a notion I have,' he responded. 'Excuse me – I've business to do.' And he'd dived back into his kitchen before I could stop him.

A bedraggled woman came in, hair poking out from under her bonnet and a general air of beginning the morning before last night was properly over. Cora was annoyed. She would not have opened up so soon if I'd not come round.

'Give me a pint, my dear,' gasped the woman. 'I've had a shock. Someone told me about a poor bitch cut up in Whitechapel Road—'

'Goodbye, Cora,' I called out, and legged it down Commercial Street to Whitechapel police station, which I entered with a trepidation caused by past experiences I'd had there.

I got through the crowd and to the desk. I asked the sergeant, a tall stringy fellow with a black moustache, 'That woman killed, what was her name? My sister's missing.'

He shook his head. 'At a time like this, everybody's sister is missing, or their mother or their daughter. We haven't yet identified the woman.'

'Her age, then?'

Deducing that my sister was probably in her twenties, he kindly said, 'Thirty-five or forty, no younger.'

The dead woman couldn't be Mary, I thought, or Rosie Levi for that matter.

'I don't think it's her,' I said. 'But as I'm here, will you help me?' And I launched into my usual tale of widowhood and Scotland and my hunt for Mary Jane, asking if he could get the records examined for any clue as to her whereabouts. I think he was attracted to me in spite of my untidy appearance, for he willingly went off to organize a search, then returned, and asked me to wait. I found a seat opposite the desk and assumed a composure I did not feel, for the place made me uneasy.

I waited while the station's clients came in and out – a captured pickpocket and the woman who had laid hold of him, two drunken sailors arrested for fighting, a woman with a baby in her shawl, crying out to the police to find a lost child – a whole parade of the accused, the accusers, policemen. A respectable-looking woman in a blouse with a diamond brooch at her throat came in, paused, shocked no doubt by the smell and the noise, then rushed to the desk, pushing aside a group consisting of policemen, a thieving apprentice who had taken a brass ingot from his master's workshop, and the indignant owner. The lady began, insensately, to ask about a spaniel she'd lost the day before in Hyde Park. She'd been to nine police stations, already, she said. The policeman, the apprentice and the robbed master yielded to her. The apprentice spoke on and on to his employer in a mumble – this would break his mother's heart, his sister was ill, he was sorry, he would never do such a thing again. Meanwhile the sergeant said to the lady, 'Well, madam, I expect the police are doing all they can, but you'll have been told of the traffic in stolen pets.'

'That's exactly why I'm here,' she exclaimed. 'An officer told me a Chinaman might have eaten him.'

'I wouldn't think so myself, really, madam,' the policeman said.

'Can you investigate? It's a most terrible thought. My husband and I are most distressed.'

'Indeed you must be,' he said. Meanwhile the thieving apprentice was talking his master round. The delay, as the sergeant dealt patiently with a member of the respectable classes, had proved useful to the boy.

'I do understand your distress, madam,' said the policeman. 'I should be upset myself if I thought anything like that had happened to my own pet animal. But we've never had any reports here of a Chinese eating a dog. They're most respectable and hardworking people on the whole, so I think you can rest easy on that score. Though if we did,' he added, 'I wouldn't be hopeful of laying hands on the villain; for there are thousands of Chinamen in the East End, you know, and they all look pretty much the same.'

There was a stir as a sailor dragged through the doors with a girl in a petticoat and shawl, her boots unlaced. He hauled her right up to the counter, exclaiming, 'Rifling my pocket, the bitch.' The policeman holding the apprentice let go of him and went to intervene. He got him by the shoulder. The sergeant behind the desk reproved, 'Wait your turn and watch your language with ladies present.'

'Lady! She's no lady! She's a common thieving whore,' cried the sailor. 'Lay hold on her, not me.'

As this went on the apprentice and his master, after a quick whispered conversation, evaporated from the police station.

'That's not the lady I was referring to,' said the sergeant with a glance at the woman who had lost her spaniel.

Another policeman came in with a piece of paper in his hand and gave it to the sergeant. He glanced at it and seemed to sigh. My eyes fixed on it. I could just read a name, Marie Jeanette Kelly. The sergeant put the piece of paper on the desk. The sailor was still clutching the girl, who was crying out, 'I never done nothing, I swear it. He wouldn't pay me, that's all. He's the robber. It's him – he's the thief.' The lady with the lost dog had flinched back and was grasping at her blouse near the throat with a long, well-tended hand. She glanced in alarm round the room at the waiting men and women while the shouting girl, still with last night's rouge and powder blotching her nose and cheeks, kept on struggling and protesting.

'All right. We'll hold her,' the sergeant said to the sailor. 'And you sit down and wait your turn.'

The other woman said rather quickly, 'Sergeant – I hope you'll look out for my dog. He's called Buffie. And here is my card.' She went to the door looking neither right nor left. The girl was taken off crying and yelling denials, the sailor left the counter and sat down. The sergeant looked at me, and at the piece of paper.

'There's a record of a Marie Jeanette Kelly, fined twelve and sixpence by the magistrates on 22 August last Wednesday week for causing an affray with another woman outside the Ten Bells public house. She gave her address as Donaldson's Buildings. That's just off Middlesex Street. Does that help you, Mrs Frazer?'

'It does. It does indeed,' I said with enthusiasm. I was delighted. Mary Jane, following the old tradition of not giving her known name in court, had, I guessed, uninventively fallen back on her baptismal name. It seemed very likely she was the woman had up for fighting only nine days before. She must still be nearby.

The sergeant looked at me cautiously. 'It's not a nice neighbourhood, madam,' he warned. 'I would advise you not to go there unaccompanied. Perhaps a male friend or relative would go with you, or go himself and spare you the experience altogether.' I knew Donaldson's Buildings, though I didn't say so.

'I shall certainly do as you suggest,' I told him. Not all Whitechapel coppers are ignorant bullies, though many are. They are licensed to be so. Their job is to keep the poor under control, as everybody knows. This sergeant though, was a conscientious man, with thoughtful eyes, which he turned on me.

'Don't get your hopes up too much,' he advised kindly. 'This may not after all be your sister and if she is not, the disappointment might be very distressing for you.'

'I know,' I said.

'I wish you every luck, but,' and I think this was the point he really wanted to make with me, 'sometimes young women such as your sister seems to be do not always welcome rescue.' He looked at me gravely. 'Some of them will have none of it. That hectic life – I believe you have some inkling of what I mean – has a strong appeal, however undesirable it seems to most ordinary people. It can become habitual, as with alcohol or some strong drug, and it's hard to step back from—'

I shook my head. 'I only hope that will not be the case with Mary Jane.' Then I took my leave, walking across Whitechapel Road where a Salvation Army band was playing, to Middlesex Street, with Petticoat Lane Market in full swing, and all the Jews out, and so down a little, poor street, and through an alley to Donaldson's Buildings. It was one of the worst of spots, a court surrounded by houses, not even very old, but sadly worn. There, at midday, men leaned against blackened walls cut by narrow doorways, smoking pipes in the sunshine. Women sat out of doors watching pale children, some shoeless. A thin girl in rags drew water from the pump at the end of the court, turned to carry her bucket home. The slabs with which the court was paved were littered, and they stank with years of dirty water and the contents of chamber pots being flung out of windows on them. This behaviour was not considered right, but people did it all the same. There were the usual couple of thin dogs turning over a pile of something in a corner by a wall. There was the usual sound of a baby crying its head off. A chicken squawked in a back yard, but otherwise, there was silence. It was the silence of real poverty, augmented by the silence of people, though no doubt perpetually at odds with each other, watching the approach of a stranger. For this would be a place where few stopped, not even the postman. In fact, none of the houses had a number, just a coloured rag trailing from a window, a symbol, circle or triangle, painted or scratched on the door.

There were gratings in the paving by the buildings. As I stepped beside them I looked down by chance and clearly saw, for the light was fairly strong, the attenuated figure of a woman covered with a blanket lying below in a heap of straw. Her face was white as snow. She looked near death. Worse, beside her, a small heap in the blanket moved a little, there was a small wailing noise. I felt chilled, shivered, moved on towards a woman sitting at the end of the court on a kitchen chair, rolling cigars on a board in her lap and placing them in rows in a wooden box. A girl of about six sat beside her on a scrap of mat, doing the same. Their fingers flew. Neither looked up as I drew nearer, although they must have known I was coming towards them. Aloft, I heard a window open, behind me, a door.

'Excuse me,' I said. 'I'm looking for my sister, Mary Jane Kelly. Can you help me?'

Her eyes were red-rimmed. She looked up at me, face closed. 'I don't know anything about her,' she said. From the corner of my eye I saw a couple of men coming closer to listen. I turned to them, saying roughly, 'See here – I'm the sister of Mary Jane Kelly. I only want to find her. Can anyone tell me where she is? Or fetch her to me? I don't care which.' They gazed at me stonily. I held on tighter to my handbag and looked them straight in the eye, feigning meekness and candour. 'I'm back from Canada,' I explained. 'I haven't seen her for eight years.' I was hoping no others were coming up behind me. The eyes of one shifted, I turned slightly to follow his gaze. There were indeed three men behind me, closing in, but, to my amazement, half-way across the court and coming towards me with his usual cocky gait, chin slightly up, was Jim Bristow.

'Well, Mary my love, my dear,' he said. 'What are you doing here in these degraded haunts of the poor? Aren't you shocked? Aren't you scared of these regions of vice and crime, where the word "home" is only a hollow mockery and the voice of religion never heard?'

'A policeman told me Mary Jane was hauled up for

fighting ten days ago and gave this place as her address,' I burst out. I'd been careless, over-confiding, I realized, as the woman rolling the cigars raised her eyes briefly at the mention of the police, then fell to working faster, while the two men near me stiffened, moved just half a pace closer.

Jim, however, seemed quite calm. That is to say, he played the part of a man who is quite calm. 'There was no call to go to the police, Mary, not when I'd told you I'd help you. Ten o'clock, Ten Bells, didn't I tell you? And after all the trouble I went to, climbing through your bedroom window – didn't you like it? You seemed to, my dear – and now you go running to the peelers without a word to me. You've upset me now. Silly girl.'

My back was still turned to the court, as I wondered how many people, gathered by small signals, were accumulating behind me. Here was Jim mocking me, suggesting by his stance and all he said that he was my man, but that I'd been disobedient and displeased him, so now he might not defend me. He'd quarrelled with me for going to the police, and although by no means everyone in that court would be a criminal, no one would dare stand up for anyone who attracted official attention to Donaldson's Buildings or its occupants. That is what is known in the East End as not minding your own business and there are punishments for it. Now I had to be obliging to Jim, who had helped to get me into this trouble. There was no point in enquiring further for Mary Jane.

'Well, Jim,' I said apologetically, courting his favour, 'I'm sorry, I really am. Truth to tell, I got so impatient to find my Mary Jane, I just did what first came into my head. Can't we go to Mrs Mundy's alehouse now, and you'll tell me where she might be?'

'All right, dearie,' he said, linking his hand swiftly under my arm. 'I'll forgive you this one time. So let's off for a drink and chat.' And he nodded to the men who had come up to me, we turned, and walked through the people, a big woman with a couple of hulking sons on either side, a ferret-faced little man, hardly more than four feet high, leaning against a wall with his hands in his pockets, watching, a crew of tattered, out-of-work fellows, a couple of saucy girls with big combs in their hair, a group of pinch-faced lads of nine or ten, already brutal, for innocence is a condition which does not last long in places like these. Jim glanced at several as he led me out of the court, me trailing, he strutting in the accepted manner.

Back in the populated streets I shook off his arm, saying querulously, 'I might have found out something there if you'd not come along.'

'You might have been pushed out roughly under a hail of cabbage stalks and peelings, or worse,' he said. 'And I wouldn't think you'd still be holding that heavy handbag you're carrying, either.'

There might have been some truth in this. I had to admit I'd taken a risk, though I still thought I might have got away with it without him. Still, to mollify him I told him, 'You're looking smart today.' It was true. He wore fresh trousers, light brown in colour, a clean shirt, bright blue waistcoat and a linen jacket, freshly ironed.

'A bit of luck,' he said. 'A man feels better for a fresh set of clothes and a few sovs to jingle in his pockets.' And as if to prove this, he jingled the money in his trouser pockets and laughed. 'You were pretty glad to get out of Donaldson's Buildings, eh, Mary? You must be thinking you ain't got no place round here no more. Am I right?'

'I can't go about as I used to, that's true,' I had to admit. 'Here! This isn't the way to Cora Mundy's.'

For without my knowing it, he had led me back to Aldgate, instead of in the other direction. He stopped outside the underground station. 'I told you I'd see you tonight,' he said, 'so tonight it is.'

'What about Mary Jane?'

'Mary Jane, Mary Jane, that's all I hear from you. How about your Jim? Think for a minute about him, who's always loved you.' He stared me in the eye. 'See you tonight,' he said, and kissed me, then disappeared into the station. He turned and called, 'Come in a hansom. They still haven't laid hands on the bloke what murdered that woman last night.' Then he left, always being the one to leave, never to be left, that was always how he got his advantage. But he had to seize a little more. From the stairs going down he called, 'That's why you need me to protect you.'

Meanwhile, a girl selling straggly Michaelmas daisies from a tray strung round her neck heard his words to me. 'That's right,' she said, 'you take care, love. I tell you, I won't rest till they've caught him.'

They did not catch the murderer or murderers, or even discover the identity of the dead woman, Mary or Polly Nichols, until the following day, through, it was said, two flannel petticoats she was wearing stamped 'Lambeth Workhouse', from which apparently she had absconded some months earlier wearing the clothing they had provided. They then found her estranged husband, a printer, who identified her. It seems she had been married to him at twelve years old and borne five children, all living. The couple had lived together for over twenty years until, seven years before, he had pushed her out of the house for drinking, as, subsequently, had her father, a Camberwell blacksmith, for the same reason. Thus she'd fetched up in the workhouse, then run away, got a job as a maid and stolen from the family, to get money for drink, I suppose, and, only months before she died, ended up on the streets in Whitechapel, dossing in a lodging house in Thrawl Street. In spite of the life she'd led it appears she was a pretty woman, dark, with nice grey eyes. Though she was forty years old, everyone who saw the body put her at ten years younger.

A man named Charles Cross found her dead at about three in the morning as he was going off to work. He was walking down by the coalyard fence in Bucks Row when on the opposite side he saw the body lying in the road by the gates of the stables.

She was still warm when found, so she'd not been dead for long. When they took her to the mortuary she had on an overcoat, a brown wool frock, black stockings, the two workhouse petticoats and brown corsets. All she had in her pockets was a comb and a bit of mirror and a handkerchief. She was wearing or carrying all she had in the world, I suppose. Seemingly, she'd been seen up and down Whitechapel High Street all that night and into the next morning, going hither and yon drinking. She'd told a friend at half-past two in the morning, 'I've had my lodging money three times today and I've spent it. It won't be long before I'm back.' Then, of course, she'd reeled off to find another client to give her the money for lodgings. She'd found him all right, but an hour later, or less, he'd killed her, horribly. Her throat was cut from ear to ear, twice, right through to her neckbone. Her trunk had been slashed down and across several times, so the intestines were poking through, and small stab wounds had been delivered to her private parts. It was said a smallish knife, no longer than eight inches, had been used.

It was said that the murderer would have been covered in blood, but I thought he need not have been. If his victim had stood up against a wall or fence, facing forward so that he could take her from behind, he could have cut her throat then. The blood would have gushed forward. When she was dead, he could have set about his ghastly evisceration, getting very little blood on him, except for his hands. Anyway, I hoped he'd cut her throat before proceeding with the rest of his business, for then at least the poor bitch wouldn't have known everything else he was doing to her.

However, when Jim left me at the underground station, I knew none of this, only that a woman too old to be my sister, or Rosie, had been killed and cut up. And at that time, of course, folk still thought the murderer had been someone she knew, or else a gang from the Old Nicholl after the few coppers she'd earned against the stable gates. Indeed, as I stood there, my mind, I don't know why, was running not on the murdered woman but on that woman dying on dirty straw with her baby in a cellar in Donaldson's Buildings.

It was past dinner-time, but I felt I'd had a whole day's worth of woe and trouble already, with Mary Claire cutting me off like that, and my panicky rush to see if my sister had been murdered and the tricky visit to Donaldson's Buildings. Of course, I'd had my gun on me in my big bag as always, and I suppose at a pinch I could have pulled it out and threatened the men who'd surrounded me. Even so, it had been a bad encounter.

Mary was, or had been recently, in the East End. What should I do next? I felt I needed to get away for a bit, in order to think, so took a cab back to Fleet Street, changed into my good rust-coloured silk dress, and a pretty yellow hat, and went to St James's Park, less than a mile off, to see if the band was playing. Perhaps I'd even visit the theatre later before plunging back into the morass of the East End to meet Jim at the Ten Bells at ten that evening, as he'd insisted.

As I walked through Trafalgar Square I remembered sleeping there among the destitute the night before I left for America. They would attempt to clear it on some nights now, I'd heard, but the poor and weary kept returning to sleep there, guarded by Nelson and his lions.

This question, Jack Armitage had told me, for he was a thoughtful man who read his paper every day, had become more crucial to those who mattered since a few years back a big march of unemployed men had got out of hand after a rally and broken into shops, and so forth, doing thousands of pounds' worth of damage. Worse still, only the year before another big march in support of the Fenians had been broken up by the police, with much violence, even before they got to the Square to rally and demonstrate. Days later, 120,000 of them marched right through the centre of town to Bow, to bury a man killed on the public demonstration. The East End turned out to cry and lament, as it always will. It was a scandal supporters of the Fenians should be allowed to march about in open support of them, said Jack. Ever since I'd left, he told me, they'd been setting bombs all over London and killing people. They spoke of recruiting more police, Jack also said, but in his opinion if this public disorder continued, not to mention the bombing, the Home Secretary should call out the army to restore order.

As I stood among the pigeons, all seemed quiet. Still, it was inevitable that London, the heart of the country and the Empire, would be the focus for troubles and discontents of every kind, whether the culprits were anarchists, Fenians or just the poor. Worse, in that city, the province of the wealthy is encircled by the neighbourhoods of those in greatest want. Rich and poor live cheek by jowl, they can't be prevented from spilling over each other's borders. From the East End to the parks, squares and prosperous streets come beggars, robbers and the destitute, while into the slums comes a strange mingling of prosperous men – those hunting whores, landlords and their agents seeking rent, and social reformers, all taking the diseases of the poor back home to distribute among the rich. A recipe for disaster.

As if to confirm some of these notions I, recently

returned from the slums of the East End, was suddenly, to my utter astonishment, accosted by a tall gentleman who raised his silk hat to me and said, 'Mrs Frazer. What a pleasant coincidence. You won't believe that only a moment ago I was thinking of our voyage together.'

Preoccupied as I was, I had difficulty in arranging my expression suitably, for this gentleman was lifting his hat to me on the very spot which had once been my old beat. Almost automatically I put on a compliant whore's smile, as if about to say to him, 'Hullo, my dear, are you all alone? Would you like some company?' – or to smile, of course, if he said it to me first. In those days, whoever spoke first, the outcome would be the same, a linking of arms and off to a dirty house off the Strand I knew, a dirty bed and money on the mantelpiece when the business was done.

He looked a little startled at my first expression, blank, brazen and shrewd all at one time as I suppose it was, by no means the face of Mrs Mary Frazer, respectable young widow of an engineer. However, I managed to recover myself quickly enough, I hope, remembering who he was and who I was supposed to be. So I greeted him politely in the character of Mrs Frazer, and with a genuine surprise similar to his own. It was Marcus Brown, my fellow passenger from the ship, but a somewhat different Brown, now out of his travelling costume. He seemed taller, richer and more important, although younger, in his black frock coat and tall hat. He wore black gloves and a black cravat. He was in mourning. What kind of man was he? I asked myself, realizing that in order to deflect his attentions aboard ship I'd been careful to ask him no questions about himself.

'A coincidence indeed, Mr Brown,' I said.

'And to think,' he said, 'I had just reflected that you must be in Scotland by now.'

Had he? I thought. I must have made a strong impression

if he was still considering my movements. 'I should be there,' I returned, 'but on arrival in London I met with an irresistible appeal from the husband of a sick friend to go and take care of her for a little while, and, of course, I was glad to do so. I was thinking about her as I walked, which is why I failed to recognize you at first.'

'The friend is improving, I hope.'

'She'll be worse before she's better, as I think they say,' I replied, indicating that my imaginary friend was suffering a trying pregnancy.

'So – while you're at liberty, may I offer you some refreshment? Have you had lunch? I've been detained and have had none. I'm hungry for food, and company, too, for this morning it was my uncle's funeral. Can I prevail on you to join me?'

I had no easy way of refusing, although I was not very keen to go.

'The Café Royal may suit us,' he observed. 'It's very near.'

So that was where we went, I offering condolences on his loss, he accepting them, and so on and so forth. We got a table in the café and took our seats.

He looked at me with very large brown eyes. 'And did you settle the business you came to do?'

I nodded.

'Then, since you are sick-nursing and I have had rather a trying morning, I think we should have some oysters to rally us.' But I asked for soup and a cutlet of fish. The waiter brought a bottle of wine and, as Mr Brown carefully tasted it, I studied his mouth. There was something in its broad shape and, indeed, in the whole formation of his face which puzzled me.

At that moment up came a fair, rosy-cheeked man of about thirty, the same age as Mr Brown, I guessed, in a dark suit with a red flower in his buttonhole. He carried a silver-topped cane.

'Hullo, Marcus,' he said, sounding a little surprised.

'Cecil,' responded Mr Brown, in a less than welcoming tone. 'And how are you?'

'Very well,' said this Cecil. He paused. 'I was going to call in at Montpelier Square—'

'I'm playing truant from there for a brief moment,' explained Brown, unashamed. When you come to think of it, wherever you go, high or low, a man who has just buried his uncle is usually expected to be on hand to pour a drink, produce a handkerchief or smelling salts when needed, open the door to callers and be ready to discuss the best side of the lamented. Yet here was Brown, ordering oysters, lunching out with a lady, or so I'll describe myself, while presumably expected at home to play his part.

'Look in later if you like,' said this cool character.

'Well, condolences, anyway,' the man called Cecil said. He was not being asked to sit down, I noted.

'It was expected, of course,' Brown said, not very gravely. Neither of the men seemed very upset or even prepared to pretend to be. Either Mr Brown's late uncle was a man mourned by few, or the pair were hardened cynics; I couldn't judge. Nevertheless, the arrival of his friend Cecil rather confirmed what I had begun to suspect about Mr Brown, which was that he was a bit of a wild one in a quiet way, his friend being somewhat more so, I guessed. On the voyage he had been a little subdued, but here in his native element his true character was more obvious, not, perhaps, to everyone, but certainly to me, a woman whose stock-in-trade was taking the measure of men.

Brown introduced me to Cecil. 'Cecil Curtis, an old friend – Mrs Frazer, a travelling companion on the voyage from New York.' Curtis made a small bow, summing me up from the explanation as an acquaintance of Brown's with no claim to any particular respect, and taking the introduction as an invitation to sit down.

'Have you not had luncheon already?' Brown asked in a cold tone.

'A mere bite,' Curtis said confidently. 'I'm hungry as a hunter. You can order my luncheon. I believe you're in a position to do so.'

'I hope I am. It's all in a tangle, Cecil,' said Brown somewhat curtly.

'Yes – well,' Curtis replied disbelievingly.

And so the waiter took Brown's order, and I found myself sitting uncomfortably between two men who were virtual strangers to me in a restaurant, when what I had intended was a gentle stroll in the park.

We exchanged pleasantries, but, sitting in this quiet restaurant, where people spoke and laughed and china and cutlery clattered gently, my head flooded with memories of the last few days, dreadful images of rushings through dire streets, Mary Claire's obdurate face as she told me, 'We've no need of your assistance – we came to the parting of the ways many years ago.' I recalled Jim Bristow's hands on my face in the darkness, the story of that horrid murder in Bucks Row.

I got through the lunch on nerve, speaking of this and that, of Canada, of gardens (the garden of Brown's house in the country, recently inherited from his uncle, had, it appeared, gone to rack and ruin) and of travel (Cecil Curtis had recently returned from Biarritz and was just off to Scotland). All the while, I could not rid myself of a feeling of darkness, melancholy, a suspicion of threat, though all the time I was conscious of the effect of my looks on both men and relieved that my yellow bonnet, though simple, was a mite smarter and more becoming than those of the other ladies present. The woman's mind is a curious thing.

It can reflect on ten matters at the same time, if it has been sufficiently well educated in so doing. My education had taught me that, if not much more. So even as my mind dwelt on gloom and ruin, I was noting my own appearance just as if I had a mirror in front of me. I also received, during our harmless conversation, an impression that the two men resembled in certain ways the remittance men English families dispatched to our wild Canadian shores to get them out of the way. Especially, I thought of poor Joey Fitzgerald who had died frozen in his shack. Well, a madam such as I am learns more about men in a year than a respectable woman can in a lifetime, that's for sure.

Meanwhile, I felt very tired. As Cecil Curtis obligingly described the landscape and nature of life in Aberdeen, the city where, I alleged, the late Mr Frazer's parents lived, and to which I was going, I found myself saying, 'After so long in Canada I begin to wonder if I will ever feel completely at home in Great Britain again. I'm half minded to return to Canada.'

The two men looked at me in some confusion, as well they might. They may have concluded I was declaring I did not fancy the life of an Aberdonian widow, or even look forward to the prospect of a Scottish remarriage.

After a pause Marcus Brown observed, 'I certainly noticed during my stay in America, Mrs Frazer, that there is more freedom for women there. The lives of the women in remote areas may sometimes be hard, by our standards, but perhaps because they are hard, they have more independence. In some ways, too, because of their value, they are more respected. Not as we respect our ladies, perhaps, but simply because of the vital part they play in life. They are rarer, too,' he said with a smile to Cecil Curtis. 'Even a squaw may in Canada sometimes marry a white man and if he improves his position, she may through him gain a substantial position. Her children may establish themselves as thoroughly respectable.'

Cecil Curtis did not take to this remark, disbelieving the facts and finding them, even if true, thoroughly unpleasant. I also found Brown's conclusions less than accurate. I recalled the Indians drifting into town, drinking themselves into the gutter, and those shacks on the outskirts of town where the Indian women lived, sometimes with white men, sometimes abandoned by them, gardening their little plots, rearing chickens and ragged half-breed children. Still, something of what Brown said was true. There were respectable marriages between some white men and Indian women. And in all probability, I thought, in a society where there is much to do and opportunities of all kinds for those who will seize them, it might be easier for a half-breed child from the saddest of conditions to make a decent life, than for a child born in the London slums. This I said.

'So it is a society in which women and half-breeds thrive,' Curtis said, half joking, half contemptuously.

'And the Irish,' added Brown.

'Well, thank God we still control such places,' Curtis told him, 'or anarchy would prevail.'

I agreed with him, saying, 'Safety lies in firm government from the top, I believe.'

'Who does not?' he said. 'Yet I sympathize with your desire to return to a country where you were happy. But how could a lady alone in such a place manage for herself? What society will she have? Who would protect her?'

I smiled at him. 'A woman's whim,' I declared. 'I am between two worlds, certain of neither.'

The meal concluded and I prepared to leave. 'I must leave you now. My friend is expecting me back. Thank you, Mr Brown, for a very pleasant lunch.'

'Do stay for some coffee,' he urged.

'I dare not,' I said, 'but perhaps you will both visit me soon. At tea-time, perhaps? I've taken lodgings near the house of my friends. Their home is quite small, so I thought it better to live elsewhere rather than become a further burden on the household.'

I gave my address and we agreed that they would come to tea on Sunday in two days' time. I could offer no less at that moment, but planned, after the tea, to lose them somehow. Easily done. In any case, by that time I should probably have found Mary and be preparing for our return to Canada.

I passed the afternoon in the park, listened to the soldiers' band, had a light supper of scrambled eggs in a teashop and was more than ready, indeed, very excited, to join the crowds going into the Savoy Theatre for a performance of *The Mikado*. I had wondered whether to go to the play of *Dr Jekyll and Mr Hyde* at the Lyceum, but, tired and gloomy as I was, I needed nothing to freeze my blood, a cheery operetta was what I fancied.

The ladies and gentlemen going into the stalls were an extraordinary sight for one fresh from Canada – the ladies' silks and satins, their jewellery and hair decorations, the cut of the men's evening clothes, all spoke of a condition of extraordinary prosperity in the nation. Being dressed in day clothes myself, I was up in the balcony, but I had a good seat and could see well. Lesser beings were even higher up, in the gallery. I much enjoyed the bright costumes and scenery, the silly, light-hearted plot and the music, coming out of the theatre into the London darkness quite carried away and excited and humming those pretty tunes, as far as I could remember them, 'A wandering minstrel I', and the melancholy 'Titwillow', and the jolly 'Three little maids from school', sung by three little Japanese maidens in silks, their faces painted in the oriental style.

I was a bit late for the Ten Bells but thought Jim would wait for me. However, he had not. He'd said, the landlord repeated with satisfaction, 'A man who's any kind of a man don't wait much more'n ten minutes for his tart to turn up.' I was half relieved. After such a long day an uneasy encounter with Jim would have been hard to endure. I was disappointed not to have got any further with my search for Mary Jane but I reckoned that, if Jim had any information about her, he'd find me again. He'd probably do so even if he had no news, being secretly fascinated by me, my escape from him and my prosperity.

So I returned to my lodgings, very weary, and went to bed, where I had a long sleep which, however, was not very refreshing, as it was again interrupted by dreams, this time of visions of the poor creature slumped against the stable gate, gutted, with Mary Jane's face, mask-like and superimposed on her own. I saw again the mother and child, close to death in the basement of Donaldson's Buildings. There was raucous, high-pitched singing:

> Three little maids from school are we,
> Pert as a schoolgirl well can be,
> Filled to the brim with girlish glee,
> Three little maids from school.

The next day I spent like a bear in its winter lair, for I knew by now, after three days and nights in the city, my nerves were nearly destroyed and suspected that if I did not try to rest a little my body would soon follow suit. I had grown accustomed to the frontier, with its openness, its huge skies and long silences. There would come, of course, sudden eruptions of violence and drama – who would expect the peace of the convent in a brothel? There would be revelations of a landscape hostile to man, someone frozen to death, a family starved on a homestead, a child killed by a snake, a wolf or a bear. Yet, soon enough there was a return to the quiet domination of nature, the silence of prairie and forest. My return to this overladen city, old in crime, had affected me. It seemed to me that here not just the speech, but all the surroundings were laden with signals and messages, double meanings and obscurities. What did they say sardonically in Canada? 'It's only when you understand that anything said by an Englishman has two possible meanings that you can begin to concentrate on the third.'

That day, I rested, letting the fog of events clear from my brain. Dora, bringing me a little piece of plaice for my dinner, began to tell me of the murdered woman, whose identity was now known. I assumed her employer, the tobacconist, had encouraged her to pass on the gossip she acquired at the kitchen door, but I cut her short. What difference did it make who she was, except to her? She wasn't William Gladstone, or Henry Irving, was she? Just a woman, to begin with, and another East End tart, to make matters worse. She was a nine-day wonder. Who cared who she was? Her family, if she had one, would not long mourn their outcast. No policeman would lie biting his pillow all night, worrying about not having caught whoever killed her. I thought, she could just as easily have been the woman I'd met two days ago in the dosser in Flower and Dean Street. Poor Bess! I remembered her straggling hair, looking, in the dim light, like the hide of an old dog, the bad corset not disguising fallen breasts and a belly slackened by childbearing and the life she'd led. Some might think she'd hardly find it worth while to take her sore feet in old boots round the neighbourhood in search of trade, but some – not me – might be astonished at what kind of woman a man will be prepared to take, when need strikes. I know anything will do. More than that, some men get satisfaction from having an old whore up against a wall in an alley stinking of urine. They rejoice at the sudden heat and quick release, where no respect, love, consideration, or even joy is expected on either side, just a couple of coppers transferred from his hand to hers, and that's that. After all, they've been told often enough that the sexual act is degrading to men and even more so to women, so naturally they believe the courtship, billing and cooing and all the rest are just window-dressing to enable decent women to participate in the crime. It's a relief for your respectable grocer or Member of Parliament to get the filthy business done outside his own home and then go back to the nest, not obliged to offend his wife, bother his head with 'my loves' and 'darlings', or run the risk of adding to his burdens with another little mouth to feed.

The whore has another advantage, too, for some: to avoid disease and pregnancy, she prefers to be taken up the backside, and this is what many men prefer. Nevertheless, the lord who can't perform with anyone but the lowest of the low, the man who'd prefer a boy but won't admit it, the respectable fellow sparing the delicate feelings of his wife and avoiding any further additions to the family, and the market porter fancying a twopenny-halfpenny stand-up before he begins his long day all have one thing in common – they despise whores.

So there's no need for a whore to be desirable: it's enough that she's there like the man who empties your dustbins, or the maid who takes away your chamber pot in the morning. And nobody cares much if she dies. For sure, this affair did not bring the Police Commissioner or the Commissioner for the CID back from their holidays post-haste – they were both away then, and for the following month.

It was hard to get rid of Dora. 'They're saying it was her pimp that done it,' she said, lowering her eyes in mock modesty at the word.

I had been reading and put down my book. 'Dora,' I instructed, 'take your horrid tale and nasty speculations back to the kitchen, where they belong, if you please.'

She bit her lip and went off sulking. I knew perfectly well the dead woman could have had no pimp. She drank, and her earnings were too small. There would have been no profit for a pimp, no chance to take well-dressed ease in pubs and coffee houses, pipe and newspaper in hand, no coins to jingle in the pockets. Even pimps have their pride. To take the earnings of a well-paid whore is a mark of rank; to take pennies from an old one degrades a pimp in his own eyes and in those of others of his calling.

Meanwhile, Sunday came, and Mr Brown and Mr Curtis arrived in the afternoon for tea. I had arranged my things carefully, sent Dora out for the last, late roses of summer and made the room very charming. I wore a lace blouse, a blue silk skirt, kid boots and black silk stockings. I had on a lace petticoat, cream, with flounces which showed a little as I picked up my skirt to walk. Dora seemed much impressed by my appearance and two frock-coated guests.

I poured the tea and handed bread and butter to the manner born. Poor Joey Fitzgerald had given us our etiquette lessons on dark winter afternoons at Esmeralda's. How we'd laughed, as the Indian girls in their chemises with their plaited hair played at fine ladies going to the opera, with table-cloths hanging down behind them for trains and cloaks, or Dolly O'Halloran learned the court curtsy in her drawers and pantoufles. Oh, I could remember, as I rang the bell for Dora to bring up fresh tea, how Joey'd coughed and drunk and coughed again. I remembered us flinging more logs into the stove, while the snow came down through the darkness outside the window, and Joey said, 'Remember, ladies, when you're guests at the dinner table of the high-ups, you must never, in any circumstances, discuss politics, money, religion, the relations between the sexes or health – yours or that of others.' At which he fell to coughing again and this time there was blood on the rag he clutched to his mouth, and he cried out, 'Wind up the phonograph, for God's sake, let's have some music.' He would always want *Carmen*, which has some good tunes, you must admit, but was too doom-laden for a man in his condition. The girls, for the most part, favoured ballads about mothers and angels and little dying children, except the Indians – music was all Greek to them. I'd always attempt to play him something more cheerful, but it was *Carmen* he really loved and I can never hear that music without thinking of his short life and lonely death. It's a hard world. Yet if he'd lived I couldn't say what future he'd have had, for they wouldn't have him at home in England and he'd never have found a place in a Canadian cattle-town. Anyway, it was from Joey I'd learned the skills of the genteel tea table with a roaring stove, whisky in the cups and a cowboy fondling a girl in the corner.

I did my best to keep the conversation going. It wasn't easy for we did not live in the same world, Brown, Curtis and I, nor had either of these gentlemen any form of trade or profession to enquire about. Consequently the conversation was slowish, though I'm sure I looked very charming as I poured the tea. We spoke of shooting – Brown had shot himself a couple of buffalo in Wyoming, of which he was proud, though my own thoughts are that such a thing might be excellent fun in the USA, where the Indians are on reservations and well provided for, but it has bad repercussions in undeveloped spots like the Canadian prairies, where they are not. If the buffalo do not breed, the Indians starve, and go without clothing and all kinds of things, for the buffalo is all they have, and though they may be uncivilized and dirty they are still men. Nevertheless, I congratulated him. We also spoke of the opening of the Canadian Pacific Railway and the driving in of the last spike in the track. I had come up a mountain in November 1885 to attend this humble ceremony at Eagle Pass in the Rockies. My feelings were mixed since it represented the end of my connection with the building of the Canadian Pacific Railway, the enterprise on which I had founded Esmeralda's. Nevertheless, even though it meant the end of a ready source of income, I was moved by the ceremony.

We spoke of books and the theatre. On hearing about my visit to *The Mikado* Mr Curtis told me he would have enjoyed accompanying me, had he known I was going, while Mr Brown regretted that being in mourning he would not have been able to. I referred again to the independence of mind bred in the Dominions. We spoke again of shooting: I confessed with a blush that I had shot at a deer, and miraculously hit it. I had unmiraculously shot a starving female bear once, too, as it was trying to get in the kitchen door for food one spring. I suppose it had cubs. I did not mention this, assuming that bear-slaying women might in their circles be considered less than charming.

At six thirty the gentlemen rose to leave. Mr Brown told me he was going to his house in the country that evening and, very much to my surprise, added that if my sick friend could spare me for a few days, he was sure it would do me good to spend some time in the fresh Kent air, and I would be most welcome to visit. I replied I should be pleased to do so, if my friend could spare me.

'We will be a quiet little party,' he assured me, 'only my mother and sister and perhaps two old, close friends.'

'So much nicer,' said I, earning a smile. Of course, I had no idea of going there, not a bit of it. Marcus Brown had nice eyes, and a friendly way with him, but I had no interest in him, in holidays, or paying visits. I'd put my money in a safe bank, found Mary Claire, and got no pleasure of it. Now all I desired was to discover Mary Jane and be off back to Canada, with or without her. Marcus Brown squeezed my hand a little; so, oh ho, I thought, that's the way of it.

It must have been ten o'clock when I wrote to Dolly

Halloran about the goods I had ordered and which were now awaiting shipping. This was in case the items arrived before I did. I instructed her where to put the pianola, addressed the letter and placed it on my mantelpiece.

Not many days after that, I was lying quiet in linen sheets smelling of lavender, the mild air of a country midnight filling the room, when I awoke to hear the sound of a stout oak door opening on well-oiled hinges. A low voice enquired, 'Mary?'

'Marcus?' I exclaimed, though softly for fear of waking the others in the house. 'Is anything the matter?'

'No – only that I want you,' the voice came back, and with that my host, Marcus Brown, was by my bedside, and bending to kiss me.

As he took me, in the complete darkness and quiet of a country night, I was on the verge, I know, of feeling desire. Startled, I scarcely noticed what happened until he, my host, was done, and when he had, I admit it, I wept and did not know why. This moved him. 'You've no cause for shame or remorse,' he told me. 'You are a young woman, a widow. What you feel is natural. You are accustomed to relations with a husband. It is a hardship to men, and to some women too, to forgo such things.'

It was a kindly speech, though it had no bearing on my true situation. I could not tell him that what I had felt, or thought I'd felt, was to me far from natural. I believed the internal scarring caused by my complaint and the savage treatment of it had removed my womanhood. What I had felt indicated to me that my body might perhaps be restoring itself, in spite of what the doctor had told me – and that if it was, I was not sure I welcomed the restoration. Sexual passion puts a woman at a disadvantage. She has much to lose. Her face and body are her stock in trade; trade demands a cool head. A woman who truly yields gives too much and often gets too little in return. A cold woman can use her power to get what she wants; a hot-blooded one can lose all for a moment's pleasure. In addition, I thought, even as Marcus dried my tears, if some internal recovery was taking place, might it not also lead to a pregnancy, taking me back into the world where a woman's passion leads to conception? And that's a bore and a blow to most women, not to mention a danger, unless the husband wants an heir, when it is a matter of the business side of matrimony. Even then, heir achieved, the matter can't be stopped. I doubt if even the Queen of England truly wanted to bear ten children and certainly she's said to have complained a great deal about the pain. For lesser mortals it's all pain and worry and of course, with the confinement, fear for your life. Still, for the moment, I had no anxieties on that score for Mr Brown – Marcus – had, like a true gentleman, withdrawn in time to prevent his seed from entering me and once I had stopped crying and he had dried my face with his hand-kerchief he'd said sweetly, 'There – are you better now? See – there's nothing to worry about. All is well. You can trust me.' So we lay talking for a little while and then he got up, kissed me and left, in case as he said, in case he fell asleep and was discovered in my room by the maid next morning.

After he had gone I reflected that his arrival in my room ought not to have surprised me so much, for all London is close to all the rest of London. The gossip in the pubs of Whitechapel often concerns the affairs of the mighty. Servants' gossip trickling down is the source, I suppose. This talk always proves that those in high places act much the same as their inferiors in matters such as purloining items from each other's houses, dipping into the till and adultery.

So, small wonder that Marcus, attracted by a lady who did not discourage him, and restless at night, decided to do a little corridor creeping. That should not have come as a shock, I thought, as I lay there after he had left, hearing only a little breeze from outside. The shock to my nerves came when I recognized that I had nearly responded to his lovemaking.

It was events in London which had led me after all to accept Marcus Brown's invitation. I'd spent Monday roaming the streets putting out word for my sister, with no result. By evening I was jaded and discouraged, choked by the dirty and unwholesome air of London in summer, where dust rose from every crack and smoke belched out continually from kitchen fires, ships in the river, trains, factories and workshops. The place was all smoke and smells, much worse in the East End of course, where there were close on a million people trying to live, especially worse in Whitechapel, which they'd crossed with railway lines to spare better parts of town. Even in the West End the nuisance was always there, if there was no wind to blow it away. That day there were sullen, heavy skies through which the sun sometimes broke, and a kind of brooding, stormy atmosphere. Eventually even the animation, bustle and entertainment of the city ceased to move me. I was in this mood when I ran into Jim Bristow eating some cockles out of a tin mug by a stall in Whitechapel Road. 'Oy!' he cried, grabbing my arm as I passed. 'What about a trip to the music-hall? Make a nice change for you. I'll bet you haven't had a night out at the halls for years. Come on, I've got some gelt,' and he patted his pockets.

I was despondent. 'You're very flush these days.' A woman carrying a crate bumped into me. Behind her, like a train, was a string of four or five children holding hands, the first clutching her skirt. 'How the poor have to live,' Jim remarked dispassionately, following her with his eyes as she moved through the crowds with her string, glancing behind her anxiously from time to time. 'Let's hope no one snaps up one of her ducklings for dinner before she gets home. Anyway, thanks for your kind enquiry. I'm flush 'cos I've been playing fan tan down Limehouse with the Chinks.'

I thought he was boasting. 'That's a very good way to get murdered,' I said.

'They're all right, the Chinks,' he claimed, 'as long as you know how to treat them. And there's a big Chinaman with a big knife on a stool by the door to prevent things getting out of hand.'

'D'you smoke opium with them?'

'Only to be sociable. When in Rome, do like the Romans do,' he replied. 'Anyway, there's a good bill at the Cambridge, performing seals and all, so how about it? Your pretty face is like a wet weekend. It'll cheer you up.'

So we set off, Jim grasping my heavy handbag and offering to relieve me of the weight, me refusing, and we headed, in the end both holding on to my bag, up to the Cambridge in Commercial Road and caught the second house just as it was starting. We sat in the stalls, in the smoky, jolly atmosphere, plenty of orange peel flying, and watched the promised seals, also a dog ballet with the animals dressed up in gauzy dresses and a low comedian in a check jacket and a bowler hat. Then came Bella Bedford, the Little Cockney Nightingale. She might have been a Cockney, but she was no girl, just a very small, heavily rouged woman tricked out in a short skirt and pantalettes. There was a chorus, all spangles and tights, much cheered. Last on was Harry Upton, a respectable gent in a top hat and flashy waistcoat, who gave us 'Work, boys, work, and be contented'. Sardonically or not, workers or not, the audience joined in enthusiastically. 'For that man you may rely, Will be wealthy by and by, If he'll only put his shoulder to the wheel.'

He'd launched into an old favourite, 'We don't want to fight', when I turned round and spotted, right at the back by the bar, behind the rail separating the bar area from the seats, my friend Rosie, in décolletage leaving nothing to the imagination, and a big purple hat covered in lace, arm in arm with a girl in scarlet. She'd already seen me. She pouted at Jim, now belting out 'By Jingo if we do', raised her eyebrows and gaped, miming amazement. Then a couple of men in top hats blocked my view and I turned back and gave it my best, bawling 'We've fought the bear before, And while we're Britons true, the Russians shall not have Constantinople.' As the audience cheered and stamped, full of patriotic fervour, Jim, by dint of furtively squeezing my breast, attracted my attention, and tugged me up out of the stalls. We went into a pub a few doors down. Without asking me what I wanted he got me a glass of port. 'There you are,' he said. 'Feel better now, don't you?' Well, truth to tell I did. 'There's nothing like a singsong,' he went on. 'That's a gloomy one, isn't it?' He began to carol the Little Cockney Nightingale's finale, 'Only a violet I plucked from my dead mother's grave as a boy'. A large man in a black suit said, 'Shut up.'

'It's a real tonic, and no mistake,' I said, to be obliging. 'I thank you, Jim, but what I want to know is, where's Mary?'

'I don't know what you're going to do with that girl when you get her,' was all he said.

'Give her the chance to get out of here,' I said. 'Look at it. Trapped rats. Everybody's after everybody else for their last crust. This place is like a bloody kettle, just waiting for the lid to blow off. I promised my mother before she died—'

'Stow it, Mary,' he said. '"Only a violet I plucked from my dead mother's grave as a boy",' he sang again.

'You've got no feelings at all, have you, you bastard?' I exclaimed.

'No. No more than you have,' he said. 'There's more to all this than you're saying. I know it, you know I know it. Now – you tell me what's up, I might help you.'

This was the most I'd got out of him during our encounters.

'Help yourself, more likely,' I said.

'Mary,' he said reproachfully, 'how can you say that? What could I hope to gain—'

'Jim,' I said, 'if you know where she is, tell me, I'm imploring you.'

He only said, 'Ah,' and looked at me mysteriously. I stood up and moved rapidly to the door. I didn't want a brawl in the pub, the slappings, pullings about and swearing which were a kind of routine, ignored by most bystanders, between men and women in those parts, where a woman would wear a black eye to prove her husband loved her.

I was in a cab and back to my lodgings, quickly. This was not the end of it. I was in bed and dozing when there came the noise of stones being thrown up at my window. I looked out – Jim was below. Rather than let him disturb Dora, who must have been in bed, I crept down and let him in. He followed me upstairs, pinching my bum and trying to get hold of me. When we got in the room he fell on one knee, crying dramatically, 'Now, my darling, why did you disappear like that? I love you, Mary Kelly, my darling, I do.' His arms were round my knees.

'Jim, you bastard, leave me be,' I said. He was pushing me towards the bedroom. We lurched into a table. I wanted no fuss, no Dora, no police, but I could see he wanted to take up where he'd left off, get back with me again, then let me provide for all his wants as I had all those years before. If I yielded, just the once, he'd see the act as my signature on our contract. But there could be no arrangement, spoken or unspoken, between us – not after that incident where the little girl had died, not after the abortion I had had and, particularly, not after my disease and the cure the doctor in New York had done on me. But being no longer capable of pleasure, nor of bearing a child, hardly a woman at all where it counted – mostly Jim's doing, I might say – was a protection in some ways. Yet, as he forced me backwards, I had to consider that as long as he might have information which could lead me to Mary Jane, I couldn't afford to fall out with him. This thought, as well as the wish to have no arguments or disturbance, made me yield to him, like it or not. And so, with a flurry of tapes and strings, and buttons popping all over the place, I was finally spreadeagled across my bed, Jim in his shirt on top, and so the deed was done. I got no joy from it of course, though I pretended to. That's my trade after all, like an actress on the stage, and I don't think he suspected my pleasure was feigned and my endearments false.

I made him leave at six, before Dora got up and there were too many people in the street. 'Oh Mary,' he said from the pillow, 'don't turn me out.'

'I don't want to, my dear,' I said lyingly, 'but I have to keep a decent reputation. I'm seen as a respectable widow, here to find my sister, and that's the point.' He'd told me nothing about her. When I asked, he made protestations of love. When I asked again he fell asleep, or pretended to.

After he'd left I lay awake, feeling annoyed and uneasy. I had kept my part of the unspoken agreement I thought we had, meaning my compliance in return for his information, but though I'd complied, he had told me nothing about Mary Jane. Perhaps he had nothing to tell. Perhaps he did know something of her life or whereabouts, but was hanging on for a better bargain, this night of love being only the opening shot in his campaign. As he'd left, he'd turned his head to the mantelpiece. I thought from across the room he'd read the name and address on the envelope of my letter to Dolly Halloran. He had good eyesight and read well, though God knows how he'd picked up the skill for he'd hardly been to school. That letter would have aroused his curiosity. At all events, he had gone leaving me uneasy in my mind; and even though I knew one of his chief weapons in life was the creation of bewilderment and disorder in women, the fact was, he had employed it and it had worked. Meanwhile, I was no closer to Mary Jane and guessed I would have to find her without Jim's help. Even if he could assist me, I had an idea the price might be higher than I would want to pay.

After Jim left I got up and stood in my nightdress at the open sitting-room window, looking out over the dark roofs and smoking chimneys. I breathed in the clouded, muggy London air, heard the singing in the music-hall in my head, saw the pushing and shoving crowds, the flickering gas over the stalls in Whitechapel Road. I could almost smell the frying potatoes, the unwashed bodies in old clothes, the faint aroma of some cracked, overflowing drain somewhere – there always was one, the smell was always there – and I reflected that Jim had had me, and having had me, even as we lay in bed, had begun to take on proprietorial airs. He enquired gravely about my life and fortune, propped up on my pillows, mimicking the air of a reliable man of business. He had even put it to me that a woman on her own needed to be married. Possibly, he'd suggested, a hint of coldness in my manner was attributable to my relations with the late Mr Frazer. 'Doubtless he didn't treat you quite right in that particular department. Many men are like that, but it discourages and disappoints a woman,' he'd sympathized. He'd even had the cheek to propose lighting his pipe in bed.

'For Christ's sake, not that stinking thing in here,' I said (which would have given me away good and proper to Dora in the morning). Yet, to continue to appear obliging I fetched him a cheroot from the box on my mantelpiece at four in the morning. It all began to recall the old routine of dancing attendance on princely Jim. It brought back that old world of hurry, scurry, bangs on the door in the middle of the night, of being in the street as dawn came up and still asleep at midday, and always some alarm, catastrophe, and danger round the corner. It's a life that can't be described. Only those who've lived it can know. Looking from my window after he'd left, waiting for the dawn, I resolved to round off our trip to the music-hall, seals, Cockney Nightingale, patriotic songs and all, with that popular finale, the disappearing trick.

So early that morning I wired Brown at Knare Park and received a reply at lunchtime: 'So glad you are coming. Best train is at 3.30 from Victoria' – and I took it.

As I watched trees, fields, orchards streaming past the window, drawing further away from London, that Babylonian city, a thought slowly came to me, or rather, a question. How could it be that Mary Jane was still eluding me? I'd advertised, sped everywhere, leaving messages and promises of a reward for information. All evidence pointed towards her being around and about in the East End, yet apparently no message had got through to her. My first advertisement had after all brought Mary Claire all the way from Liverpool. Of course, Mary Jane might be abroad, or in this very countryside picking hops. She might be in prison, or ill. Yet somehow I was not satisfied with any of these explanations. But if she was about and had heard I was looking for her, why was she unwilling to meet me? Perhaps she was ashamed. God knew what the last eight years had made of Mary Jane.

Mary Claire, I thought, hadn't wanted anything to do with me, but at least I knew why. She had her small house in a long street with the brick chapel at the end where on Sundays she took her well-scrubbed family. She had her regular daily round, and probably it was the continual round of washing, starching, scrubbing and dusting which provided her with a sense of comfort and security. So long as she could keep up with her tasks, gaining the grudging approval of her husband, a strict mother-in-law and her censorious neighbours, she could believe nothing would go wrong in her little world. Well, I had to confess my own responsibility in all this, with father dead, then mother, my own sudden evaporation, leaving no message behind, must all have been a bad knock for her. So she had found for herself a life ruled by a stern God and plenty of yellow soap. Who could blame her?

But Mary Jane, a whore like myself, had no respectability to protect. She could afford to remember her parents, sisters, what had happened and where we came from. Why didn't she come? I puzzled over this as smoke streamed past the windows, revealing and concealing by turns the reapers in the fields yellow with corn, hedged around them, the little stands of trees here and there, swelling hills, orchards of trees hung with ripe red apples. It was like a picture from a children's story book, so pretty, so safe and so tranquil, so unlike the towering mountains, great lakes, unexplored forests and measureless plains of waving grass moving as the winds moved, oceans of grass – all that landscape I had left less than a month before. In Canada most places were unchanged, unvisited by man, or disturbed only by the light footfalls of the Indians. Here, every inch of ground had been ridden over, trodden, ploughed, reaped countless times. Countless hands had shaped the land, planting trees and hedges, making ditches, diverting streams, to make it what they wanted. Here were no bears or wolves or snakes, savage snows or dusty broiling summers. It was peace. We went past hopfields, the full-grown hops clinging to their poles and strings. In one a big gang of gypsies was stripping them. Their painted caravans were parked in the next field. In another some twenty or thirty pickers from London, mothers, fathers, children, were doing the same. Two men heaved the filled sacks on to a cart. A woman was boiling a cauldron of water over a fire by the side of the field. The sun was still hot; the pickers moved slowly. A woman slapped a child and I heard his sharp cry as we passed. Through the open window of the train came sweet gusts of country air; then, as we turned a corner, the acrid smell of engine smoke.

Just short of Faversham I, the only passenger to descend, got out at a little station, where roses grew in beds behind the platform. There, a short, respectable-looking man in a bowler hat approached me. Lifting his hat he asked, 'Mrs Frazer? Sir Marcus desired me to meet you and drive you to Knare Park. He sends apologies for not coming to meet you himself. A matter of family business. Shall we go to the gig?' So we gave up our tickets and walked from the station across the yard to where a little brown-painted gig, with a good-looking chestnut horse in front, stood waiting. A porter stowed the small trunk I had with me at the back, among some parcels the bowler-hat man had evidently collected in Faversham before meeting me. The bowler hat made sure to tip the porter for me. All this intimidated me more than somewhat, so did the fact that Mr Brown had a handle to his name. He must have been a baronet all the time (he was too young to have been knighted) and I hadn't been aware of the fact.

So off we clopped, soon off the big road, and going down small ones. There were well-kept hedges and copses on either side, cows mooned over fences, watching us pass. I began to wonder how much of all this belonged to Marcus Brown and felt nervous about the whole affair. For all I knew the Queen would be there when we arrived and I wasn't sure I was up to the job at all. Bowler hat volunteered, 'My name is William Edwards, madam. I manage the household for Sir Marcus – as I did for his uncle before his death.' Not much regret for the late lamented Brown, I noted, observing also that Edwards appeared a decent, capable fellow, well up to managing anything. I wished for a moment I had him at Esmeralda's, wondered if he was open to offers, decided no, he was not a man who would take easily to life in a brothel. 'I also act as butler,' he mentioned, 'my wife being cook-house-keeper. It's a small establishment. Sir Marcus's uncle lived very quietly. I think you'll find the house a very pretty one.'

'How far is it?'

'Two and a half miles, and we have a lovely day for the drive.'

He told me a good deal as we went along, though judiciously. Sir Marcus's uncle had started off as a soldier, but soldiering did not suit him and after the Crimean War he had given up his commission and bought the estate, thereafter living quietly for thirty years, farming, putting his tenant farms in order and modernizing the house. 'When I came to the house as a boy,' Edwards told me, 'there was only one tap in the kitchen and a pump in the yard. Every drop of hot water required for the household had to be heated over the kitchen fire.' Edwards himself had begun as a kitchen and garden boy at sixpence a week. His son, he said, was at a polytechnic in London studying science, while his daughter was an apprentice seamstress who lived in Faversham with the family for whom she worked. On hearing that I had just returned from Canada he remarked solidly that his son, once qualified, planned to emigrate.

The sun was almost down when we turned off the road and along the drive. At a certain point it curved, revealing a gem of a house, all red brick and old windows, quiet and glowing in late sunshine. It seemed huge to me, though I suppose by the standards of houses of that kind it was not. At the back of the house a garden ran, on a slight incline, down to the farm fields, one golden with corn stubble, one green, where sheep grazed. A small river ran through.

At the end of another field I saw a boy with a stick urging a group of cows through a gate. Behind that were more fields. Further back still, there was a church spire just visible amid some trees, four or five miles off. To one side of the house – I could not see it then – lay a sunken garden.

We drew up in front of the house, where roses grew in beds. Marcus came out to meet me, with his mother. I suppose the warmth of Marcus's greeting was enough to make Mrs Brown dislike me from the word go, though I dare say even without that she would not have warmed to me much. She and Marcus resembled each other, but in his case that appearance had worked out as a brown complexion, with a ruddy tinge, big, rather merry eyes and a generous mouth, whereas with his mother the same face was sallow, the same eye was wary, warning and disappointed, the same mouth pinched with heavy but concealed obstinacy.

I was taken to my pretty room, where vases of roses had been placed. Having washed and changed into a grey dinner dress suitable for a widow and nothing to frighten the horses in the street, I came down into the drawing-room to meet the others. Cecil Curtis was there. He greeted me very civilly, but I was wise to the situation now and realized my host had revealed an interest in me, and Curtis had backed off, as an old friend ought. Then there was Roger Crooke, a big, bluff man, an old friend of the family and Member of Parliament for the area, and his pale daughter Guinevere, a young widow of about my own age. She, I quickly saw, was Mrs Brown's candidate for the post of daughter-in-law. Apart from them there were only two girls, still in short skirts, with their hair down. They were Alice, Marcus's seventeen-year-old sister, and her friend Veronica.

Mrs Brown, in black silk, with a lot of jet sewn on and some diamonds, being the hostess, started straight away to make me feel uncomfortable. It took me some time to realize that it wasn't quite in order for Marcus to invite a complete stranger, and a young woman at that, into a family party at his house so soon after his uncle had died. I was longer still in realizing that an unmarried son of thirty, who has just inherited his uncle's money, land and title, could do what he liked – go into the Church, or the law, seduce all the village maidens, take off for the North Pole, whatever he pleased – but that what Mrs Brown desired was to settle him down and keep him at home by means of a marriage to a woman of a good family, with some money, who agreed with her about everything. Now, the Crookes were a very big family in the country, Guinevere Coleman had been left rich by her husband, and therefore she was the choice.

As the days passed Mrs Brown came to like me less and less. I did not come from a world she knew, my tale of who I was did not convince her; she rightly suspected me, and all the more since she, who knew her own son best, understood better than I did at the time that he was deeply attracted to me. What I thought was a fancy, such as men get, went deeper than that. Meanwhile I was all at sea. I'd been reared in East London, completed my education on the streets of Whitechapel and spent the last eight years on the Canadian frontier. I couldn't understand half what these people were saying, for the topics they spoke of and the assumptions underlying their lightest remarks were completely foreign to me. I knew no one they knew, I couldn't play any of their games, from piquet to croquet: advertising that I was a dab hand at billiards and poker would only have marked me down as a low female. Even my clothes were all wrong, being foreign and fitting in the right places instead of the wrong ones. During the day the ladies wore cotton dresses and straw bonnets and so did I, but theirs were English, mine French. So I kept quiet, appeared stupid, and in spite of the pretty country-side and charming house, began to wish I was elsewhere.

Although I had only arrived on Tuesday, it seemed to me the easiest way out of this dilemma was simply to pack and disappear. Therefore, I scribbled a wire to my solicitor, Mr Ratcliffe, asking him to send me a telegram recalling me to the bedside of my imaginary sick friend. I got it sent on Friday morning during a stroll round the village, complete with forelock-tugging yokels, condolences on the death of the uncle, congratulations to the young heir, etc., etc., from ruddy-cheeked local tradesmen. No doubt but that the Browns were a big noise in this peaceful spot, but what they took for affection, as the women bobbed curtsies and the men touched their hats, I saw as nothing but fear of a blow or hope of a bone, as with dogs.

We, that is, Marcus, Mr Curtis, Mrs Coleman and the two girls, took a pint of ale outside the local inn, sitting under a big chestnut tree. The men, that is, took the ale; we ladies had lemonade. Guinevere Coleman buttered up the gents; the girls attempted to suppress the boredom and bottled-up energy so plain on their faces. Marcus's sister had a little sly look as she gazed at me, as if she suspected I had different information to impart than the kind she had been given so far, and wanted it badly. Girls are quick in that way. Cecil Curtis and Marcus, in their white suits and panamas, sat with their legs stuck out, enjoying the sensation of being outnumbered by pretty women and monarchs of all they surveyed. I concluded they could afford this satisfaction, for they could go elsewhere when they felt like it, in the direction of fast horses and fast women if they wanted, whereas poor widowed Guinevere, and Alice and Veronica, all needing husbands, had no such freedom.

Then it was back for lunch, the heavy table in the rather gloomy dining-room presided over by Mrs Brown, who enquired as to my maiden name. I told her blandly, 'Kelly,' knowing that it would prevent the usual genealogical enquiries, for there are few Kellys in the ranks of the notable English families, and it would be a foolish person who would try to track a Kelly back through their connections to the Plantagenets.

'You are descended from the old kings of Ireland, then?' she remarked, somewhat sarcastically.

'Bog-Irish, rather,' I claimed, sick of the woman and all her works. This caused a silence until Crooke burst out laughing.

'So – what do you think of Mr Gladstone's efforts?' he enquired. Crooke was a Conservative MP and therefore an opponent of the Prime Minister.

'I know very little of politics,' I said. 'But I doubt if we'll solve the Irish question. The Irish will solve it themselves, I suppose, by emigrating and emigrating, until there's no one left in Ireland, but the rest of the world is full of us.'

He smiled at this. 'A good solution – a solution without bloodshed.'

'Then who will live in Ireland?' asked the girl Veronica, looking up in wonderment from her blackberry and apple pie.

'We'll leave it all to the donkeys,' supplied Cecil.

'Oh, you're joking,' she concluded.

'What do the women do in the wilderness, Mrs Frazer?' asked keen Alice. 'Do they round up cattle and fight Indians, too?'

'Alice, how absurd,' said her mother. 'I expect they keep house, as women do everywhere.'

I nodded in assent, for it was no lie that I kept a house, though not the kind of house Mrs Brown could imagine.

In the afternoon we went to an abandoned castle in the neighbourhood by carriage, and had a picnic tea in the grounds. Mrs Brown accompanied us, to keep an eye on Marcus, but after tea Cecil Curtis suggested a stroll and, on Marcus's instructions, I believe, tried to make sure he and Guinevere and the girls lost us in a wood, which I prevented. There was nothing obvious about Marcus's behaviour, he was not trying to corner me in dark places, squeeze my breasts or pull up my skirts, but for me that made the whole matter more confusing, not less.

It was late afternoon when Marcus caught me alone in the sunken garden. Knowing that next day Mr Ratcliffe's telegram summoning me back to London would arrive I felt quite detached, almost as if I had already left, as I sat on my old stone bench, a low yew hedge behind, hearing the click of croquet balls on the lawn further off. The laughter and exclamations of those playing reached me. 'Beast! Beast!' I heard Alice exclaim, in jesting rage. It was odd to think that when I was no older than those two big girls in their white dresses and black stockings I'd been approaching men in the street, laying my hand on their shoulder and asking them if they were lonely tonight, all for a couple of shillings. Alice and Veronica were lucky, I thought, to be playing croquet on the lawn while the cook in the kitchen got tea ready. I sat there in calm contemplation, book in hand, gazing at the small dry fountain, with the greenish bronze model of a nymph on it, and at the roses behind, mostly gone. I could hear the little cheep of a starling on a bough behind me. And then who should come through the hedge behind me but Marcus.

'Ah!' he said. 'You're in search of tranquillity.' He sat down beside me. 'Do you like my house?' he asked. 'Or are you dreaming of Canada?'

To tell the truth, over the quiet days I had found my mind returning to the vastness of that country. Here at Knare Park I felt as suffocated as I did in Whitechapel, though in entirely different ways. It was not of course dirt or foul air, or teeming streets filled with hungry animals all trying to push to the top of the heap in order to survive, which seemed to choke me. Here in Kent I felt stifled in another way. Here was a small world of unyielding order. Those who lived in it believed in their own absolute rightness, that this little corner of the universe had been created to measure and judge the rest. Comfort and complacency reigned. The surroundings had charm, the residents not.

That morning I had woken early, risen, gone to the window and breathed the fresh morning air. I looked over the lawn where starlings and blackbirds hopped and pecked in the dew, stared upwards at the blue sky, heard from downstairs the faint clatterings and bangings of the house being arranged, breakfast cooked, the clop of the breadman's horse arriving at the back door. Gazing over that still landscape of small, hedged fields, the length of willows by the river, a wagon, far off, moving down a distant lane like a toy, I was seized with delight at its prettiness. Then I remembered the place I had left, where the air in winter was like a knife and wolves in the forest howled under snow-laden trees, the snow billowed over the prairie, mile on mile. I thought of hot summers, thousands of half-wild longhorn cattle being driven helter-skelter down the main street through the clouds of dust thrown up by their hooves, to the rail head. I recalled huge brazen skies, lightning flickering over the plains, rain battering flat a thousand acres of grass. Where, I wondered, did I belong? Perhaps, stuck half-way between being a woman and no-woman, half Irish and half French, I was doomed to be an individual with no country, no place I felt to be my own.

Nonetheless, whatever part of the world I might call home, or not, it had to be admitted that in the New World there was work for all, untilled land to farm, communities to be established, towns built. This provided some chance of a better life to anyone willing to work and quick to seize an opportunity. A man there, if he was lucky and energetic, could change his life, for better or worse, which is not so easy in a country where a wagoner must stay a wagoner and his sons after him, where paupers breed paupers, washerwomen bear only washerwomen, queens give birth only to kings. There's no rhyme or reason about the condition of life in which a child is born. Whether French or Russian, rich or poor, girl or boy, fate decrees it and nothing can alter it, no matter how much tea Rosie Levi's menfolk drink in their Whitechapel kitchen, talking of rights and revolution. Yet in Canada, because of the newness of the country, a poor man will get his chance, and that's no bad thing.

Anyway, as Marcus and I sat together in the old garden, after he had asked me if I thought of Canada, I told him something of what I felt, adding politely, a woman in those circles not really being expected to have ideas of her own, 'I expect I surprise you. Yet spending so long in another part of the world prompts thoughts, unconventional as they might seem.'

'From the moment we met, you never gave me the idea you were a conventional woman,' he said.

'Thank you for your charming compliment, if you intended one,' I responded.

'Would you prefer to be called conventional?' he challenged. 'If so, you would be wrong. You are charming. That is part of your charm.'

I evaded this. 'I suppose it's impossible to prevent anyone from calling you anything they want.' I said. I had the impression, as I always do, when a man desires me, of the atmosphere thickening around me. I asked, 'And have you made up your mind yet about whether you'll stand for Parliament?' This had been the subject for debate at the previous night's dinner table, Crooke having said he was planning not to stand for the constituency at the next election and sounding out, as they put it, Marcus for the job.

'I'm turning the matter over,' he told me. But I knew

he would accept. 'Ladies, perhaps, are more fortunate than we men. Their path is clear to them.'

If he believed that, I thought, he'd believe anything. My choice had been to make a career as a milliner or a streetwalker, a common enough choice where I came from, but did he really think Guinevere Coleman did not see him as a post she was applying for, with his mother as sponsor? Men will never understand women or their lives or know them for the cheating servants they are, and, while the last woman left in the world has enough breath in her body to lie to them, they never will.

'A career as the guardian of a constituency and legislator for the nation is not to be despised,' I said.

He gazed at me. 'You express yourself quaintly sometimes.' After this he added hastily, 'Do not take this as a criticism, I beg you. I find it . . . interesting, fetching.' He went on more boldly, 'I find you fetching altogether.' More boldly still he added, '. . . Mary.' And he took my hand. I did not withdraw it. It's the same old game wherever you go, I thought to myself, and this was how it happened that he came to me that night, how I found myself, early next morning, so shaken, tearful in fact, after the deed was done. When he was gone, I stood at the window looking out just as first light came faintly on to the horizon. The shapes of birds were beginning to move and drop through the air like leaves. A small, cool, vital breeze was blowing.

I thought, Well, Mary, this week you've given your favours to two different men and neither paid a penny for the privilege. Come on, gel, what are you thinking of? And so I went back to bed and fell asleep until the maid came in with tea.

It was at breakfast that the awaited telegram summoning me back to London arrived, and not a moment too soon, for Mrs Brown's face over her porridge and kedgeree was a picture, and I guessed her suspicions of me were now thoroughly aroused. Perhaps she had heard voices, or a floorboard creak, and so suspected the night's transactions, perhaps she was working merely on instinct, but she gave me a thorough grilling over the breakfast table in respect of my mother's maiden name – 'Your mother French? That would account for your dark looks' – and of the late invented Mr Frazer – 'didn't I hear that Hugo Frazer had married in the colonies?' The temptation to tell the old bitch who I was, and who I thought she really was, grew stronger and stronger, until in came Edwards with Mr Ratcliffe's telegram, at last.

Marcus entered at that point and looked at the message in my hand in alarm. 'Not bad news, I hope,' he said.

I told him that my friend's husband had telegraphed saying she was unwell again, and would like me with her. I felt I should leave immediately. He was most upset but I think I heard his mother whisper, 'Opportune,' into her plate, which I, though not he, was meant to hear.

Explanations and farewells over, we started for the station, Marcus having said he would see me off. Mrs Brown enhanced the party by sending along Alice and Veronica with some errands to do for her in Faversham, in order to prevent us from being alone, so at the last moment the gig had to be unharnessed and its horse put with another one to pull the carriage. We all set off. I was pleased not to be alone with Marcus, for as far as I was concerned there was no point in a love affair between us and I liked him, so would not have enjoyed the moment when I told him who I was and made him suffer. Partly due to Mrs Brown's well-timed delay with the carriage (although Marcus had inventively sent the girls off to the station manager's cottage to ask about some terrier puppies) there was little time for sweet nothings on the platform. He had barely time to kiss my cheek and tell me he would be in town next week and would call on me.

Dora could be told to say I was out, I thought, as I settled down in my carriage.

As the train grew closer to London, though, I became increasingly agitated. Had there, during my absence, been any message from Mary? Would there be any communication from Dolly Halloran, whom I'd left in charge of Esmeralda's in my absence? In every other respect a sensible woman, she had a weakness for a plausible, well-set-up man and one of these rogues could always take advantage of her. If some such fellow had hit town after my departure, matters might have got out of hand. And what, I pondered, was I doing allowing Jim Bristow and Marcus Brown to lay claim to me? In the end I'd be so restricted in my actions, as they encircled me like attacking Indians, that I'd have to move to another apartment to evade them. I felt worse and worse as we entered the sad, smoky neighbourhoods bordering the railway line. In the country I had at least slept without nightmares, but as we crossed the Thames, a terrible foreboding and the old anxiety threatened to overwhelm me. I prayed I would find Mary on my doorstep when I returned and be able to pack up and leave England quickly – with or without her, but at least assured of her well-being. It was not to be.

Back in London, there was nothing but outcry, alarm and fear on all sides. On the day I returned, Saturday, 8 September 1888, another woman, Annie Chapman, was found murdered in Whitechapel at six o'clock in the morning. The body was found in a small recess beside the back door of the yard of 29 Hanbury Street, Whitechapel. The building, of eight rooms, one a shop selling cat's meat, contained seventeen people, but Annie Chapman was not a resident and had apparently gone with her murderer into the yard through an unlocked passageway leading from the street. She was a forty-five-year-old woman, mother of two children, and had separated from her husband, a Windsor coachman, a few years before she died. Up to eighteen months before he had sent ten shillings a week to the post office in Commercial Street for her. When the money ceased, she enquired and found out he was dead. After that she lived with first one man then another, supporting herself by doing crochet work, selling flowers and matches in the street, and prostitution. She had lived, mostly with a soldier who was sometimes away with his regiment, in a lodging house at number 35 Dorset Street for four months, paying by the day. On the week she died she was missing from Dorset Street, having, she said, been in the casual ward for destitute people for a few days, using it as a hospital, for she was ill. She went out drunk on the night she died, though she was seemingly no great drinker, to get money for her lodgings. The post-mortem proved that she was already gravely ill with lung damage and damage to the membranes of her brain, perhaps tubercular or syphilitic. The murderer had killed a dying woman.

Scattered near the body were the contents of the pocket under her skirt, which had been slashed open – a piece of muslin, a comb and its paper case, two pills she was taking for her complaint, in a screw of paper, and the corner of an envelope. The two rings the murderer had wrenched from her fingers, some pennies and two new farthings had been laid at her feet. She wore a black jacket, brown bodice, a black skirt and black lace-up boots, all old and dirty.

The evening before her death this poor woman had talked to a friend at her lodgings and had told her she was too ill to go out and find a customer. Later the friend found her still sitting in the same position on her bed but she had rallied herself. 'It's no use my giving way,' the sick woman had said. 'I must pull myself together and go out and get some money or I shall have no lodgings.'

This woman, a widow fallen on hard times, not an inebriate, not a hardened prostitute, but just an amateur eking out a poor living, was found lying two feet from the back of the house, her feet pointing towards the bottom of the yard, her face and hands bloody, skirt up and knees open. Her throat was cut back to her spine, her abdomen had been sliced open, her intestines still attached, part-severed and laid on her right shoulder. The murderer had cut out her uterus, ovaries, the top of her vagina and portions of her bladder and taken them away. They were never found.

They took her to the same mortuary where they'd taken the other women who had been killed, Martha Tabram and Polly Nichols. Her death put the East End in terror.

I knew nothing of this when I went to Mr Ratcliffe's office straight from the station, sending the cabbie on to Fleet Street with my trunk.

The first intimation I had that anything was amiss was when Mr Ratcliffe sat me down gravely in his own small parlour, asking his servant to fetch me a cup of tea. He regarded me gravely from his own comfortable armchair. His dog was at his feet, thumping its tail on a rag rug. 'I have news I think might upset you.'

Mr Ratcliffe had of course guessed much of my situation, as a lawyer will. From the instructions I'd given him as to messages, and the areas from which I'd hinted they might come, I believe he had a pretty clear idea of what kind of woman Mary was. Much of what he understood conflicted with, or did not substantiate, the account of myself I'd given him, but nothing of this was said between us and he never in any way hinted that I or my concerns were not completely respectable and in order. No doubt there was a point at which he'd draw the line but, for the mean while, he appeared to be quietly on my side. He had been ready to send me an untruthful telegram; we were quite confidential.

My first thought when he mentioned upsetting news was that Mary was dead.

'What?' I exclaimed.

'Not the worst news,' he assured me hastily. 'At least, I hope not. You will have heard of the death, a week ago, of a woman, an unfortunate, Polly Nichols by name? And now another woman, unidentified as yet, has been killed in the same neighbourhood. I have my servant at the police station on your behalf – I am quite sure the victim is not your sister, why should she be? – but I consider . . .' He broke off, saying, 'Are you feeling unwell?'

I was sitting transfixed in my chair, sick, dizzy, holding my hand to my breast. Thoughts ran round in my brain. There was a murderer killing off women one by one in Whitechapel. I had no doubt about that. So my sister might be his latest victim; but even if she were not, had not died last night, if they did not capture the man she might be killed tonight, tomorrow night, the next . . .

A maid brought in a teapot and cups on a tray. Mr Ratcliffe poured me a cup.

'Drink this,' he said. 'It may help you.' Then the maid returned and called him out of the room. He left, sagely, and closed the door and I sat staring at it, knowing his servant had returned to say who the dead woman was. When he came in, after only moments, I knew from his expression the name was not my sister's. I dropped my head, sighed aloud in relief.

'As you've guessed, the poor woman was not your sister. Her name was Ann Chapman.' He sat down. 'Another unfortunate. It happened in Hanbury Street, which is off Commercial Street.'

'I must thank you for your kindness,' I said. 'It was

most thoughtful of you to anticipate my anxiety and send your servant to the police station.'

He regarded me earnestly. 'It is indeed a great relief your sister is not the victim. But two women have been killed in Whitechapel in one week, both by the same hand, the police say, having found similar injuries. This is a very disagreeable subject, Mrs Frazer, you'll have to forgive me. You see, we're not out of the wood, are we? It may be that your sister is not in that neighbourhood at all. But you are, regularly, are you not? Sometimes at night?' I nodded. He said, 'Precisely. Yes. And a man – or men – is at large and has killed two women—'

'Three,' I said.

He was astonished. 'Three?' he repeated.

'Before the first woman Polly Nichols was killed they were telling me in the locality about another woman who was murdered, stabbed over and over again, near Whitechapel High Street, less than five minutes' walk from where this latest woman died.' I looked at him. 'I know women of that neighbourhood, leading that kind of life, are not safe. They are killed, often enough by robbers or even men who know them, yet this . . .'

'Three,' he said again, broodingly. 'A murderer at large. This is an awful thought.' He coughed. 'One might think a man of my profession would take the idea more calmly.' He paused, then said, as if to himself, 'They say the woman's injuries were fearful, grotesque.' Then he shook his head as if to clear it. 'Forgive me. I should not have said that. But – is that what you think, Mrs Frazer, that the same man killed all three women?'

'What else is there to think?' I said. 'Let's hope they catch him.'

'But if, as you say, three women have been killed by the same man what would be the motive? They are poor women. It cannot be for gain. Have they some secret, perhaps, that he's trying to conceal?' He thought. 'No, surely not; that cannot be the reason. The man must be insane, a religious maniac perhaps, believing he is doing God's will. Whoever he is, he must be very cunning. And,' he added emphatically, 'I must implore you to stop your peregrinations in that neighbourhood. It will not be safe for a woman alone until this individual is caught. Just imagine, if you had been there last night, instead of the other woman, what might not have happened. We must think of this man as that most frightening of criminals, the man with no motive for what he does, or none that a sane person can understand. So, until he is caught, we have to consider no woman safe.'

You could run from Hanbury Street, where they'd found the dead woman's body, to Cora Mundy's in two minutes. Cutting through alleys and hopping fences you'd only have to travel about fifty yards. I drank some tea, which was cooling now. 'You are right,' I said. I didn't mention I always carried a gun. Ratcliffe knew a good deal about me and, I was convinced, suspected more, but he was bound to take against me if he knew I was in possession of an unlicensed firearm. I thanked him again for his kindness and departed.

I would have to step up my search for Mary, and I needed to know more about the murder than Mr Ratcliffe or, indeed, *The Times* newspaper could or would tell me. I needed to engulf myself in that mix of gossip, speculation and rumour which surrounds events in neighbourhoods like Whitechapel. As when men pan for gold, a sieve full of grit and mud is watered, shaken, watered and shaken again. So from all this gossip a bright truth usually emerges, and that is often the real truth of the matter, though not always the truth finally presented by the authorities. Therefore I ignored Ratcliffe's warnings, those of a man who did not understand the environment of the East End.

In Jack Armitage's pub there was a lot of drinking and shouting. Many had left work at Saturday dinner time and, with that instinct to be together and talk which arises at times like that one, a crowd had gathered in the pub. As I had come through the streets, there had been a kind of silence. People, especially the women, were looking about them, watching strangers, as if trying to identify friend or foe. There were policemen everywhere. At that moment I felt I was closer to Whitechapel than I had thought. I had a wish to be among my own kind now this terror had come on us all.

And terror it was. The first thing I saw as I got into the crowded pub was a woman in hysterics, sobbing into her apron. Jack himself wasn't there. He was, a potboy told me, pacing the floor at the London Hospital, where his wife had been taken early in the morning. Her labour had begun the night before, but, as anticipated, had not gone well. 'They'll be cutting her open now, I expect,' the boy told me, with some relish, his mind on eviscerations.

'Look, Sarah,' a man appealed to his shaking wife when they'd calmed her down a little, 'it was just some poor old tart murdered for her few pennies. How often hasn't that happened round here?'

'There's a maniac about, Jack, killing women,' she was sobbing. 'Don't tell me there isn't.'

'That's right, Jack,' a man in a cap and coat, with a muffler, told the other. 'Don't tell her that. It ain't true. A copper told me. No woman should go out alone from now on till they've caught him.'

'Well, if he is killing women, he's only killing tarts,' said the first man.

'You hope,' said the other.

I stood squashed in a corner beside the bar, voices all round me.

'A woman in our street heard it was her daughter. She fell in a fit and they had to send for the doctor.'

'It's just that gang from Stepney pinching money from tarts.'

'It was done by a copper who did in that other one, Polly Nichols.'

A woman said, 'What do they expect, these women? Stands to reason they'll get murdered.'

'Poor souls. It's not their fault – they're only trying to keep body and soul together,' claimed another.

'Not with him about,' said a robust man's voice. 'Never mind souls, you can't even keep your body together with him on the prowl.'

There was a slap and an enraged shout. 'Show a little respect,' said a woman.

'And it ain't you in fear of being killed and ripped up,' another woman said.

And the voices went on as I stood, deathly chilled, in all the hubbub.

'Asking for it, I say.'

'My brother reckons somebody he works with did it – Joseph Smith, that's his name.'

'Only a heathen could do it.'

'He wants tearing apart, whoever he is. I'd kill him.'

'Who wouldn't?'

'Them women, unfortunate as they may have been, was all Christians, not Jews, so what do you think?' asked someone.

'He knows the neighbourhood, that's for sure,' someone else said.

'He gets away quickly, probably with blood on him, but nobody ever sees him. He's got a bolthole somewhere.'

'Must be local,' said a gloomy voice.

'Could be a nob, with a carriage waiting. He just jumps in, blood and all, and off they go,' said someone else.

'A carriage?' came a scornful voice. 'In Hanbury Street

at six in the morning? It'd attract more attention than an elephant.'

'A woman round Brick Lane heard the news and she miscarried.'

'There's organs from that poor woman they still haven't found.'

I pushed out of the pub, saying I'd come in later to find Jack. I thought I'd go back to the last address I'd had for Mary, Donaldson's Buildings, and try again for news of her. I didn't think the men there would dare to threaten me this time, even in that obscure spot. There were now too many policemen everywhere. Suppressing my queasy feelings, for Donaldson's Buildings was very close to where two of the women had been killed, I set off across Whitechapel Road, for Commercial Street, where men and women going about their business were doing so in a state of extra vigilance, as though they might see or hear something to tell them more of the crime. Annie Chapman's had been a poor, obscure life, I imagined, ending up on the streets of Whitechapel, heading fast for an unmarked pauper's grave. Now her name was travelling from tongue to tongue. She'd achieved fame, by having her guts ripped out in a back yard.

In the court of Donaldson's Buildings all was quiet. A fat woman in a black dress covered by a grey apron was furiously sweeping a tangle of peelings, the heel of a loaf, some rags, away from her front door. She gave me an earful about the habits of the people next door, which, she told me when I could get a question in, was number 11, the place where my sister had lived a month before. The tenants were pigs, who threw their leavings, including the contents of chamber pots, out of the windows shamelessly night and day. Only last night someone had done this again, as I could tell, if I had a nose. It was a battle to keep decent. She'd lived there nine years, had two sons in steady work, but the court had been going steadily down for years, the buildings being colonized by foreigners, Jews, bog-Irish, all sorts, great numbers of them crammed in like pigs in a sty, no chance to keep clean even if they wanted to. Once upon a time this had been a decent place. Poor but decent. Decent working folk lived there, who kept themselves decent, went to church of a Sunday, and work of a Monday, kept their kids shod and fed and in order. Now it was a cesspit, full of foreigners, criminals and if it had not been she was in charge of the house and had an amicable arrangement with the landlord, she and her boys would have cleared out years ago. I agreed with everything, nodding sagely and saying, 'Yes,' trying to interject an enquiry.

'Fah!' she exclaimed in disgust, kicking a rag into the heap of rubbish she was creating. 'Bloody clouts. Can you believe it? These women haven't the simple decency to keep their monthly rags to themselves. Animals are cleaner. Any animal you care to name is cleaner than that.'

'I'm looking for Mary Kelly,' I managed to say. She reached into the doorway for a dustpan and brush, began to push the rubbish into a dustpan, then tip it into a big paper sack from a warehouse.

'Mary Kelly,' she said. 'Mary Kelly – yes, I can tell you about Mary Kelly.' She'd been there with her husband – there was a wealth of scepticism in her tone as she pronounced the word – but had left about a week ago with a big trunk of clothes, not a sheet or a saucepan to her name, of course, but could anyone believe in a woman who had to borrow a kettle to make a cup of tea, pawned it, no doubt, to buy drink, or on hard times, but had a trunk of clothes, silk petticoats a-plenty, though, no doubt, not a pair of drawers to wear under them. 'Out late, up late,' she added. 'Neither of them working.'

She finished with the rubbish and pushed in the top of the sack.

'I'm her sister,' I said. 'I'm trying to find her.'

She didn't apologize for her remarks, and her expression suggested neither of us was worth spitting on, our affairs of no interest. She shook her head.

'You don't know where she went?'

She shook her head again. A woman, two children in tow, came hurrying down the alleyway and into the court. When she saw the other she broke into a run. 'Oh my God, oh my God,' she was crying. 'Mrs Severn, have you heard? I don't know where to put myself. There's another woman been murdered, cut to ribbons in a back yard down Hanbury Street, just near the brewery.'

'What? When?' exclaimed the other woman.

'Last night. I'm shaking all over. There's a madman out there. The whole neighbourhood's full of coppers. But I asked one and he says they don't know who he is. What are we going to do?'

Both women were now upset, the children staring from face to face in terror. I left the court. I was now only a week away from Mary. A few days earlier that knowledge would have been a comfort. Now, the near certainty that she was still in Whitechapel and leading the same old life frightened me. Nor was it much consolation that she had a man to protect her, for if she was a whore, as it appeared, then he was probably a pimp, so how close would he be if she was in danger? If he wasn't the danger itself, I thought.

I went straight to Cora Mundy's, entering the very territory where the woman had been killed. Here the women stood talking in low voices in knots and stared at me gravely as I went along, alone. On a corner by a wall my eye lit on two bold little villains practising disembowelling their sister on the pavement, with a stick. The victim was screaming. A young woman in rusty black and an old bonnet hurled herself from a doorway on the group, abusing the boys, threatening them with a beating.

A policeman was running towards the noise as I passed on, though it was only a little child screaming.

At Mrs Mundy's the room was crowded, but not noisy. A group of labourers stood by the bar drinking, four women were supping stout at a table, two men in bowlers, clerks perhaps, were drinking rum, and the only laughter came from three drunk Swedish sailors who were pushing each other in a corner, getting black looks. Cora wasn't there. I went up to the bar and waited. Nearby at a table was a family group, father, mother, a pretty daughter, two burly youths. The family man was saying earnestly, 'I don't care what you say. I say you two pack up here and now and go down to my father's in Suffolk, stay there in his stable, give him a hand in the fields. I don't want you about until this trouble's over. This place isn't safe for women at present.'

'Oh, Pa,' the girl protested, 'it's only street women what are getting killed in the middle of the night.'

'So far,' her father said. 'But it doesn't have to stop at that.'

Cora Mundy came out of the back room, face set like a barometer at shock and gloom. It altered when she saw me. 'Mary – Mary, my dear. I know why you're here. How you must be feeling! My heart goes out to you.' How the women of the East End loved their theatricals, their dramas, heaving bosoms, screams and sobs.

She took me in for a moment. I thought there'd been another murder, one I hadn't heard of yet, and that the victim was Mary Jane. I stood there in doubt, half believing this awful theory, but at the same time knowing perfectly well what she wanted was to clasp me as I screamed and fainted, roused up, swore revenge, sobbed, fainted again. Then she could send a boy running for the doctor, tell everyone later she had no idea I'd take it like that, but I'd gone white as a sheet, she'd barely had time to catch me as I fell, for a moment thought me dead, the doctor had said I was within an inch of my life.

As I opened my mouth to ask what she meant a robust shout interrupted. 'Come off it, Mundy. What are you on about? Leave Mary alone.'

I turned round to see Rosie Levi pushing through. She slammed half a sovereign on the bar, said to Mrs Mundy, 'Come on, get us a drink, Cora, and bring it over.' Then she took me by the arm and pulled me into the far corner of the bar.

'What did she mean, her heart goes out to me?' I asked.

'She knows you'll be worried about your Mary with this villain about, that's all,' Rosie said. 'She's making a meal of it. Well, it's not her sort he's threatening, is it?'

She pushed me through a gap in some backs and followed herself. I sat down opposite two young men and a young woman in a perky pink satin bonnet with feathers on it, which did not chime well with her reddened eyes, her blue eyeshadow above them or her pallid face.

Rosie said to one of the men, 'Trust Cora Mundy. This poor woman here, Mary Kelly, is looking for her sister round here and Cora's trying to pretend she's been done in by the madman.'

'Well, I pity you,' said the girl in the pink hat. 'Not knowing.' She coughed. 'I pity all of us – with this horror round us.'

'No point in jumping at shadows, is there?' Rosie said stoutly. 'Look at the odds. There's thousands of women in Whitechapel—'

'The odds shorten if you're a whore,' one of the men felt obliged to point out.

'Oh, God, what are we going to do?' wailed the girl.

'You've got us, darlings,' said the man, almost a boy, really. His name was Toby. He had golden curls poking out from under a smart black cap and a red and white patterned neckerchief. His friend, Tom, had long dark hair and a gold, or nearly gold watch-chain across a white kid waistcoat. The East End lads are like women; they'll spend every penny they've got on clothes to make a flash appearance, never mind the rent. Neither of these young men was above nineteen; they'd have the education of four-year-olds, be as mischievous as boys of nine and as wicked as men of fifty. In a place where all felt sobered, only they and the laughing Swedes were cheerful. I could see they'd spotted that when whores are afraid pimps come into their own. As they say, it's an ill wind that blows nobody any good.

The potman had told me Jack Armitage would be back at six o'clock, so I stayed where I was for the afternoon. Tom and Toby told how they had gone round some farms in Surrey, robbing them. 'Easier there,' said Toby. 'Folks in the country don't expect cunning robbers like ourselves. All you've got to worry you is dogs, and I'm a dab hand with dogs, I am.'

Meanwhile the crowd in the alehouse ebbed as evening came.

Tom confessed to, or boasted of, a murder conducted in the course of a robbery in Hackney. Rosie did not believe a word they said, I could tell.

Mrs Mundy came up with refills, saying, 'If this goes on, it's going to be bad for trade, I can tell you that. They're saying a copper did it.'

A boy came in with a parcel of something for Cora, a toffee apple on a stick in the other hand. He waved it about. 'Got it down Hanbury Street. A bloke's set up a stall, there's that many there. The neighbours are charging sixpence to go in and look down over the yard where the woman died. There's blood on the fence where the man escaped.'

'So they haven't caught him yet?' asked Mrs Mundy in a lugubrious tone.

'Nah,' he sneered. 'They're just getting in each other's way and falling over each other.'

'They should use bloodhounds,' Toby observed.

'Anyway,' said the boy, 'it'll be dark soon. Any of you ladies like an escort home? I'll do it for a tanner.'

'A lot of help that would be,' said Rosie. 'Push off, you monster.'

'What are we going to do?' said Ella of the red eyes, not for the first time. 'I daren't go out tonight. I daren't stop at home, by myself, neither.'

'We'll come with you, just as a favour,' Tom said.

'I'd better go up west,' she said. 'It's safer there.' She had a coughing fit.

'You've got more chance of dying of that cough than getting murdered,' Rosie told her. 'You ought to go to the doctor.'

'Come on, love,' said Toby, taking her arm. 'Come with us. We'll see you all right.' She was taken from the room by Tom and Toby, one on either side, she looking back at us fearfully in the doorway as they dragged her out.

Rosie looked at me and shrugged. 'Silly cow,' she said. 'She's wondering if they did it, but she still goes with them.'

'You don't know who to trust,' I said. 'You told me you were scared, didn't you?' She nodded. 'You don't seem scared now.'

She shook her head. 'I suppose it's worse worrying about a thing when no one else is. Then you think you're mad as well. Like I said, the whole neighbourhood's falling apart. Look here, I've got an idea. Why don't you get some handbills printed for Mary? Offer a reward. Get boys to run round giving them to people. Of course we know half the ignorant pigs round here can't read, but those who can will tell them what can't. My uncle Lemuel's a printer. He keeps the press in his back yard.

He'll do it overnight for you. On Monday he'll get some dirty kids and give them sixpence each to put the bills round the streets. We can go there now.'

'I was going back to Jack Armitage's to see if there was any news,' I told her.

'Let's do that, then go to my uncle's.'

As we left a man carolled out, 'Watch out, girls, or you'll wake up in an alley with your guts hanging out.'

A woman standing by the bar with a pint pot in her hand smacked him round the face with her old black handbag, taking him by surprise. 'You ponce,' she exclaimed. 'How dare you joke about things like that? You're a brute, you are.'

'It's only the tarts, missus,' he said with his hand to his face.

'Only the tarts?' she said furiously. 'Only the tarts?' She downed the rest of her pint. 'Men!' she cried. 'They'll stand together whatever they've done. It's enough to make you bloody well weep.'

Rosie and I left, grinning and a bit drunk on Mrs Mundy's gin. We crossed Whitechapel Road to Jack Armitage's, eating fish and chips as we went.

'Maybe I'll find a client in the pub,' muttered Rosie.

'Christ, Rosie,' I said. 'Not tonight of all nights.'

'I've got to live,' she said. There was a cold wind off the river, and it was now dark. 'He'll have had his fill of guts for the time being, whoever he is.'

Rosie gripped my arm as we went down the side street to the pub. 'Two against one, at any rate,' she muttered.

Inside, Jack Armitage was back behind the bar. 'How's the wife?' I asked.

Rosie put a gin in my hand. He shook his head. 'They had to cut her,' he said. 'The baby's all right, a great big boy.'

'She'll be right as rain in a week or two,' I told him.

'I hope so,' he said unhappily. 'My God. You should

have heard her screams when they wheeled her off. One of the nurses hit her, to shut her up. Fancy striking a woman in labour.' He was badly shaken.

'Bitches, them nurses,' Rosie said.

He looked at her sharply. 'Are you two out alone? Are you barmy?' he asked. 'Haven't you heard what's happened?'

'Haven't heard anything else,' declared Rosie.

I drank my gin. I was muzzy now. I barely understood, at first, what Jack told me: '. . . saw her down Middlesex Street last Sunday morning.'

'What?' I cried.

'Yes,' he said. 'I was going to send you a note to your lawyers, but this business with the old woman put me off my stroke. Well, we went down there to get her out of the house; she was brooding and getting more and more miserable about how she might have to go to the hospital; so we took a stroll down Petticoat Lane to get one or two little things. So, while she's rummaging on a stall down the bottom, the Aldgate end, I just caught sight of this woman I thought was Mary going up towards Wentworth Street, right in the middle of the road, strolling along, cool as you please, wearing a nice red dress with a bustle, and bonnet to match, very tasteful and ladylike – I know it was her, because just as I caught sight of her and thought that's Mary, she turned her head sideways to look at something on a stall, so I saw her face quite clear. I was only about ten yards away but there were people moving to and fro. Just then, two fellows crossed behind her and cut off my view. Then more people got in the way, so by the time the crowd had cleared I'd lost sight of her. She must have turned off somewhere. I ran up to see if I could find her, but she'd disappeared by then. I ran back and asked the old woman if she'd seen her, but she'd seen nothing but an old fish kettle she was trying to get a bit cheaper.'

I stared at him. He was a dependable man. He would never have told me this story unless he'd been as good as certain he'd seen Mary.

'There was a bloke with her,' he went on. 'When I first glimpsed her she was arm in arm with him, leaning up against him, lovey-dovey style. Then she pulled away a bit to look at whatever it was.'

'Did you recognize him?' I asked.

'No. I only saw his back, just for a moment. There was a lot of people there, as usual. But it was a clear day. I think I saw her.'

He turned away, pulled a pint for a man, agreed that murders were bad for trade. I looked round. Rosie had disappeared. 'Where's Rosie?' I asked in alarm. Jack said, pulling another pint, 'She slipped out while we was talking, with a geezer in a brown bowler – gave me a wink in the doorway. Silly bitch. Do anything for money, she would. Jewess, of course. Don't go out looking for her, Mary, for Christ's sake,' he warned. 'Pound to a penny Rosie's all right. She's one of the tough ones. But while you're searching the alleys for her, you could come across our friend with the knife.'

Then Rosie materialized behind me, her hair wispy and her bonnet disarranged. She said, 'Come on, Mary, my duck, if you want those handbills printed.'

'That didn't take you long,' said Jack. 'It's not healthy round here for you lot – why don't you take a cab to where you're going? That man in the corner'll take you.'

Rosie shouted, 'Oi! Cabbie! Over here!' adding, 'My feet are killing me anyway.'

'I don't suppose that's all, either,' Jack said.

'Stow it, Jack,' she said. 'If my money's good enough for you, so am I. Hope your wife feels better soon.'

The cabman came up and took us to where his horse was standing, wearing a nosebag. He took the nosebag off and we clopped off to a narrow street in Stepney, where

Rosie muttered, 'Here we go. Sabbath's over. They'll let me in now if it's business. Not like my mother and father. They wouldn't let me in if they were starving and I was the Prince of Wales.' Then she banged hard on a door and called out, 'Uncle Lem! It's Rosie. Let me in.' Then a stream of her language. Finally a bearded Jew in a black hat and a collarless shirt opened the door and looked at her suspiciously. 'Business?' he asked.

'Yes. Come on, Uncle,' she said, and entered the house. We went down two steps into a low passageway past a door, past an old pram with a baby asleep in it, into a kitchen at the back. Two children were asleep head to toe on a trestle bed against a wall and the rest of the space, about ten feet long, was occupied by six people. In spite of the lateness of the hour, they were all active. A woman in a long dress and a headscarf was cooking something up on an old primus stove in a corner; an old man sat, reading and smoking a pipe, on a wooden chair by the fire, where another cauldron of food was boiling on a trivet. On either side of a table two young women also in headscarves were sorting sheets of paper into various sizes while at one end a young man in a little cap was putting type into a frame with a pair of tweezers, and at the other a boy was reading a huge book written in funny characters, his finger sliding backwards along the line as he muttered under his breath.

All this was taking place by the light of a couple of hurricane lamps, one in the middle of the table, one on the mantelpiece. A babble of foreign talk stopped as we came in, the uncle first, then Rosie, and me behind. The people at the table looked up. The old man spotted Rosie and instantly turned his eyes to his paper again. Then the young man with the book, who had not taken his finger off the line, looked down and began to mumble again. The other young man looked at her with open disapproval. The woman at the primus stove, who'd swung round, greeted Rosie curtly, turned the stove off and turned back to us, hands on hips. She gave me a dirty look, too, as I stood in the doorway. The black sheep of the family, Rosie, in her bright yellow bonnet and low-cut blue dress, was home. Rosie, in the meanwhile, greeted everybody. 'Auntie Hep – Becky – Suzanna – Sol – David – how's the studies, David? Is the wedding fixed yet, Becky dear?' But she got the cold shoulder from everybody.

However, the black sheep's wool always looks a little lighter to the family when the sheep arrives holding cash in its hoof, so the atmosphere brightened a little as we sketched out my handbill. 'REWARD', it was to begin, in big black letters, saying underneath, 'For any person giving information as to the present whereabouts of MARY JANE KELLY, also known as MARIE JEANETTE KELLY, whose sister Mary Anne Kelly is searching for her, the sum of 15 POUNDS will be paid.' Then followed her description, and Mr Ratcliffe's name and address. Then, imagining him bombarded by everybody in the East End who needed fifteen pounds, I added the following words: 'Bearers of information not given seriously and only in the hope of payment will be reported to the proper authorities and prosecuted.'

I left money for the handbills and the boys to distribute them, and we departed, Rosie getting a fairly cordial farewell.

In the dark street she asked, 'Going home, Mary?'

'Where else, at this hour? You'd better come with me, there's a murderer on the prowl.'

She shook her head. 'I've rent to pay. See here, Mary. All I've got to do is find a cab, go up west, pick up a toff, take him to Mrs Murchison's where there's plenty of people and I'll be safe as houses. You coming?'

'No.'

Neither of us had a coat or a shawl and we were both

shivering. A policeman with a lantern walked down the opposite pavement.

'Going to catch the murderer for us?' called Rosie provokingly.

'It might be better if you went home,' he said.

'Why? Can't you protect us?' she responded.

'We'll get him. Have no fear,' the policeman said, and went on his way.

Rosie shook her head at me in the darkness.

'They'll get him,' I said.

'I wouldn't bet on it,' she replied and strolled off in search of a cab. She had a nerve, Rosie Levi.

On Monday came a letter effortfully written by Dolly Halloran in Calgary. After some domestic details of liquor supplies, a rotten portion of the verandah replaced, the regular visit of the doctor from Banff ('All well,' she said), she went on in this way: 'The Indjun girl called Kid got herself pregnant again so this time I threw her out but guess the others have been feeding her from the back door at night for she is still hangin about and will not go back to her farther, maybe for the reson he will not have her. The profitt for the week you left hear was 29 shillin for there was cowboys in and trappers celebratin their departur for the mountins, and a side of beef, which we ate and made some jerki. For the next week it was 30 shillun, but will be lower when the trappers went away for the winter. I have got men to split kindlin, about 70 logs, for the winter, Harriet is complainin of a cold but I pay her no mind, and ther is a new girl I mite take on, says she is French and cals herself Adely, but she is mostly Cree I think. This would make ten girls to seven room, as you know, but she is a good girl, only 18 but not silley, you put me in ful charge of the house on leeving, but I must hav your advise. There was a fight saturday, beggs broke his leg bein thrown down the stairs by Flash and Marie. But nobody payd no mind, the redcotes looked tother way. Wether good, tho windy it is not cold and Mr Hamilton sends his best reggard, as I do and will you do me a big favor Mary as you love me which is send money from London to my family in Donegal as the mortgige is nearly up and it will be sooner than from hear. I cannot bear to see ar farm go back to Capt Armitage and the family starve. So do it please, Mary do, as you love me and pleas do come back soon. Mary as that all goes well I'm uncertain it is a big wurry and a stragne on me looking arfter all mysef wich I do not complane of at all but miss you bein gratefull for your true presense and the good laffs we allways have, and Jack Berry is still pressin marrige on me so you see my plite. So I leav you with all love and blessins to you and hoping that you found your sisters. Come back saf my freind, your Dolly.'

This communication gave me pause. I had been away a fortnight when Dolly wrote and already she was feeling the strain of office, so to speak, while the prosperous rancher who was in love with her was pressing his suit, and she, no judge of Indians, planned to take on a girl she knew nothing about. Takings, too, were low, which must mean that bills were too high, or some not paying because the girls were letting them get away with it.

I reflected that I had been in London for almost two weeks and had found one sister, though had been rejected by her, while the other, though nearby, still eluded me. Perhaps the handbills would find her. Meanwhile I was getting more frantic. I could feel London dirt sinking into my skin and my soul. I felt invaded by that old London atmosphere of greed, lies and betrayal. It was like that yellow-green fog they call the London particular, which writhes into houses through cracks and crannies and leaves all it touches dirty and greasy. Yet the city was full of glamour and enticement. Everything was here, the cruelty, dirt and want, and the entertainment, the luxury, the variety, and a frantic, exhausted vitality, like that of the tarantella, that dance where people cannot stop dancing until they drop dead.

I slept that night and dreamed again of that monster pursuing me through the streets and alleys of the great, grim city under heavy, filthy skies. Walls dripped blood as I ran in a panic closer to the dark waters of the Thames and found the dark ship where my sisters stood, waiting for me, beckoning to me. Yet I could not reach them. My pursuer seized me as I stood on the dock, I saw the two white-clad figures, open mouths as they screamed – and woke, terrified. As I lay in bed with a clammy brow I thought, I must not stay in London too long. If I did something terrible would happen to me.

Next morning I set about, through Mr Ratcliffe, unravelling Dolly Halloran's business over the mortgage her family had with Captain Armitage of Donegal, but it was not as simple as it seemed on the surface. For although it appeared to be just a matter of paying the thirty pounds owed to Armitage he began to struggle not to receive the money. It emerged that he wanted to seize the farm – more of a patch than a farm in fact – because he planned to divert a river running through the property into his own grounds to make a water garden. So it turned out to be a complicated, tricky business with letters to and fro and duplicity on all sides.

I kept out of Whitechapel for a time. *The Times* said after the murder of 'the woman Chapman', as they called her, that the ordinary prudence of a murderer couldn't be counted on in the case of this man as he was a madman. Yet it wasn't fear of death that kept me away, nor the stricken silence of the streets (which soon enough ended, human life being what it is thereabouts, too demanding and agitating to allow any mood to last long). What it was I do not know, unless the feeling I've described, that the place was reclaiming me, and I knew it could, one way or another, kill me.

I shopped, I visited the theatre, bought books, Marcus Brown called and wrote. I told Dora when he came to the door to say I was with my sick friend, and I did not reply to his notes. Jim Bristow sent an ill-written love message by a dirty boy. I sent it back to Mrs Mundy's, saying I was in Liverpool with my sister Mary Claire. He seemed to accept this for there were no further messages. So I led an even life for nearly three weeks, but I was not easy in my mind and the dreams went on.

The days grew cooler, the nights began to close in. The grass was weary, the trees turning orange and brown and a big sun was low in the sky.

One late afternoon I was in Hyde Park, listening to the band. Fashionable men walked to and fro. Summer was over and the well-off were coming back to town. Nurses hurried perambulators and children in sailor suits with hoops and boats back to their homes for tea. But the Whitechapel murders had penetrated this peace and prosperity. Sitting in my chair in front of the bandstand I heard a well-dressed woman talking to a companion behind me as the band stopped for an intermission, the soldiers in tunics shaking moisture from their instruments, the drummer tightening his drums.

'What a shocking thing,' came one woman's voice.

'Of course, the victims are all women of a certain kind,' came the other.

'But can we be sure that will continue to be so? He may widen his net.'

'The police will catch him. At any rate, my dear, it's unlikely he'll start to prowl about Grosvenor Square at night. I'm sure we have nothing to fear.'

The other woman thought she had, but 'It's the servants I'm afraid for,' she said. 'One's never quite sure where they're going – or who they know.'

There was a pause. 'Hm,' said the other consideringly. She must have been imagining the scullery maid letting in a murderer by the back door. I'd had the thought myself, about Dora's lover, but had dismissed it. I didn't think him a homicidal maniac, and I did, after all, sleep with a gun under my pillow.

Meanwhile, the bandsman had climbed back on to the bandstand and raised his baton. They were playing tunes from Gilbert and Sullivan.

'So charming,' sighed one of the women, terrors forgotten.

'Was that a drop of rain?' I heard the other say.

> 'Three little maids who all unwary
> Come from a ladies' seminary
> Freed from its genius tutelary . . .'

'Three little maids from school,' both women sang with the band enjoyably, under their breaths.

I turned and copped a look at the ladies behind me, both in their thirties but young-looking, with pleasant expressions. They were fresh-faced after holidays in the country and wore nice tailor-mades. Small bonnets were firmly set on well-coiffed hair, their hands were in tight gloves, their umbrellas and handbags were tidily about them. They didn't seem likely candidates for murder in an alley. The women who had died, and those who might die yet, if they did not catch the murderer soon, were poor prostitutes whose only comfort was a neat gin and a chat, maybe a bit of love from a man as poor and beaten as they were.

The victims were women past their prime, half-forgotten mothers of children they had half forgotten themselves, abandoned by their husbands when their looks went and the drink took over, unprotected even by the law. They had nothing but the clothes they stood up in, and the coppers, if any, in their pockets. They lived between lodging houses and the alleys they whored in, standing up against fences and walls. They had nothing, they were nothing, except to the few who knew them, and if a man ripped one of them up in the dark – angry lover, thief or maniac – and left them lying out in the open like a slaughtered animal, their carcasses were worth less than any pig's in a slaughterhouse. If one of these women appeared now in the park and sat down beside one of the ladies behind me to listen to the band (which she never would dare), to those ladies she would seem less than an animal, dirtier, more depraved, her life more horrible than a beast's. Those prosperous women came from houses barred and locked, dogs and servants there to keep guard, streets well lit, policemen patrolling, looking for those whose appearances suggested they had no business there. They were safe; a guinea or so to an East End mission at Christmas took care of conscience. But, in any case, what could they do but live as they did? They had one thing in common with the whores, they were not men. They seemed rich, but probably owned nothing. Anything they did possess would be firmly in the hands of men, husbands, fathers, bankers. Their fears of murder, I thought, were like a shadow of something else, the fear of men in general, who could do what they liked.

They sang by turn, 'One little maid is a bride, Yum-yum.'

'Two little maids in attendance come.'

'Three little maids is the total sum,' and then together, 'Three little maids from school!'

I got up and walked slowly from the park, enjoying the long composed view, the pond, the fresh breeze. That night, within the space of one hour, the man people now called Jack the Ripper killed two more women in the East End.

★

Elizabeth Stride, a pretty woman, Swedish by birth, was forty-five and had separated from her husband, by whom she'd had two children, about six years earlier. She'd been living on and off with a labourer in a lodging house in Flower and Dean Street, working when she could and whoring when she couldn't work or needed extra cash for a binge. She was killed at the back of a big house in Berners Street off Commercial Road, where men the neighbours called 'bad Jews' went, those who did not adhere to their religion. They published a magazine from the annexe at the back of the building, near where the body of Mrs Stride was found dead at one in the morning. She had a flower pinned to her jacket and was holding a paper of scented cachous to sweeten her breath, just as if she'd been out with a lover. Her throat was cut. She was not mutilated, unlike Catherine Eddowes, whose body was discovered only three quarters of an hour later, in Mitre Square, half a mile away.

Catherine Eddowes was forty-six and had parted from her common-law husband after fifteen years of marriage eight years earlier, having had three children. She lived mostly with a regular lover, a market worker. When found by a policeman who had patrolled the area only fifteen minutes earlier, she was sprawled flat, one leg aslant, her skirt pulled up showing hideous abdominal wounds, her face almost unrecognizable. Her throat had been cut, eyelids and lips slit, parts of her nose and cheeks had been cut away. Her trunk had been slashed open from the breast to thigh, and from this great jagged wound the murderer had cut out, and taken away, her uterus and one kidney.

She was the woman I'd met at Mrs Mundy's the day I arrived in London.

*

More work for the Old Montague Street mortuary. Real panic ensued now and not just in the East End. This was when they took off the play of Jekyll and Hyde at the Lyceum. The Conservatives were calling for the Home Secretary to resign, as he'd not caught the murderer. More police flooded in, partly to protect the Jews from riot, for they were being blamed for the murders. Yet still Jack the Ripper went free.

Letter to George Lusk, Chairman of the Whitechapel Vigilance Committee:

> From Hell. Mr Lusk. Sir, I send you half the kidne I took from one woman, presarved it for you, tother piece I tried and ate; it was very nise. I may send you a bloody knif that I took it out if only you wait a while longer. Catch me when you can Mr Lusk.

That night I was awoken by strange noises. I got out of bed and pushed up the window. Fleet Street was full of policemen. There were two wagons full of them with others standing on the running boards. There were ten mounted men, going down Fleet Street in formation at a fast canter, and on the pavements other policemen were running. Dora was shouting from the upstairs window, 'What is it? What's happening?' Other windows were going up elsewhere, other voices were calling out. A policeman racing down our side of the pavement stopped, looked up at Dora and me and cried, 'Two more women found murdered nearby. Stay at home, for the love of God, until we catch him.' Then he ran off. Dora screamed, and above in the window I heard her boy consoling her.

I put on my wrapper and sat in front of my empty grate until dawn, thinking about this new and almost unbelievable horror, and what it meant. Of course I didn't know if Mary, or Rosie Levi, or anyone I knew had been killed, nor could I until the bodies had been identified, which might be some hours.

This madman was still at large. It looked as if nothing and no one would stop him in his career unless he was caught, red-handed, by the police or informed on by a person who knew who he was. Meanwhile I had booked my passage for America. I would leave in two weeks' time, for I could not, and would not, stay any longer. I had business to conduct in Canada. I had now done all I could to find Mary. I had followed her tracks as far as I could – now she would have to find me. But if she was hiding from me in the East End, and I still believed she might be, then perhaps now fear would make her reveal herself.

I cooked my own breakfast early, a shaky Dora coming down a little later. The horror of last night's information induced us both to drop our mutual irritations and suspicion.

'Has the boy gone?' I said, nodding at the ceiling.

She said he had. 'I can't stay here no more,' she said. 'I'm so frightened. It's getting worse and worse. And,' she said defiantly, 'you'd better not go out at night no more.' She added 'madam' as an afterthought.

'I'm going back to Canada,' I said. 'I'll give you my address.' She stared a bit at this, but made no comment.

Then the breadman banged on the back door, handed over a small loaf and said, 'This is the best I can do. Your bread comes from Whitechapel, two of the bakers didn't come to work this morning – their wives wouldn't let them, they wanted them by them.'

'What happened?' I asked him.

He looked very discouraged. 'Same story. This time, two old . . .' He evaded the word and went on, 'Caught in dark spots. One woman was very sorely used. Very sorely, they say.' He shook his head. 'They don't seem to be able to catch him.'

A moment later my landlady, Mrs Cooper, came in with a tall, uncomfortable-looking fellow, her brother-in-law.

'Who was that man you were talking to?' she demanded.

'The breadman,' Dora responded, looking pointedly at the small loaf on the kitchen table.

'Well,' she said rapidly, 'Mr Ellman and I have checked the locks and shutters and that, as far as I'm concerned, is that. This is no place for a woman to be conducting a business. I shall return when this is settled.' She was in a panic, opening and closing the clasp on her handbag. 'I don't know what the police are doing. This man should have been caught weeks ago. But I'm certain there's no safety for women in London any more.'

Dora broke in: 'I can't bring myself to stay here any longer, madam, especially with an empty shop below. I shall have to give notice, with respect—'

This startled her. She broke in. 'What? You want to leave? Where will you go? This will be very inconvenient. Mrs Frazer will have no attendant. Someone else will have to be employed.'

Dora looked at her hopelessly.

She rattled on again, 'Well, that's as may be – I must be on my way. I have other things to attend to.' And with that she turned and, trailing the lanky Mr Ellman behind her, hurried off.

There was the sound of the shop door opening, a rattling of bolts and locks as the couple retreated through the premises in haste. Dora shrugged hopelessly. It was obvious that if she left, she would be going without pay or a reference.

'Where will you go?' I asked.

Then there was a knock on the door at the side of the shop. She went to answer it. A tall boy in knickerbockers and big boots came into the kitchen, startled and embarrassed by two strange women in their wrappers. He held out a piece of paper to me, at arm's length. 'Father asked me to bring this round to you. The maid found it on the doormat early on. It must have been pushed through the letterbox in the night.'

It was a note, written in pencil on the back of what looked like an old bill. It read, 'Mary. Things have gone too far now it's time you knew the truth. Your sister is at 26 Dorset Street Millers Court. Dont go there by night for fear of murder.' At the foot of this note, written in fluent handwriting, was the signature, 'A Friend'.

The boy – I suppose he was Mr Ratcliffe's son – went off. I stood clutching the note in the chilly kitchen. It smelt of the truth. I had almost no doubt Mary was in Dorset Street.

'Dora,' I said, 'I have to go out quickly. Get me a bath.'

She began to fill the big kettle. 'No,' I said, 'just bring up the water. I'll have it cold.'

Upstairs in the boxroom, as she filled the bath from a bucket, I told her, 'I'm going to leave my address in Canada for you on the table. I have a business there, employing many young women. If you ever think of making a change, write to me.'

My tone, urgent and commanding, brought her up short. She straightened, still holding the empty pail, looked me in the eye, and said bluntly, 'You're very young to have a business. What sort of business would that be?'

I was in a desperate hurry to get to Dorset Street before the bird had flown. I didn't have time to fence with her. 'What sort of business do you think it is?' I demanded. 'Now, fetch another pail of water.'

Very startled, she walked off obediently, then turned in the middle of the sitting-room to make another enquiry, I suppose.

'Look sharp, Dora,' I snapped.

Suddenly she looked terrified. My mask had dropped, startling her, and I think she was making some fearful connection between me and the Whitechapel murders. In ten minutes she'd be round at the police station laying some incoherent information against me. Everyone seemed to have lost their wits this morning. No wonder.

'Oh, don't bother with the bloody bucket, Dora,' I said. 'Look, here's the address and a sovereign for yourself.' I scribbled the address, went back into the boxroom. I threw off my clothes and stepped into the icy bath and began to sponge myself down.

She babbled uncertainly from the doorway, 'There's Red Indians there.'

'What the bloody hell do you think is here?' I asked her ferociously. 'I suppose you feel safer in London – after what happened last night.' I was shivering now. I got a towel and put it round me, still desperately cold. 'Don't stand there with your mouth opening and closing,' I said, going into the bedroom. 'Run out and get me a cab and tell it to wait at the kerb. Then pack up my trunks when I'm gone and I'll consider your services to me terminated. And if I find anything missing when I unpack, even a hairpin, I'll settle you for good and all, you can rest easy on that score. Don't worry your head about it. Whether I'm in Canada or Africa or at the other end of the earth, if you rob me, I'll see to your punishment.' As I'd spoken I'd put on my underclothes. Now I got into a brown woollen dress and was slipping on my boots. Dora disappeared.

I sat on my bed and looked again at the note. 'Things have gone too far now . . .' It was well-formed writing, firm and fluent. Why did it look familiar? I turned the note over. It was written on the back of an account from a Whitechapel brewery for three barrels of stout, delivered to Mrs Mundy, in Brushfield Street. Cora! I thought in astonishment. No, not Cora. She could barely write. This was from Harry Mundy. I'd seen his scribble, on newspaper edges, lists on bits of paper, many times. But why would he, or he and Cora in combination, send me information anonymously, yet make it pretty plain where it came from? It could be no accident. Harry was very intelligent. His idea must have been to get the information to me, yet to be able to deny it, say the bill had been picked up and used by someone else. Yet, if money-hungry Harry wanted to deny having supplied information which might lead to a reward, then it was because fear of reprisals from another quarter outweighed his never-flagging desire for cash. So someone else was involved or more than one, and Harry was afraid of whoever it was. Unless it was a hoax of Harry's, but I couldn't believe he would be so stupid as to play such a nasty, pointless joke on me at such a grim time.

I was fearful as the cab went east through the banking and business areas, and I was feeling a little dizzy, too, and took it for a sign of nerves. These unstoppable murders, all taking place in one square mile of London, seemed to be filling the atmosphere with fear and mistrust. Sometimes it was as if no individual were responsible; the very air we breathed was a miasma, carrying plague. And again, since all natural order had broken down, was anything to be trusted? Even a note, probably from the hand of Harry Mundy, a straightforward person in his way, might be from someone else, might be a trap. The address I'd been given was in the next street from Mundy's alehouse, but five minutes away in one direction from the house where Martha Tabram had been stabbed over and over again on a landing, and another five minutes away, in the other direction, from where Annie Chapman had been ripped open in a back yard. What confidence could I have in the message? Was it a trap?

My cabbie, a taciturn man, stopped his horse outside Liverpool Street Station and said, 'No further.'

'No further? Why not?' I asked.

'I couldn't take a woman alone down there,' he said. 'Haven't you heard there's been more murders?'

'Not there,' I said.

'He may have moved off a bit because of the coppers,' the driver said. 'But Commercial Street's his base. That's where they'll find him, if they do.'

'I'll walk it, then,' I said, getting out.

'On your own head be it,' he replied, pocketing his fare and whipping up his horse.

I walked down Brushfield Street. It was only eight o'clock. Clusters of dark-clad women, the respectable, stood on the pavements, talking in low voices. There was none of the febrile excitement a revolting crime can often bring to the streets. Even the children seemed subdued. The only life was a dog which had evidently snatched a chicken from someone's yard and was consuming it in a heap of flying feathers in the angle of a building. The women watched me as I went along, well-dressed, neatly shod, with my big bag. I began to bang on the door and shout for Mrs Mundy. 'Cora! Cora! It's me – Mary.' They were in, must have been, but asleep, or pretending to be. I went on shouting, my voice seeming to echo in the silence of the street, while the women watched. Finally a woman slid up to me, holding a baby. 'Do you want some help, dear?' she asked.

'Are they in?' I asked.

'Haven't seen them go out.' She frowned. 'Have you heard about the murders?'

I said I had.

She shook her head. 'I wouldn't stay around here if you haven't got to.'

Two policemen walked round the corner opposite us. We both looked at them. 'They can't stop him,' she said flatly.

'Well,' I said, 'I'd better be getting along.'

There's a point where, if a man's beating up a woman, as often as not when it gets bad enough the woman gives up pleading, or shouting angrily, crying for help or fighting back, and just lies there, taking the kicks and blows like a poor old horse who can't drag his load any further. He can't go on, the driver could beat him to death, nothing will make him move. The women here, after this new shock, were like that. And every time a man walked past, they looked at him, long and hard. In such a situation each man's face speaks of vice, secrecy and depravity. The eye of fear and suspicion sees everyone as guilty, milkman, chimney sweep, policeman, judge, doctor, tram-conductor. Three of the murders had taken place at the week's end. The murderer could be a respectable employed man, taking himself from a factory or warehouse, even from the Bank of England or the Old Bailey to find his terrible pleasure.

I went round into Dorset Street. Two tired whores, in finery, caught another coming out of the door, with an empty milk can. They grasped her one on each side and spoke into her face, urgently. I saw the expression on the face of the woman with the milk can change to one of horror. Her mouth dropped open. She started to shake and looked ready to faint. They went off together, arm in arm, three whores, to fetch a drop of milk for their tea at nine in the morning.

'D'you know Miller's Court?' I called.

They all turned back to look at me. 'Through the arch,' one said, pointing a little further down.

Through the arch was a court, with no exit at the far end. Five or six small houses stood on one side, on the left someone had cut off the back parlour of the Dorset Street house and put a door in the side wall. Beside it were two windows, making a one-room apartment. There was no one about. A dirty net curtain covered the windows but it was caught up a little on one side, by some object on the window ledge inside the room. I went and looked in.

To cover the inessential features first, it wasn't a bad room. It might have looked squalid to my suitor, Marcus Brown, my landlady Mrs Cooper and many others, but by local standards a twelve-foot-square room inhabited by one person is luxury. I saw a fireplace, full of ashes, opposite the window through which I was peering. Beside it was a table covered with a cloth. On this were a couple of plates, a kettle, a pair of little, tidy red boots, very smart, and hanging from the table, pinned down by a flat iron and a jug, a petticoat with lace, drying. And these were the signals which, as I stared, made me know my anonymous informant had led me to my sister's lair, for as an Indian can trail an animal by tiniest signs, knowing the terrain and the animal as well as he knows his own hand, so we know each other, if we know each other well, by little habits and ways of doing things. The manner in which the boots lay and the drying petticoat had been secured, even the placing of the kettle, told me Mary Jane lived here. I was shaking as I stared, and here I come to the essentials of the case.

The bed was to the right of the door, under the window. And on that bed, bold as brass, perfectly at home in shirt and trousers, and barefoot, dreamy, staring up at the ceiling, lay – Jim Bristow. The hand far from me held a pipe, smoke curling up. The hand near me, just below the window, idly caressed a large, villainous-looking black cat with a torn ear, which had had more fights than hot dinners, I'm sure. As I stared, watching that hand stroking the beast, the cat saw me, turned big, empty green eyes towards me, held my gaze. I felt as if I were sinking into those pitiless, animal eyes. My knees shook. I straightened up, my head was spinning, I took a few paces, fell against the damp and unforgiving wall of 26 Dorset Street, expecting my head to steady, but it did not. I realized I was fainting, tried to go into the street and fell, I believe, in the archway leading into Dorset Street.

PART III

NIGHTMARES came. A hot, hot night. My mother's stumbling steps as she came up the stairs. The door opened. Bloody cloths soaked in an enamel basin on the floor on a boiling hot night. I was on the merry-go-round at Victoria Park, round and round and round I swung, fearful of falling. A night in the barroom of Esmeralda's, the piano playing, the card game going on, a woman in a scarlet dress downing a whisky, straight, at the bar. I open the door for dawn coolness, but it will never be cool or light, ever. A shot rings out. At the music-hall Rosie Levi tells me she knows a murderer but will not say his name. Wouldn't you like to know? she mocks. The ship in the river sways to and fro at anchor. We know the murderer, Mrs Brown tells me confidentially, in the sunken garden, but it would be unsuitable to make his identity public. The dried-up fountain with the little statue suddenly bursts. There's water everywhere. Three little girls in white frocks with hair ribbons in their long hair sing a silly song, swaying to and fro, seductively, like music-hall singers. Three little maidens, all unwary. I'm turning down Thames Street past the women, past the pubs, shouting, 'Quick, he's after me, he'll kill me, you, too,' but no one can hear for the clanging of the engines coming to the fire. Calgary's on fire and all burned down. St Katharine's Dock is on fire. London Bridge is burning down. Blood and fire. Calgary's on fire. It's burning up, horses stampeding, the good women of the town and their children all running to Esmeralda's for shelter (only Mrs O'Rourke still nods to her former hostess; the rest have returned to snook-cocking and, if vulgar, sniffing at the whores). And the fire sweeps on, taking wooden house after wooden house. A boy weeps for a yellow cat. Stampede. I'm running away from the murderer, but somehow into the flames. My sisters are calling me from the ship in the river. It's hotter and hotter. I shall have to turn and face him. He puts his knife in my stomach. The lamb's fleece is bloody. We used to scream on the wall looking down into the abattoir. Three little maidens all unwary, come from a ladies' seminary. Blood and fire, flood and fire.

Then, some time later, I suppose, I wake from the fever, see a green arched ceiling, gas-lamps, metal beams overhead, hear a moan, a sentence I cannot understand. Then, I'm afire again, but drowning, down in the sea, tangled in weed, Thames weed, I see my sister's face, floating towards me. She swims past, laughing at my struggles. I cannot breathe. 'It was very nise. Catch me if you can, Mr Lusk.' I cannot breathe. I hear rasping breaths. Mine. A cargo of oil has been released from the hold of a docked ship. Fire sweeps the water. I break the surface, aflame.

Still later, a voice says, 'Drink this.' Now, I'm swimming in the river, a hot day, pelicans line the banks. A flight of them sweeps overhead.

Ahead of me now, I see a window, the frame painted green, the centre, where the glass should be, solid dark yellow. As I watch, it moves, the yellow, and waves about. I sleep, or faint. Later the voice says again, 'Drink this.' I feel water on my lips and tongue. I want more, but it goes. I think I saw a hand, square, pink, rough and clean, with big reddened knuckles, a wedding ring embedded.

Now I'm hauled up, not very gently, and gazing at a woman's face. A forty-year-old face, big nose, a few broken blood vessels in round cheeks, a pale mouth, and above it, a starched white cap. She spoons some rough food, porridge or the like, into my mouth. I eat it, to oblige, though I don't want it. 'Lie down,' she instructs and pulls me flat again. I lie flat, very tired, but hearing voices, 'Nurse! Nurse!' There's a moan. My breath rasps in and out. There's the crash of metal from somewhere, footsteps running. 'Bed four,' a voice orders. Feet pass. There are green metal arches above me. I'm in hospital, I tell myself, and that's all.

'What's your name?'

'Mary Kelly.'

I slowly returned to my normal senses and found myself on a hard bed in coarse, clean sheets, in a long ward, with beds for about fifty women. From the nurses who swiftly fed me, fetched bedpans, washed me roughly, I discovered I was in the London Hospital, had been there for nearly six weeks, since I'd been collected from the pavement where I'd collapsed. I'd had double pneumonia. 'We thought you'd die,' said a friendly young nurse, handing me a tray with some sad boiled fish and mashed potato on it. I was desperately trying to piece myself together. I fell asleep again, without eating, as she spoke. She roused me, and made me eat.

That day the almoner, a pale woman in a stiff black dress with a white collar, a big bunch of keys at her waist, arrived. She woke me and she took my name and address. I was still grappling for myself, trying to recall who I was, what I was doing there. As I told her my address in the city I suddenly remembered seeing Jim Bristow on that bed in Dorset Street.

'You were very *clean* when you arrived,' she said, it seemed critically. 'Have you any family or friends you can go to?' she asked. 'You need nursing. Have you any money?'

No one knew I was here. 'My bag,' I said in alarm.

'You had no bag when you came here,' she said. 'I'm afraid someone may have taken it as you lay on the pavement.'

There was no information it seemed worth giving to this woman, who to me was like someone I half dreamt and who, on her side, I suppose, saw in a hospital bed a skeletal young woman, some ruined milliner or shopgirl, unsought daughter, a piece of human flotsam cast up on her hygienic shores, to be cured and thrown back into the muddy waters she came from.

'Mr Sloane and Dr French will be here to see you later.'

They tidied me up. I slept. I was awoken by a senior nurse, when the ward was quiet. Behind her were two men in black suits, doctors, she told me. The older one had a black beard, cut to a point, a black moustache, a silk cravat. This was the surgeon, Mr Sloane, a dandy. Screens went round. He pulled up my gown and prodded my stomach. To my horror, before I knew it, his big fingers were going inside me. I resisted. 'Now then,' he said, looking at his colleague, 'it won't hurt if you relax.'

In the next bed a woman was sobbing for her amputated leg. 'Oh no. What'll I do? My leg. Where's my leg?' she moaned. A big trolley of used dressings came past, wheeled by a pale nurse, only about sixteen. There was much noise and a choking smell of disinfectant.

'Feel it,' he continued, talking to the other doctor. The second man, in turn, poked and prodded. The fingers came out. 'An ovariotomy will answer the case here,' said the bearded man. 'Or, if need be, the more radical operation.'

'What?' I asked weakly.

He looked at me, without seeing me, rather as you might observe a cat coming into the room while talking to someone else. 'You've been rather a naughty girl, my dear,' he said. 'But we can put you right, don't worry about it.'

I brought out some words. 'It's my lungs, they said.'

'Ah, but why?' he asked, as much for the benefit of the other doctor as for mine. 'Why, we have to ask ourselves? What produced this general weakness? Prior examination suggests a venereal history, an interrupted pregnancy, possibly more than one. Never you mind, my dear,' he assured me, 'we'll put you right.'

All this time the nurse stood by. 'Tomorrow,' he said. 'She's a strong girl.'

The nurse nodded. 'Good afternoon,' they said. She ducked a near-curtsy, and responded, 'Good afternoon, Mr Sloane, Dr French.' She was gone and the screens pulled back and moments later it was almost as if nothing had happened. I was so very tired that I wished to believe nothing had, and so I slept a little, but when I woke to the sound of a rattling tea trolley I asked the nurse who came with my cup, 'What was the doctor here for?'

'To see how you were, I dare say,' she said.

'They said they'd put me right – tomorrow,' I persisted.

'Ah well,' she said, thinking. 'Well,' she said more briskly, 'they will then, won't they?'

'What?'

'Put you right,' she said. And she turned away. We were all paupers here to them. The better-off went into clinics or were nursed at home. We were just poor women with muddled lives, too many children, husbands drunk or out of work, or without husbands at all. The nurses themselves were respectable spinsters, many working only for the money. Some were dedicated, but often more to the idea of service itself than to the patients.

It was the woman lying next to me who helped. A

blanched face against a snow-white pillow turned to me, a tired, low voice said, 'I heard you got Mr Sloane operating on you.' She was a washerwoman, married to a longshoreman, and had been brought in when she collapsed with gangrene. They'd cut off two of her toes and she was waiting to see if they'd take off another.

'Operation?' I whispered, terrified. 'What operation? It's my lungs . . .'

The ward was dark, with only two nurses there, one at either end, sitting at desks in the gloom with little lamps to see by. The woman whispered, 'It can't just be your lungs. This is the surgical ward. I heard them. I thought he'd come for me. I hope he never did nothing while I was under.'

'What do you mean?'

'Well – my parts, like. Female parts. I felt down there. I think I'm all right. My husband wouldn't like anything like that.'

'What will he do to me?'

'Why,' she said, 'he'll cut your inside out. Womb and that. He's famous for it, operates on society women, writes books about it.'

'But – what for? I don't need surgery. It's my lungs . . . my lungs . . .' I must have been babbling.

'It's for your own good, I suppose,' she told me. 'He does it for the fashionable women so they won't have no more youngsters.' She paused, said with an effort, 'But in your shoes I wouldn't want to go under the knife. Not here. Not for that.' She paused again. 'Not his, anyway,' she added. After another pause she added, 'He's fond of the knife, Sloane.'

'I don't have to—' I said like a child.

'He says you've got to,' she told me, like a mother.

The nurse came up. 'No talking. You must rest now.'

'Nurse,' I said, 'Mr Sloane . . . in the morning . . .'

'That's right. You're on his list.'

'But I don't want –'

'Kelly,' she said, 'Mr Sloane says you need this ovari-otomy. That's what it's called. Your insides aren't as they should be. That's why you're here in this ward. You're in good hands with Mr Sloane, of that I assure you. He's much in demand from titled ladies. And you won't have to pay. You're lucky, so don't be a silly, ignorant girl, and stop complaining.'

'But I don't want an operation.'

'You should have thought of that, when you did what you did,' she told me, and went back to her desk.

In the dim light from the nurses' lamps I could see the fog putting its fingers under windows, creeping along the floor, tendrils, like seaweed, waving in, dissolving, thick-ening the air. Sounds from outside, in Whitechapel Road, were muffled. I must have lain for hours, weak and terrified, not knowing what to do. Did I really need to go on to the operating table? Was I going to die if I didn't? Would I die if I did? They would not let me refuse. I might cry out and fight, but the pad of ether would come down on my face, early tomorrow morning, and they'd have their way with me. If I survived the operation I would be ill again, trapped in this place, at everyone's mercy, unable to leave for a long time. Could I escape? I was wearing a coarse hospital gown. They would never bring my clothes and I did not know where they were kept. I had been in bed for so long and I felt so weak I was not even sure if I could stand.

Much later, it seemed, a nurse came and raked the stove, rattled more coke on to it. Someone moaned. Another woman cried out, 'Johnny! Help!' I was in hell, I thought, and it came to me, as it would have done to an animal, that I must escape. I had no thought now but of not being there in the morning to see the half-light of

November coming through the windows, feel the suffocating pad over my face, have the knife cutting into me as I lay unconscious. It was my death I feared.

The nurse who had tended the fire went back to her place. I watched, secretly, my head just raised from the pillow. But she did not stop at her desk; she went out. The other nurse seemed occupied.

I got out of bed. My legs began shaking violently, but steadied as, quietly, in the shadows, I crept from the ward by the door the nurse had used and closed it behind me. In the semi-darkness created by lowered gas-lights I slipped down the stairs and found myself in a huge, tiled hall. Cowering in the shadow beside the stairs, I saw big doors to the outside. A chair by the door, for a porter, was unoccupied. As two nurses crossed the hall in caps and cloaks, I stayed hidden, vastly relieved the exit to the street was so close, anxious in case I was caught before I got out. I was in a nightdress, without shoes, trembling with cold, and I had no money. Then the doors to the outside banged open and in came two policemen, dragging in the dim light a woman with blood pouring from a wound in her head. 'Porter! Porter!' called one. 'Christ – where is the man?' The woman, swearing, was trying to get away from them.

'Damn this, Fred,' said the other policeman. 'There – can you hold her? I'll go for someone.'

As he ran off the woman suddenly collapsed and lay on the floor in the gloom, like an abandoned doll. The other policeman dropped down and crouched beside her, still holding her arm.

I was ready to run for the doors when two nurses came clattering in from somewhere, ran to the woman and bent over her. The policeman said, 'I think she's a goner.' But one of the nurses, as she leaned over to attend to the woman, had slipped off her cloak, to leave her arms free. I ran silently on my bare feet from the shadow of the stairs, caught the cloak up from the floor and was in the street and down an alley on one side in a flash. There I crouched, gasping for breath, in the angle of a building. I heard cries and the sound of a policeman running. But the feet went past along Whitechapel Road while I leaned back against the cold damp wall, sucking in freezing fog.

I sank down on the narrow pavement, in a doorway. I was alone in that still, yellow air, weak, barefoot, penniless and with my old lodgings some two miles off. I could hear shouts and footsteps from Whitechapel Road. 'Get away from me, Bill,' came a woman's cry. Boys in a gang ran past. 'Which way?' 'Up Eddie Clutterbuck's – he's got some—' and they were gone. Nevertheless, I thought it must be late, from the sounds. Past midnight, perhaps. I breathed in and out, trying to steady myself. I had only to make one more effort and I could find help. All I had to do was slip across Whitechapel Road unobserved, take to the dark streets and alleys on the other side and within ten minutes, little longer, I'd be there in Dorset Street, close to Mary's lodgings. And if she wasn't there why, a minute off, there was Cora Mundy's.

The thought of this short trip, though, put me in a terrible state. The police were after me for absconding from the hospital in a stolen cloak – they'd have me back for that operation, under arrest, too, if they caught me. And at the back of my mind, of course, was the question of whether they'd yet found that slaughterhouseman, the killer of women. I was afraid. I, who had travelled vast plains and been thousands of feet up in unexplored mountains as the first snows came on the pines – I was afraid.

I remembered the big Indian disappearing so silently, flowing like water into the forest. If you looked for him a moment later you could not have seen him among the tall trees. He would return just as invisibly, suddenly appearing at the wagon, holding a bird or animal dangling in his hand. And that was all I had to do, just slide into the streets, slip along like a shadow from wall to wall, doorway to doorway, like an Indian. That was all. Yet I was afraid. I had arrived here prosperous, healthy – and armed. Now I was sick, penniless and utterly defenceless, no better off than those the murderer had chosen as his victims. Never mind, I told myself. It will soon be over. And forcing myself to my feet I crept along cautiously and peered round the corner to see if anyone was coming.

Because of the fog I could see only a few yards ahead and around me and that dimly, but there seemed to be no one about in Whitechapel Road so I went swiftly across. Once off the main road where the street lights were fewer I would be less visible. For the rest, who in that neighbourhood would think twice about a barefoot woman in a cloak slinking about at night like a stray cat? Even the lights of Whitechapel Road were dim in the yellow fog, as if veils had been thrown over their lamps. Further up were naphtha lights and a smell of fried potatoes. Some poor man trying to sell food to people at midnight, in thick fog. I ran left, swerving towards the street to evade the doors of a pub. There I had to shake off a couple of sailors, run from them in fact, on freezing and now bleeding feet, very tender, because I had been in bed so long.

Just before I got to the turning I wanted to slip into I heard a coachman crying, 'Whoah! Whoah!' to his horses and a big black coach slowed down in the street beside me. The coachman was hunting prey for his master inside, no doubt, for the passenger could not have seen me through the fog. What a terrible pair they must have been, to be out looking for bedraggled tarts in such weather. But I ran into the alley and leaned against a wall, gasping for breath, listening for the sounds of the horses' hooves to go. Then, before I felt ready to move on, I went anyway, limping now, but still travelling as fast as I could, hearing my own breath whistling horribly in and out.

I twisted and turned through the narrow streets. Once I heard heavy footsteps behind me and my heart jumped in my chest. If the man meant me some harm I could not fight him – I was too weak – nor outrun him. He came behind me steadily all the way to Brick Lane. It was a little better lit and I was glad of that, now I was further from the hospital. The danger now was less of a policeman, more of some stray man, God knows who he might be or what he would want. I had no money, no weapon, no health and no one to care for me. What difference was there now between me and Martha Tabram, Polly Nichols, Annie Chapman, Elizabeth Stride and Catherine Eddowes?

At last I got into Dorset Street, where Mary lived. It was empty as far as I could see. I hobbled along, hugging the walls, until suddenly a man caught me from behind and pushed me against a wall. His breath smelt of violets. 'Let me go. I'm ill,' I gasped.

'So you say. So you say. You'd say anything but your prayers.' But I remember his big hand coming on to my brow, which must have been beaded with sweat, and he took his hand away and went off himself, fearing to catch the infection he thought I carried.

I found the archway and went through it to the room where my sister lived. The window was broken now and had a rag stuffed in it, which I removed. The only light was from the fire opposite. At first all I saw, by firelight, was someone, a man, crouched over the fire pushing some objects into the flames. All I observed of the bed, which was right under the window where I stood, was that there was something on it and that something was so horrible my mind rejected it, had to reject it. One more glance, then I turned my head away, seeking some object which would convince me I was alive, in a real world, that this was no nightmare. Thus I stared at the bricks beside the window, old and yellow, then forced myself to look again at that bed, beneath my eyes, on which lay a body so hideously mangled that at first it was only recognizable by the arms and legs. Thank God the light was dim. One arm dangled over the side of the bed nearest me, over tumbled, soaked bedclothes. The face, turned upward, was so cut about it seemed barely a face at all. Inside that room, bending over the fire, was a man who had cut a woman's face to raw meat and eviscerated her. He had carved off her breasts.

I fell back, nearly fainting, against the wall beside the window. I must run back through the alleyway into Dorset Street and scream, 'Murder!' But even as I leaned there the door grated open and that monstrous man, in a black coat, came out quickly and half-ran past me. I dared not shout now. There was no one in sight. He might kill me before anyone heard my cries.

As he turned the corner, deliberately slowing his walk, I crept after him. Now he was walking swiftly but calmly, a man in not too much of a hurry in his respectable dark overcoat. If anything he looked too respectable for that neighbourhood at that time of night. He could have been anybody. That is the horror of such monsters. I quailed as I thought of those bloody hands, jammed in the pockets of his coat, and of what else he might be clutching, what grim mementoes of his crime.

He was moving in the direction of the Ten Bells, the pub on a corner only a little way up from Spitalfields Market. It might still be open and if it was, there I could get help. On the corner opposite the Ten Bells, too, lay Christ Church, that massive soot-blackened edifice designed, surely, to placate some fearful God. Around it many homeless people slept in the churchyard, even on nights such as that one. Advancing slowly I prayed for lights in the pub, a crowd, people.

That was when, on the corner outside the Ten Bells, I saw him turn right round in the dark. He sensed he was being followed, the villain, the animal. That instinct was how he had escaped so often before. I fell back against a wall and thought he'd not seen me. Then he rounded the corner. A few paces forward and I could see lights in the windows of the Ten Bells. I hastened on, pushed open the door of the pub and gasped in the direction of the few people there, 'Quick – the Ripper – he's here. Follow me.'

My voice sounded to me thin and weak. As I left the pub I was suddenly afraid that I had not been heard, or had been taken for a madwoman roaming about, whispering terrible things into the night, then disappearing. At any rate, I heard no shouts behind me, no banging of the pub door to indicate people were following me. Nor was there anyone outside, no poor creature giving up any hope of better shelter for the night and seeking refuge among the tombstones, no tart looking for a last customer – no one. It was the dead hour of the night when even in that area few are abroad, all must sleep, cowering in whatever cranny they can find.

The man had turned in Fournier Street and I was spent. I knew too that the longer I followed him the more likely it was that he would spot me. I remembered that the vicarage of the church lay beside the side wall of the great building, in Fournier Street, not a hundred feet from where I was. I would bang on the door and hope the vicar, or a servant, would be alert enough to raise a hue and cry. I could do no more.

What I had forgotten was that between the church and the vicarage were the large wrought-iron gates, wide enough to admit a hearse. They must have been unlocked for as I went gasping past I was seized. One hand went over my mouth, I was borne back, stumbling to keep my footing on the damp flagstones, and there he threw me back. My head hit the church wall as I fell. Next I knew, he had his hands round my throat and was choking me. I felt one hand release me, while the other continued to squeeze my throat. I felt a fumbling in his pocket, heard the click of his knife on the paving stones. He was ready to kill me with it. As I tried to roll over to escape him both his hands were round my throat again, tightening. I lost consciousness, smelling his foul breath in my nostrils and imagining my own body, dead, limp and ripped, lying by the church wall like a bloodied doll.

The hands must have slackened as the murderer heard, or just felt, the woman approaching. It was only a glimmer of a white face I saw, with a dark shawl round it. It came closer. I began to struggle. As the hands tightened round my throat, to silence me I suppose, I managed, I think, to croak her name. She must have heard. A voice cried, 'Mary!' She launched herself towards me. There seemed to be another figure behind her. Suddenly the madman's grip loosened, then fell away. I sank to the slimy paving, gasping, nearly unconscious. As I revived a little a terrible anxiety swept over me. I managed to raise myself from the ground on my elbow and look sideways to where, a few feet away, two figures – men – struggled on the ground. I crawled towards them, saw a knife in the air held by the man on top, ready to descend. The other man's hand grappled for the knife from below. Then I saw a woman's skirt and long shawl, her arm and hand, trying to grasp the knife. I heard metal clang on to stone nearby. The knife had been dropped. Still sprawling, I felt for it all over the greasy paving, my fingers meeting shiny clumps of rag, paper, all manner of things. Then I found it and got my fingers on the handle. The men were still fighting. I heard dreadful gasps, the sounds of struggle.

I had the knife. I crawled to my sister's side. Jim Bristow was pinned on the ground under the madman's body. His eyes bulged, for the man had him by the throat. The other man's breath sobbed also, for both Jim's hands, in turn, were round his throat. It was like the act of love, the one man on top of the other, the gasping, the wrestling and twitching of the bodies. I raised the knife and brought it down, feeling it go through coat, flesh, into nothing. The murderer's body bucked against it. I pulled out the knife, gasping with the effort. I pushed it in again, through coat, flesh, and this time struck bone. I pulled myself forward a little, leaned in, pressed half the weight of my body on it. His body bucked again, resisted, sagged, with a sigh. He was spent. He had often spent himself with a knife, as a woman died. Now it was his turn.

Jim rolled him off and lay, hauling in long breaths. Mary and I were both on our knees, I with my head drooping, near-unconscious again. I barely knew where I was or what I had done. Mary was saying, 'My God. Oh, my God,' over and over again. Jim sat up, still breathless, and croaked, 'That must be him.'

The body lay face down in the dark. I heard Mary and Jim turning him over. 'He's young,' I heard her say. I crawled the little way to the body and gazed down on the face of the killer. The blue eyes were open. Horribly, the eyelids flickered. The blanched face, a pimple by the lip, the red-brown, slightly curling hair, were those of Churchill, Brewer's corrupted clerk.

What trouble lay behind the mind of the well-cared-for widow's son? What in God's name, apart from Brewer's training in seducing women for the rent, had brought him to murder? There's a kind of darkness in all our minds we can never admit to; the sources are different, the feelings are different, but there's no one, whoever they are, man or woman, who doesn't carry their own evil seed saved up inside them. They deny it, but know secretly it's there, pray it will never find fertile ground, sprout, grow and bear wicked fruit. Churchill was one who, in youth, before he had any chance to make something better of himself, had been introduced to vice, whose whole training had gone against the vice, and in the conflict between desire and a conscience perhaps too strictly trained had become bestial – no, worse than a beast, for no one but a man who has a brain and can suffer conflict, and have perverse thoughts, can make himself so atrocious.

And there he lay, the monster, dead, or so I hoped, and there was Jim, flat on his back, and Mary and I kneeling.

Jim was up. 'Drag him into the shadows of the church wall,' he said in a low voice.

'I can't,' I said. Everything was spinning round me.

'I'll drag him. You drag her,' he told Mary. She pulled me up and supported me as I staggered to the wall, then slid me down, so that my back was against it. I was shaking and could not stop. I heard Jim hauling back the body of the dead man a little further off. Mary stood in front of me. 'Bastards,' I said, though my teeth were chattering violently. 'A pretty pair you are.'

Jim arrived. 'I saved your life,' he mumbled.

Mary Jane, tougher than either of us, said, 'Who is he?' nodding in the direction of the corpse.

'What's going on?' said an old man's voice weakly. He was along the wall, a little way off, a bundle of rags and lice, trying to shelter.

'Shut up or you'll regret it,' hissed my sister.

'He's killed a woman in your room. He's the Ripper,' I told her.

'Oh, my God. It's poor Amelia,' Mary said.

'Who's dead? Another one?' said the cracked old voice of the bundle of rags.

'Shut your bloody face or I'll kill you,' Mary said fiercely, then she said to me in a voice getting higher and higher, 'She borrowed the room. Is she dead? What's he done?'

'Shut up, you stupid cow,' said Jim to Mary in a low, violent tone. He crouched down, pulling her after him. So there we were, terrified and hissing at each other in the darkness against a damp wall, with the dead body of the

208

murderer not three feet away. Meanwhile Jim whispered, 'This is no bloody good. A woman dead and here's another corpse. What are we going to do?'

I was saying, weakly, 'He *is* the Ripper,' when the final horror came – he wasn't dead! A groan came from where the body was lying. Mary clutched my arm convulsively – a grip of iron. 'Oh, God. Oh, God, he's not dead,' she moaned. 'Jesus Christ help us – what can we do?' At least the old man was quiet, terrified.

Jim was apparently calm. 'Go and sit on his face, Mary,' he ordered in a whisper, but his voice shook.

'I've got in enough trouble doing what you said,' said Mary, with a sob. 'I can't. You can't make me.'

'Go on,' he urged. Then he sighed a frantic sigh and crept off on his hands and knees in the direction of the dying young man, the insane killer, the tormented beast, Churchill. There was a scuffling noise, then a terrible silence. Jim crawled back in the darkness. There was a pause. 'It's done. He's better off dead,' he said.

'All right. Let's get away now,' hissed Mary.

'Yes. A body in your room, and another here, then a manhunt and who knows what the outcome of all that will be? We could end up heroes or on the scaffold, convicted of two murders. Two? Four, five, six murders. I don't want to hang,' he whispered. 'Nor do you, I suppose.'

'Get rid of him, then.'

'Easy said,' Jim told her.

There was some singing in the street, not twenty yards away. 'Let's leg it,' urged Mary.

Now came a steady pacing. 'Copper,' said Jim, who could tell the tread.

It passed. Jim whispered, 'Look, there's that old geezer there and God knows who else. We've got to get rid of the body.'

'It means the river,' I said in a low voice.

But it was over half a mile to the Thames, past the pubs, the people, the patrolling police.

'Hang on,' Jim said. 'There's a cart works behind here.' He was off quickly and quietly.

Mary and I hung on, shivering, with our corpse. I clutched my cloak round me, tried not to make a noise as I coughed and coughed.

'You all right? Where've you been?' she asked.

'In hospital. Where've you been? That's the point.'

'I was going to find you. Jim thought . . .' She seemed ashamed. And had reason to be.

'You've made a fool of me,' I wheezed. 'Both of you. And Jim's made a bigger fool of you.'

'I know it. He kept it from me at first, that you were looking for me. Then he said . . .' She sighed. 'All I want now is to get out of this lot. And Amelia dead. My God,' she murmured. 'Mary Anne, I'm sorry I let Jim talk me into keeping quiet about where I was. He could see you had money, and he wanted some and you know what he is – persuasive.' She broke off. Then she said, 'I saved your life, though.'

There was a rattling noise. Jim was back with a handcart. 'Help get him in,' he said. We got the limp corpse into the cart as quietly as we could. Jim threw some sacks that had been at the bottom of the cart over him. 'You two had better hide where you can. I'll do it.' He took the handles. 'Save me from the scaffold if I'm caught,' he said, and I could tell he wondered if we would. It would be easier not to, and he'd foxed both of us, one way and another. It's a rotten trick to sleep with sisters, rotten to get one to deceive the other, but he was a rotten bastard, headed for the gallows from birth. When all was said and done, he knew it, and so did we.

Nevertheless, after he'd trundled the body a little way, we agreed between ourselves to follow and see what happened. I was shuddering with cold, my feet like ice. He saw us behind him as he pushed the cart across Whitechapel Road. The gas flared, there were people about and a couple of policemen, plus a police wagon, sorting out a pub fight. He did not dare come near us, or call out, for fear of attracting attention. He cut from alley to alley, where it was dark, creaking along. We shadowed him.

Down by the railway goods depot a couple of cheery young men called out above the sound of shunting engines, 'Look out, mate. There's a couple of tarts behind you.' We crept down Tower Hill, under the looming walls of the Tower, and at the bottom we turned off, found a set of little steps going down to the water off a quiet street, got the cart down, heaved the body into the dark gurgling water and the cart in after. Then we ran.

They saw me back to London Wall, the border dividing the dark area of London from the light. There we separated, Jim having handed me two sovereigns, the first and last money I ever got from him in my life.

This is how, I believe, the man called Jack the Ripper met his end. They never found his body. They have never found out who he was, as far as I know. He wasn't anybody, by the time he died, just a man gone so far wrong he was no longer human, who killed six poor women no one would otherwise have bothered about.

I give my account now, and sign it with my own name. Possibly this is the last time I will ever use it. Once I was Mary Anne Kelly, now I'm Mary Anne something else, tomorrow I shall be somewhere else, someone else, and later perhaps somewhere else and someone else again. What's in a name, when all's said and done? In recalling those terrible events of a few months in the year 1888 I feel fortunate to be alive, unlike those other obscure, needy women fixed forever as victims by their names,

Martha Tabram, Polly Nichols, Annie Chapman, Elizabeth Stride, Catherine Eddowes and the one who even now is not known by her proper name, but is called Mary Jane Kelly.

PART IV

POSTCRIPT BY ROBERT NAUGHTON JAMES

As THE publisher of this account, which was given to me by Jonathan Jessop, who is probably the grandson of the writer, I feel I ought to make some explanation about its provenance and authenticity. I must point out that this book is not published as an incontestable historical record, although I myself believe it to be one. My own choice, as a would-be publisher of the document, was whether to wait perhaps many years until it was fully authenticated or to act on my own gut instinct, that it *is* a true account, and publish it as it stands for the interest it's bound to hold for readers. Clearly – I did the latter. Meanwhile, I'm indebted to several historians dealing with the period and in particular to my friends Mr and Mrs Richard Whittington-Egan, who have advised me on the crimes committed by the murderer known as Jack the Ripper. They and others concede that Mary Kelly's story, given here, may well be true, that errors of fact made by the writer could be ordinary errors such as we all make when dealing with our own, everyday experience, and that possibly in some cases the writer has used false names to conceal the real identities of those involved ('Jim Bristow', for example, and 'Mr Sloane', the surgeon at the

London Hospital). But the experts all say this story is quite likely to be a true account of the Whitechapel murders by someone who was there, and deeply involved.

As far as I'm concerned there is no logical way of separating the provenance of the story from the issue of authenticity so I shall begin by saying that when I began to read, just over a year ago, this bulky set of papers – which, from the appearance of the paper and ink and the handwriting, careful copperplate of the kind taught in Board Schools at the time, seemed to be very much of the late nineteenth century – I soon lost any feeling that the story was not what it seemed to be. I can't predict the final verdict. Nevertheless I genuinely believe this is a true piece of autobiography by a woman involved in one of the most fascinating crimes of the nineteenth century. Tests are being conducted, facts examined which will support or call into question the validity of the information, but what convinces me, as an ordinary reader, certainly no expert, is that never, over one hundred years, has any writer on the subject of the Whitechapel murders concentrated so much on the victims, so little on the detective story side of the affair, i.e. the identity of the murderer. I believe that only a woman, and one intimately concerned with the victims (she and her sister both potentially victims themselves) could have told this story in such a way.

If I am right and this is Mary Kelly's story, it was written, obviously, after November 1888, when the last murder was committed, and almost certainly before 1895 when she, by then Mary Brown, wife of the Marcus Brown referred to in the tale, suddenly and without warning left her home after seven years of marriage. She never returned. The pages of Mary Kelly's story were found in an old suitcase among family effects from Knare Park, Sir Marcus Brown's home in Kent. All the evidence points to Mary Kelly and Mary Brown being one and the same, which of course means that Mary did not return to

Canada immediately after the last events described in her story. Instead she must have accepted a proposal of marriage from Sir Marcus and ceased at that point to be Mary Kelly of Whitechapel, becoming, if only temporarily, Lady Brown of Knare Park in Kent. (A further validation of her account is the fact that Sir Marcus was returned to Parliament in the election of 1892. She mentions the prospect of this, of course, in her narrative.)

The papers published here were among her belongings, packed up hastily and consigned to the attic by her husband after her departure. Understandably enough, left suddenly with the two children of the marriage by his wife, he would not have wanted traces of her lying about the house to remind him, or them, of her disappearance. He later divorced her for desertion, remarried, and began a new family.

In any event, it was not until 1925, just after the death of Sir Marcus, that his daughter Caroline Jessop (Mary's child, if that is what she was) went to Knare Park with her cousin's wife to supervise the clearing out of the house, which was to be sold. Caroline's brother had died on the Somme in 1916, Sir Marcus's second wife was also dead.

In a dress box in a trunk in the attic, Caroline discovered the pages of Mary Kelly's story. They lay among other items presumably belonging to her, from gloves to the contents of her desk, and including the appointments of her dressing-table, even the silver-backed hairbrush we read about in her narrative, still with the owner's long black hairs caught in it. Caroline and her cousin thought it was obvious that at some point Sir Marcus had made the servants sweep the house clean of his former wife at great speed. The impression was of items packed up rapidly and thrust away out of sight.

The two women also had no time to spare. Caroline was a mother, her cousin pregnant. Both women wanted to be home. So they did not disturb the two trunks containing Caroline's mother's property, merely marked them to be sent to Caroline's house in London to be sorted out later. Whether Caroline Jessop read her mother's story later when she had time to go through the trunks, or simply kept it without reading it, no one knows. Her son believes she may never have read it, merely kept it, out of sentiment, possibly planning to read it later and never doing so. Apart from anything else, her husband Stanley Jessop was in the Foreign Service and the couple were usually abroad. In 1949, returning to Britain from Prague, both died in an air crash. Jonathan Jessop suggests that when he found the story in his mother's effects he might have been the first person to read it since Mary Kelly composed her account at Knare Park in the last decade of the nineteenth century.

Why she did so at all is one of the many mysteries surrounding the whole affair. But then, why did she abandon a comfortable home, a kindly husband and two young children? Did she feel she must leave a record of the events? Did she write in a peculiar mood of nostalgia? Or was this her farewell to a pleasant life as a country wife and mother, before she took off without a word? She seems to have been a woman with a restless nature, unaccountable by ordinary present-day standards, unaccountable, perhaps, by the standards of her own day.

So – the tale discovered, another question arises. Why did Jonathan Jessop wait so long to reveal what he found? He says frankly that as a young man, a diplomat like his father, making his way in the world, he was convinced that if the story Mary Kelly told was accepted as true – and he as her grandson – it would do nothing for his career prospects. I'm sure he was right to imagine the matter could have damaged him. Afterwards he would always have been marked out as the grandson of a Whitechapel prostitute, 'the tart who killed the Ripper'. He would have carried that bizarre label, whatever his merits or achievements might have been. He would always have been bedevilled by this one extraordinary fact about him – that he was Mary Kelly's grandson, no basis for a solid career in the Foreign Office. At any rate, as he points out, he would never have known if this fact had been detrimental to him.

As he got older, more senior, and had proved himself, this consideration might have been less worrying but, as he would be the first to say, as his status improved, he grew more sensitive about his reputation.

So for many years the moment never seemed right to make such a revelation. And rightly, it seems: even after his retirement Jonathan Jessop was busy. He was chairman of a recent Home Office committee on the manner of dealing with complaints against the police, a sterling piece of work, much praised, but, as Evelyn Jessop, his wife, pointed out, what would it have looked like if he had suddenly emerged as the grandson of a self-confessed prostitute and unofficial executioner? Would he have been thought suitable to undertake the business? You can imagine the headline – RIPPER KILLER'S GRANDSON HEADS CRIME TEAM. Of course, the existence of Mary Kelly's manuscript was no secret to friends and was actually something of a family joke by then, but public attention would have been a different matter.

And then the whole story came up again. When he made ordinary efforts to trace his grandmother and discover what had happened to her after she disappeared from Knare Park, he never found any evidence of her remarriage or of her death in the public records. He took it she must either have changed her name, and lived on under the assumed one, or else gone abroad and presumably died there. At that point the life and death of Mary Kelly, as far as he was concerned, became a mystery which would never be solved. Until, astonishingly enough, in 1987 he got a call from a firm of lawyers in New York enquiring if he were indeed the grandson of Mary Kelly, formerly Lady Brown of Knare Park in Kent. They had found Jessop by contacting the owners of Knare Park, who knew from whom it had originally been bought. In this way the firm had traced Jessop. The matter was, they said to his astonishment, connected with the will of an old bachelor, Frederick Hamilton, who had died at the age of ninety on a farm in Vermont, where he'd been living for many years. Hamilton had left the amazed Jonathan Jessop his fortune, a large one, more than five million dollars. That's to say, to be accurate, he had left in his will five million dollars to be divided among the children and descendants of the children of Sir Marcus Brown and his wife, Mary.

At the time Jonathan Jessop had no idea why this old man, a complete stranger, had left his family such a vast sum. Naturally, as soon as they could, the Jessops went to Vermont on holiday to see what they could find out. On investigation a peculiar story – another peculiar story involving Mary Kelly – emerged. Frederick Hamilton's money had been left to him by a woman, Mary Kelly Hamilton. He and two old ladies, one calling herself Mrs Hamilton, the other Mrs Thomasina Chesney, had bought the farm in Vermont in the late 1930s. The old ladies had died within six months of each other, only a few years after their arrival, and the middle-aged Frederick Hamilton had gone on living in the house and farming the land, capably enough, for the next thirty years. When he got old, he let the farm but continued to live in the house. The local story was that he knew what he was doing with the land: he seemed used to farming. Although he was reticent about his past, he did say he had come from Canada to help his mother in her old age, adding that she had left him there when he was very young and he had no really strong filial feelings for her.

At the local inn where Jessop tried to pick up information, further gossip was sparse. A lot of the story had been lost over the years and Jessop got the impression the local people were reticent on general principle: there might have been more they could have told him, if they'd chosen to. However, drinks all round in the bar elicited one further comment about the career of the Vermont Mary Kelly. This came from a woman, lifting a glass to Jessop in thanks, who said, 'I guess all that money came from this.' When Jessop asked her what she meant, she replied, 'Prohibition. I heard Frederick say once or twice it was Prohibition that set his mother right. Makes sense doesn't it? If she came from Canada, too, originally and had connections there, she'd have been in a good position to run booze over the border.' When the Jessops considered the matter it did seem possible that if Mary had gone back to Canada when she left Knare Park she might have extended her interest in saloons and brothels into bootlegging in the USA during Prohibition. From her account she was no stranger to bootlegging, having begun it in her frontier days.

Jessop, staggered, ordered another round and then another. Apparently they made a night of it at the inn. Next day a drinking companion led him to the three graves in the town's quiet little graveyard. There lay Frederick, his grave still unmarked, and, not far off, the much older gravestones of Mrs Mary Kelly Hamilton and Mrs Thomasina Chesney, widow of Arthur Chesney of Ontario, Canada. Who they really were we may never know. We can speculate – was the mysterious Mrs Chesney really the other Mary Kelly, who was supposed to have died a victim of Jack the Ripper? Or the endearing Rosie Levi to whom our Mary was planning to offer employment? Dora, the maid? Or someone else completely? Which one, if either, was Frederick's true mother? We don't know. It's unlikely we ever will. At present, there's no getting to the bottom of the story and probably there'll never be.

This odd finale to the history of Mary Kelly's manuscript persuaded Jonathan Jessop to give me the story purportedly written by his grandmother to publish and I am delighted to be able to do so. It's a strange document, from a strange hand, providing much material for research and speculation. But I really believe, partly because of the language the author uses, a mixture of the literate speech of the time and lapses into argot, or what we would call street-talk, partly because of the attention, as I've previously remarked, on the women slain rather than the slayer, that there's every reason to believe this is an authentic and remarkable account of events at the time of the Whitechapel murders.

Robert Naughton James,
Bagley and Green, Publishers.

BIBLIOGRAPHY

Begg, Paul, *Jack the Ripper*
Berton, Pierre, *The Last Spike*
Cunningham, Phyllis, *Costume in Pictures*
Davison, Peter, *The British Music Hall*
Ewing, Elizabeth, *Fashion in Underwear*
Fishman, William J., *East End 1888*
Gray, Jannes H., *Red Lights on the Prairies*
Honeycombe, Gordon, *The Murders of the Black Museum*
Howells, Martin and Skinner, Keith, *The Ripper Legacy*
Hudd, Roy, *Music Hall*
Jackson, Richard, *Popular Songs of the Nineteenth Century*
Knight, Stephen, *Jack the Ripper : The Final Solution*
Laver, James, *Costume and Fashion*
Rumbelow, Donald, *The Complete Jack the Ripper*

The Times, August–November 1888
Underwood, Peter, *Jack the Ripper*
Whittington-Egan, Richard, *A Casebook on Jack the Ripper*
Wilson, Colin and Odell, Robin, *Jack the Ripper*